ALIEN THREAT

To Bill,
One of my best friends for
The last 70 years
Dick Blide 4/27/13

Richard W Blide

ISBN: 1475285590
ISBN 13: 9781475285598

Cover picture by professional artist and illustrator, Pierre Mion
www.cedarknollbooks.com

CEDAR KNOLL
BOOKS

Other books
by Richard Blide

Heartfelt: A Memoir of Political Intrigue, Passion and Perseverance

Acknowledgements

I wish to thank my friend, Pierre Mion, a professional artist and illustrator, for painting the cover picture for this book and my wife, Patti, for support and help in editing.

*This book is dedicated to my wife, Patti,
and our daughter, Leslie*

Table of Contents

Strange Beginnings

"After traversing the starred vastness of the Milky Way Galaxy for nine years, we're finally approaching our destination. Before us sits a star, which we had named Bugger. Before we left home, we determined that it was orbited by eight planets. The one that was most likely inhabitable was the third rock out from its star. Now we're within its solar system. It's gradually increasing in size, and we can see wisps of white stretching across a globe of blue. It had already been determined that it contained water, and this seemed verified by what we're seeing now. Closer still, we can see areas of green and brown. Now we've penetrated its atmosphere, and a panoply of wonders is unfolding before us. We've discovered a veritable treasure trove of geographic and biologic diversity. It resembles home. Now we have to find our predetermined landing site."

An earlier shower had left the budding branches dripping droplets of rain. Daffodils were beginning to bloom. It was cloudy and chilly, not an unusual spring morning in Washington, DC.

The Brownstone did not stand out but blended well with similar homes on Capitol Hill, an area containing residences of some of the more affluent of the government's employees.

After checking his morning email, Peter Bradford picked up the New York Times and settled into his library's Morris chair. He liked early American furniture, particularly a more sparse style, perhaps not the most comfortable, but then he was more a practical than a sensual person. His butler, Manfred, was stoking the fireplace, creating a pleasurable atmosphere for relaxing on a Sunday morning.

Much of his life had revolved about the government, particularly these later years, serving now as the National Security Advisor. He had wanted to stay at the Institute he had founded some years before to continue the research and writing about military history that had become his passion. The President, a life-long friend, had asked him to take this position, and knowing that one does not turn down such a request without a good reason, he had not. The nation, now in the throes of two wars — fear of terrorist attacks and an economy in recession — left Peter with little free time these days. So, to have this Sunday morning to himself was especially enjoyable.

A lean six two, in his mid-fifties, with thinning brown hair graying at the temples, Peter was an impressive figure. But what made him stand out were his piercing blue eyes with bushy eyebrows that gave the impression he could see right through you. He was an intellect, kind, and surprisingly somewhat introverted, but once you got to know him you could hardly help but like him. He had a paternalistic attitude toward his younger colleagues. A troublesome problem now was osteoarthritis in both hips which was becoming increasingly painful.

The phone rang. Manfred rose from his fireplace chore and answered, "Ah Michael, it's good to hear from you. Yes, your uncle's right here. Sir, it's your nephew." Peter put down his paper and took the phone.

"It's good to hear from you Michael. How are you doing?"

"We're very busy now doing a lot of overtime work. The corporations are pounding the doors to get our new cloud software."

"Sir, the reason I'm calling is to let you know that a good friend of mine will be contacting you shortly. You'll find him to be quite unusual, in fact extraordinary. So, I want to assure you of his integrity. He has a mission he wants to discuss with you. I'll let him give you the details. You can trust him as much as you trust me. His name is Cephid Aenid."

"This is quite unusual, Michael. Can't he go through the usual channels?"

"His employer knows of you, and made the explicit request that Cephid contact you directly."

Peter was feeling pressured. "Who's his employer? I don't understand the reason for his request."

Michael could understand his uncle's reticence. "He asked that I provide no details. He'll answer all your questions, when he sees you. I've known him for several years, and he is one of my best friends. I know it's a strange request, but I assure you that he's trustworthy, and I guarantee his integrity. I believe that his mission is important for our country."

"OK, Michael, I'll have my secretary set up an appointment."

"So, how has the government been treating you, sir?" Michael, an intellect too, and a highly regarded IT executive, was usually light-hearted, but on this occasion he sounded quite serious.

"Work has been going well. For the most part, I get my way except for Herbert in Defense. He gives us all a hard time. It's just his nature. I think he actually believes he's keeping us all honest with his nit-picking ways."

"Well sir, I have to run. We have some new, promising products coming to market, and my boss wants to get a leg up on the competition. I'll tell you more about it later." Peter heard a click, so he hung up.

Musing for a few moments, Peter recalled that his wife had died five years previously. His closest living relative now was Michael, the only son of his brother who had since passed away too. The two of them now were as close as father and son. With his wavy black hair, good looks and outgoing personality, Peter often thought of Michael as a reincarnation of his own father.

Just a few minutes later the phone rang again. Manfred picked it up. "Bradford residence, whom may I say is calling?"

"This is Cephid Aenid. May I speak to Peter Bradford please? I believe he's expecting my call."

Manfred handed the phone to Peter, "A Mr. Cephid Aenid, sir."

ALIEN THREAT

"Hello Mr. Aenid. My nephew, Michael, said that you would call. What can I do for you?"

"Sir, I represent a foreign government, and I'm here on a very discrete mission. I would like to set up an appointment to see you privately, preferably not at your office, perhaps at your home. It's very important that no one know of this first meeting. My mission is of a peaceful nature, and there's no danger to you. I expect that you would have your security people present."

After pondering for a moment, "Mr. Aenid, this is quite unusual. What government do you represent? You'll have to give me further information as to the nature of your mission and why this can't go through normal channels. I'm sure that you understand, as National Security Advisor, I have to be careful. Why have you contacted me rather than other government officials? The State Department might be more appropriate." Peter was somewhat irritated.

"Sir, my government chose you as our initial contact, first because security is of the utmost importance, and secondly, it was felt that with your background and experience you would best understand our mission." Mr. Aenid came across as matter of fact.

"You'll have to give me a better indication of the nature of your assignment, or I'll have to deny your request."

"Sir, our mission relates to space exploration. We have considerable knowledge in this area of which you are unaware. Your scientists would be most interested in what we've learned. I can't reveal what power I represent, particularly over an unsecured phone. But again, I want to emphasize that our intentions are entirely peaceful."

"Perhaps you would be better off contacting someone at NASA who would be more closely aligned with your interests."

"As you know, our contact with you is through your nephew, Michael, who felt that you would be our best contact within your government. We chose the USA because you are a democratic republic and are the reigning super power in this world. We're looking for you to give us guidance in broadening our contacts within your government. Once you become acquainted with our mission, you'll better understand our need for secrecy. And sir, there's someone else you can contact to verify the validity of our mission. David Standid is a scientist with an outstanding reputation who works at Sandia Labs in Albuquerque. He can vouch for my integrity as well."

4

Becoming curious but cautious, "Let's make a tentative appointment for this coming Saturday at my home at 9 a.m. Do you have a number where I can reach you to confirm this meeting?"

Mr. Aenid responded with his phone number. "I'd like to bring Standid with me as he's an advisor to our government. He'll be able to answer any scientific questions you may have." Peter agreed and they disconnected.

Standid, a U.S. scientist, an advisor to a foreign power, Peter mused. He thought further that he must get another opinion before setting up a meeting under such strange circumstances. *Who better to contact than the President.* In his present position he frequently met with George and, as it was, he conveniently had an appointment for the next morning.

President George West shook Peter's hand. "Good morning, Peter. Please have a seat. "Standing six feet with short clipped gray hair, not yet balding, President West was trim and agile. He had a twinkle in his brown eyes and a smile that ingratiated him to people. He and Peter had met in college, as opposing basketball players, and although they were from different schools, they had become friends. Peter did not use the President's first name on formal occasions, but he did so when they met privately.

"George, yesterday I had a call from a Mr. Cephid Aenid who said he was a representative of a foreign government, but he would not say which nation. He wants to see me privately—*without* other government officials present—preferably at my home. The meeting is to be held in the *strictest* confidence. His mission relates to space exploration. I suggested that he contact State or NASA, but he insisted that the first contact had to be with me as those were his instructions. I don't understand why me, but he said that I'd been chosen for security reasons and because of my broad background. He had no accent, which seemed strange for a foreigner. I couldn't guess his nationality. My nephew, Michael, called to let me know that Mr. Aenid would contact me. He assured me that he held him in high esteem, and that his mission was very important for the United States. I hesitate to see him under such circumstances, but I don't want to dismiss him without good cause. I would normally disregard such a call except for Michael's insistence on the significance of the meeting. He would never make this request unless he felt it was extremely important."

The president rose and walked over to a window. With a frown on his face, he pondered the situation, while looking out on the White House lawn. "Peter, I know you wouldn't bring up this situation unless you thought it important. We have known each other since college days. I trust your judgment. So it's your decision. However, I *insist* that you take every precaution and beef up your security." He returned to his desk.

"Thank you George. I'll take all necessary precautions."

"If I may change the subject, Peter, is there anything *pressing* on the national security front? I have a heavy schedule today."

"No sir—" a smile broke out on his face "—things are unusually quiet for once."

The president rose indicating the end of the meeting, "Contact me after your get-together with Mr. Aenid. It sounds like an intriguing situation. The misses and I will be up at Camp David for a few days, so you can reach me there if necessary." The president accompanied Peter to the door where they shook hands before parting.

Peter had his secretary call Mr. Aenid to confirm their meeting.

It was another gray day in Washington. It had rained that night and the humidity was still high. Cephid and David were approaching the Bradford home. Both were slight of build, a little less than six feet tall, and appearing to be in their early thirties. There the resemblance ended— Cephid, blue eyed and fair-haired— had a Celtic appearance while David— brown eyes, black hair and a darker complexion— looked to be Mediterranean in origin. Both, with sharp features, would not be called handsome. Neither one would stand out in a crowd.

They stopped before the steps that led up to the house. "David, let me let me do the talking. I'll bring you into the conversation when we come to anything scientific. I'm glad you could fly in from Albuquerque for this meeting. I told Mr. Bradford of your association with Sandia Labs but nothing of your background."

"That's fine with me. My boss said someone from Washington had called requesting information about me. He said that he had praised me to the hilt. It's hard to hold back and just go along with the pace they're setting. At times I would just like to throw a blockbuster of an idea at them and see what would happen. But that would raise a lot of suspicion."

"Well, David, you may soon get your chance to speed things up if our talk goes well. Now, let's get this show on the road."

They climbed the short stoop to the doorway and rang the bell. Two men were conversing nearby. They assumed that they were part of Peter's security.

The door opened, "Good morning sirs." Manfred looked at them with a smile and raised eyebrows. Cephid explained who they were, and that they had an appointment with Mr. Bradford. "Come in please, we're expecting you."

Cephid and David stepped into the entry hall and were immediately approached by another individual.

"Gentlemen, I'm a security officer. I have to check you for concealed weapons."

Both men assumed the expected posture with arms raised. The officer frisked them and removed rather strange looking weapons from each. He gave them a disapproving glare but said nothing. Manfred, who had been standing to the side then ushered them into the library.

"Good morning gentlemen," said Peter Bradford as he rose. "I hope you didn't mind the search, just a routine precaution around here."

"Not at all, sir, we expected no less. Sir, this is David Standid, an engineer from Sandia Labs in Albuquerque, and I'm Cephid Aenid. We appreciate your accommodating our request for this private meeting. I'm sure you'll understand shortly our need for the utmost secrecy."

Peter smiled. "I have to say that I'm anxious to discover the nature of our meeting. Although space exploration isn't my bailiwick, I do have a good grasp of our program at NASA. Please have a seat."

Peter looked at his visitors more closely. Then a curious expression appeared on his face, as if he didn't quite know what was going on. He had never before experienced a situation like this, and he was in a dilemma on how to handle it. He decided to be patient and see how it played out.

Cephid sat down and leaned forward. "Mr. Bradford, what I am about to tell you will probably stretch the limits of your imagination, but let me assure you that I will be able to substantiate every word.

First, I did mislead you *somewhat* in indicating that I represent a foreign government."

Peter stiffened. Cephid continued. "I represent a people you have never met nor seen. This might sound like science fiction, but we are from another planet, not one in your solar system, but one in the Milky Way Galaxy. If you recall your astronomy, we are on the Orion spur, the same as your Earth. We are further out on the Spur than you, in fact, about four light years distant or 24 trillion miles."

Peter looked bewildered and pale. Cephid continued. "We have been on your planet, Earth, for about 35 years, studying your people, cultures, and languages, everything to better understand your ways. We felt we had to do this before contacting you to help bridge the gap between our civilizations. It's just now that we feel confident in contacting you and making our presence known."

Peter, pale but with some of his composure returning, said, "How could you arrive and be here this long without our discovering your presence?"

Cephid smiled. "Our civilization is much more advanced than yours, perhaps by a millennium. Our stealth technology is far superior to yours, so it wasn't difficult to come here undetected. However, remaining undiscovered has been more of a problem. We have made contact with some of your people over the years, and they have remained silent at our request. As you can see from the two of us, we raise little suspicion; we try to remain plain, just a part of the crowd so to speak. David, here, has worked at Sandia Labs in Albuquerque for a number of years without raising any suspicion. He remains rather aloof and eccentric to help conceal his real identity, but his resourcefulness has been a boon to the company which has earned him considerable respect."

"This is really too much for me to handle." Peter held his hands up. "Why are you here? What is your purpose? I presume you don't have dishonorable intentions or you wouldn't be sitting here now."

"Sir—" Cephid paused and looked at David who gave him an encouraging smile. Peter was still looking pallid and uncertain. "We are a *peaceful* people and we mean you no harm. Earth is the first planet on which we have found an advanced form of life in our galaxy similar to our own. Later, we can give you a detailed description of *our* planet and people."

Still looking stunned, Peter's color was starting to return. Cephid continued, "Before I go further, I want to give you a message from our leader, President Palid Lindid, which should help calm your anxiety. Perhaps that's where I should have started. But first, for many centuries now we have invested considerable time and money in exploring our galaxy, particularly around our own solar system, but now we are ready to expand our efforts further out into space— as shown by our being here. In this effort we have decided it would be advantageous to have satellite stations some distance away from us from which to expand our search. Earth presents an *ideal* first station. Our leaders want to offer the United States the chance to work with us in this effort. This would be a great advantage to your people in that we would give you the benefit of our advanced knowledge. That is the message— to invite your country, and hopefully other nations on Earth, to participate with us in the peaceful exploration of space. " Cephid paused. He could see that Peter was sweating, and wanted to say something.

With his voice rising, "I'm not sure that we want to make this great jump into the future. It could be very upsetting to many aspects of our life. People might not understand what's going on, or even want to undergo these changes."

"We have thought of that. Our intention would be to do this gradually. We could monitor how these changes are affecting your people, adjust accordingly, and back off as necessary. Our intention would be to initially concentrate on our space program and the technology involved, which wouldn't directly affect the lives of your general population, but we would keep them abreast of our progress. This would give them an idea of what they can expect in the future that would affect them more *directly*. We know that education of your people will be an important part of any transition to a more advanced society, especially if the process is sped up."

Cephid could see that Peter was becoming more relaxed. At that moment he got up, went over to his desk, and picked up his pipe. Cephid waited, presuming that Peter needed some time to think. Having filled his pipe from the humidor on his desk, Peter picked up a lighter, lit his pipe, slowly sucking in his breath to get the tobacco started, all the while staring at Cephid. Peter then ambled over to a window and stood looking out. He gave a barely audible grunt, turned and retraced his steps to his Morris chair. "This is the strangest story, by far, that I have ever heard in my life. But ... somehow I believe you."

"Let me give you a little more information about us to make you feel more comfortable. Later, we plan on showing pictures, videos, anything you request to show you what our planet and life are like. You'll find us quite different in many respects, but on the other hand, you'll see that we share many of the same qualities and interests."

"Our planet is called Xyrpta." He pronounced it X-erp′-ta. "We have a solar system similar to yours. Our planet is almost twice the size of yours. A total of ten planets circle our star. Our population is now *half* the size of yours. Unfortunately, we went through a war where we lost many people. That was two and a half centuries ago, and we have now recovered physically but not population-wise. Xyrpta is essentially one country with many states. As we became more globally oriented, our countries slowly combined to form our present single, *unified* nation. We are a free people. Our leaders are elected, but I have to say that our present rulers have been in office for a considerable time. However, as you'll see, it's quite *different* from your government, perhaps an advancement that you'll eventually undergo. We have a strong military but use it now for defensive purposes. Because of the prolonged war, we give defense and security the *highest* priorities, so that we will never again have to go through a devastating war experience."

It was apparent that Peter wanted to interrupt. "Why did you pick the United States, and what do you expect from us?"

"You are a super power in your world, and your government and people are the most like us. We're asking your country to join us in this space project. However, we realize that this will likely become a *global* effort, requiring the help of many other countries. You appear best suited to accomplish the goal of establishing a unified global program with which we can work."

"That's a tall order. As you probably know, virtually all the countries in our world are *fiercely* independent. I don't know that we can expect much in the way of cooperation."

"We looked at the excellent cooperation that exists internationally among your astronomers and astrophysicists. In science you already appear to have a good start. I think that, when other countries see what we have to offer, they will want to climb on board."

"Well, we'll have to see. One aspect that'll be difficult, I'm sure, is the politics that will arise from this situation, particularly in the present, when one party is against anything that the other party favors no matter the goodness of the cause. I know that we'll have a difficult row to hoe."

Peter took advantage of a break in conversation to ask if the gentlemen would like some coffee or tea. Both declined but Peter asked Manfred to bring in coffee none-the-less.

"Sir, we have another surprise for you, the last one today I assure you."

Peter said wryly, "I don't think you could surprise me any more than you have already," He showed a little smile. It was obvious that Peter was starting to warm up to these two gentlemen. David had said not one word, but he had nodded in agreement and smiled appropriately in support of everything said by Cephid.

"I don't know about that, but I'm sure that this'll be the second biggest surprise of your life." Cephid gave a reassuring smile. "I believe I mentioned that, while on earth, we have tried to adapt to your way of life, so you would be more accepting of us. One of those ways is our appearance. On Xyrpta we have humans but they look significantly different— which I'll get to later. We have four extremities, two eyes and a nose and mouth like you. However, both David and I are *not* human. It took us nine years to travel from our planet to yours. That would be impractical for humans. Although we traveled to your Earth, we have no realistic way of returning home." Peter frowned. "To put it bluntly, both David and I are what you would call robots (bots), but of a *very* advanced nature."

Peter blanched, put his pipe down, and leaned forward. He said nothing, just waited. This explained his initial uncomfortable reaction on meeting these gentlemen. They had seemed strange, not real, in a way he couldn't explain.

Cephid continued and said, "David, show Mr. Bradford your middle finger." David grabbed his left middle finger with his right hand and bent it. There was a sharp crack. David walked over to Peter and showed him his finger lying by itself in the palm of his right hand. There was no blood. Peter swooned. David then took the finger, snapped it back in place and rubbed it for effect. Then he showed his hands to Peter. Both appeared whole.

Peter said, "This could be just a charade. He has an artificial finger. I saw no blood or even a wound."

"David, stand up and take off your coat and shirt."

David did so, which showed a lithe physique but lacking in detail. Cephid turned him around so his back faced Peter. He ran his finger over David's back, pushed on the area, and it popped open as if on a hinge.

Cephid said, "Mr. Bradford, come over here so that you can see the inner workings of an advanced robot."

Peter rose gingerly and took a few steps, "My God, it's a circuit board."

Cephid explained, "It's similar; we're made of an advanced, light, very strong metallo-plastic material. Our joints, facial and other motions are controlled by nano- motors. Our limbs and joints can accomplish every movement that yours can and then some. Our most advanced part is our brain. I think that you'll agree that our conversation, bot to human, has been as good as what you could expect between two people. But we do have some limitations— no rib markings, our fingers show no creases, we have no whiskers and no hair on our bodies except on our heads. If you look closely, you'll notice that our face can smile but can do little else; our eyes have irises and pupils but don't change size— they are actually cameras which send pictures to our brain."

"We bots were made in the image of the humans on Xyrpta, and that's how we appeared when we arrived on Earth. It was then decided that it would be best if we appeared more like you Earthlings, believing that this would make us more acceptable to your people. We sent back to Xyrpta details of your human's body, and they in turn, configured a new bot made in *your* image. We eventually were able to produce these bots here on earth in a laboratory we had set up. The end-product stands before you. I came from Xyrpta and looked like an Xyrptan, but then I was reconfigured in an Earthling's image. Bots back home are mostly left to look like machines, metal and plastic, but some of which are given thinking skills."

Cephid closed David's port and asked him to redress.

Peter sat down and put his chin on his hand. His brow furrowed. "I just can't believe that you aren't human. It boggles my mind. You are very intelligent. You speak well … I think that I'm likely in a dream and that I'll awaken shortly."

"You're in no dream, Mr. Bradford. You're on the verge of a *great* adventure, more than you could ever dream. You have within your grasp what no one before you has ever experienced— an opportunity to bring to your people a *millennium's* worth of advancement in *your* lifetime."

At that point Manfred came in with coffee and some sweets. "Do robots eat and drink?" Peter asked, raising an eyebrow to them, while helping himself to a cup of coffee.

David answered, "We need neither food nor liquids for sustenance. Our energy is battery-powered and long-lived. However, we can both eat and drink so as to appear sociable. In the end we have to flush our system of the debris."

"I have to end this meeting shortly." Peter shook his head. He had been running his fingers through his hair and it stuck out oddly. "But, first, I have two last questions. How did you arrive on our planet?"

Peter noted that their speech was without emotion and was mechanistic. "The type of space ship we use is determined by the load and whether it's live or inanimate. In the early years the Xyrptan Space Agency sent exploratory missions to your planet because our studies suggested that life existed here. When this was verified, we initially came in a small spaceship that was similar in some respects to what your NASA uses, but with significant differences, which we can describe later. Our initial visit was to set up a virgin outpost so we brought just the bare essentials— a dozen bots in storage. Bots and the equipment were packed together like *a can of sardines*. They remained inert during the trip, and then two were activated to land the ship. Subsequently, our spaceships arrived fairly regularly over the years until we had built a rather large compound, much like a human's ranch. If all goes well, I'm sure that you and your friends will eventually visit us. It will boggle your mind."

"My last question, where do we go from here? Do you have directions from your leaders on how we are to proceed?"

"We would like *you* to organize and set up meetings with the appropriate sources in your government to facilitate accomplishing the goals we mentioned. With your stature and your broad contacts, we felt that you would be in a good position to do so. We need you to convince your people of our good intentions and of the value of our project. Once you have the attention and approval of your government, we expect that they will contact other countries, perhaps through your United Nations, to get a global initiative started. A lot of ground work will have to be done."

"I took the liberty of telling our president of this meeting but no one else. I have videotaped it too."

Cephid nodded approval.

"I'll talk to him and send the video over for his viewing before I meet with him, which will be *soon* in view of the importance of our meeting." Peter rose signifying the end of their session. How do I contact you, your people, and your government?"

"For now all communication should go through me. I'll be in contact with our leaders to inform them of what we accomplished today. I have what you would call a *photographic memory*. My superiors can download your words and my retained pictures from my brain that will be as accurate as your videotape. In addition, they will have the benefit of my thoughts that transpired during our conversation. We can't give you access to our communication system, as yet, but I expect that this will occur eventually if everything goes well. You can contact me at this number," and he handed Peter a card.

I have one last question. Michael, my nephew, first contacted me and said you were *good* friends. Does he know that you're robots? Does he have knowledge of your mission?"

"Yes sir. Michael has been my closest human friend on earth, and he has been an *invaluable* contact for us. He knows that I am a bot, and he is aware of our mission. We think very highly of him. If we can move forward, we expect that he could be an important intermediary."

Cephid smiled. "I'm sure you'll have difficulty persuading your people that this is all true. David has a gift for you and your people."

David handed Peter a bar of metal, measuring about 4x1x1/2 inches.

"This is a piece of metallo-plastic material. Among its many unusual properties is its strength *which* is much stronger than anything you have on Earth. Give it to your scientists to analyze. I'm sure they'll be astonished. Whatever happens, whether we are able to move ahead or not, it's yours, and we'll give you the formula and how to produce it to show you our good intentions. It's no small gift."

They all moved into the hall where the security guard was waiting. He handed them their weapons.

"I can't resist asking one *last* question. As you might imagine, now that I am beginning to accept all that you said, I have a thousand and one other questions. How many of you are on Earth, and have any of your humans arrived, or do they plan on coming to Earth?"

"We have no humans here nor do we have any intention of making that move in the near future. We have about a hundred bots on Earth, mostly in your country, but also some abroad. You are the only government we have contacted so far. We plan to contact others eventually, particularly if our talks don't go well. Our humans do travel to neighboring planets but they do not engage in more distant space travel. Bots can do a better job without the care of a living person and all that entails."

Manfred opened the door. Peter said, "Gentlemen, I'm at a loss for words to describe your visit. I expect that we'll see each other soon," Peter had a big smile on his face. Cephid and David returned the smile. No one thought it necessary to shake hands as they departed.

Attack

Peter called the president at Camp David immediately after the meeting. "We just completed our meeting, a really *remarkable* session. I'm sending a video over to you by courier, so you can see it as soon as possible. You'll have a hard time believing that the two men I met are robots. They came from the planet, Xyrpta, in nine years, which is 24 trillion miles from Earth. "Their mission is to entice us into partnering with them to explore space. After you view the video, I'd like to meet with you to prepare a response."

"I'll set aside time tomorrow. And tomorrow is my birthday, Peter. You wouldn't be trying to pull an elaborate birthday hoax on me would you? Mary will call and give you a time for the meeting. I know you'll keep this under your hat for now. If this got out before we're prepared, it would cause worldwide confusion. This boggles my mind as it must yours."

"Sir, I couldn't come up with a hoax this elaborate."

The President's secretary called Peter's number shortly thereafter. Manfred took the call and said to Peter that a meeting had been set up for two days later.

On Monday Peter went into his office early. Michael had been on his mind last night. He couldn't wait to talk to him about the bots. Manfred had made a copy of the video, and he wanted to view it again before he called. He was still amazed at the events that had transpired just two days prior.

His secretary got through immediately. "Michael, I'm glad I was able to reach you so quickly."

"I left word for them to put you right through whenever you call. I'm sure you have many questions. Cephid called me yesterday and said that everything had gone well. I hope they didn't disappoint you." Michael gave a little laugh.

"On the contrary, it was the biggest surprise of my life. How long have you known them?"

"Cephid contacted me and several scientists around the world several years ago. Since then, he and I have become good friends. He's almost like a brother. I've met several of his fellow bots, and they are just as remarkable."

"Can you tell me anything further about them, about their quarters here, or about their civilization? I'm meeting with the President shortly, and any additional information would be appreciated."

"Sir, I'm sorry. They requested that I give out *no* information. They want it all to come from them. I suspect they don't want any distortion caused by a third party."

"Michael, the red light on my phone is blinking. I have an important call coming in so I have to go. Nice talking to you." Peter clicked to the other line.

"Sir, you have an incoming call from the President's office." Peter's secretary sounded worried as he clicked to another line to hear the President's secretary.

"The President wanted me to call and make you aware of an incident occurring *right now* at the airport. You can catch it on TV." She hung up.

Peter reached for his TV paddle and turned on a local TV station.

Cephid had accompanied David to the Baltimore-Washington airport that morning where he was going to catch a plane back to Albuquerque. He wanted to talk to David about their meeting two days before. Cephid had paid the taxi driver and the cab was just pulling away. As it did so, a black limousine slowly approached on the other side of the street. Both bots were always hyper-vigilant of their surroundings and kept an eye on the approaching vehicle. When it was abreast of them, an arm protruded from the rear window, and shots were fired at them. Cephid and David both instinctively ducked behind a parked car as bullets whizzed past them. The limo braked, and three men jumped out. With weapons drawn, they raced to nearby parked cars. Shooting continued as Cephid and David drew their weapons and returned the fire. The few passersby ran for shelter.

Cephid fired and a thin stream of blue light arced sideways around one of the vehicles. Cephid heard a yell. David fired his weapon and a shooter lurched from behind a car and fell to the ground. The third man started running toward the limo which had started moving. The bots withheld their fire to avoid hitting pedestrians in the park behind the runner. As this man ran— he looked to be Chinese — he hurled something across the street. Cephid dove for the ground and David landed on top of him.

As the car sped away, an explosion erupted close by that shook the ground. Cephid heard a grunt from David and he became a dead weight on him. He crawled out from underneath and surveyed the damage done to David. It was considerable. A finely striated, cream-colored gel-like material gaped through a large opening of what remained of his head. Cephid realized that it was a wonder that he, himself, still remained intact. He had some tears in his clothes and a few lacerations to his artificial skin but no internal damage. On the other hand, it was clear that David was irreparable.

By this time a crowd had started to gather and gape. Sirens blared in the distance.

Cephid reached into David's armpit and pressed a button. David slowly began to vaporize, a wisp of smoke emanating upward.

Two bodies lay on the walk across the street. Cephid ran over to them, checked their pockets and removed what looked like billfolds from each of them. He rose and began walking away. He glanced across the street. David had completely disappeared. He heard gasps from the small crowd that had gathered. Several yelled at him to stop, but he didn't. The last thing he wanted was to be here when the police arrived. He caught a taxi, and as they pulled away, two police cars passed them. The cabby asked what had happened. Cephid said he thought there had been a robbery. He returned to his abode uneventfully.

Peter saw the scene after the attack and heard the newscaster describe what had transpired. One passerby, who had remained hidden nearby, described what he had seen. The eerie part was the description of the body disappearing. The newscaster gave him a dubious look.

Perturbed, Peter did not know how this would affect their plans. He would have to contact Cephid to see if he was all right, and ask who the attackers might be.

As soon as Cephid returned to his apartment, he checked the billfolds that he had confiscated from the dead thugs. They contained only a driver's license and a few bills. He suspected that the licenses were forgeries. He wondered who they could be and who had sent them. Then there was the Chinese man who had escaped. This was very worrisome. Their well-kept plans for secrecy appeared to have been breached.

Next, he would need to notify his superiors of the recent events. He went into his home office, which consisted of a small room with a chair and desk. A laptop sat on the desk, which, in turn, sat on a black box. He had a multi-tasking printer, a router and a small TV. He sat down and removed what appeared to be an inkpad from the drawer of his desk. He opened the pad, put his index finger into a groove, and then remained silent for over fifteen minutes. He was downloading the recent happenings from his brain to his superiors via a sensor connecting his brain and index finger. This was a task he did each evening, but this was a special circumstance necessitating an immediate communication. In turn, he could expect instructions on how to proceed.

Not long afterward the phone rang. Cephid could see that it was Peter Bradford. "Hello, sir, I expected that you might call."

"Cephid, are you all right? I was just watching TV about an attack at the airport. The report was so extraordinary that it made me think of you guys. A bystander said that an injured man— who appeared to have been shot— was attended by his friend. He said the injured party disappeared in a wisp of smoke. I heard another witness give a similar story, but he said that the body appeared to have risen and gone to heaven. He thought maybe it had been the second coming and resurrection of Christ. The newscaster surmised that both reports were unreliable. Having just met the two of you, I suspected otherwise."

"They reported that there were two dead bodies, but so far there has been no identification and the attack remains a mystery."

"David and I were attacked. This came out of nowhere. David was destroyed, and I had to make him disappear to remove any evidence of our presence. However, someone else knows that we're on Earth, and that's quite disturbing. I've contacted my superiors, and they have their suspicions and will investigate. The two dead men appeared to be no more than thugs, but a third man, who appeared to be Chinese, got away. It's clear that David and I were the intended victims of the attack. I frisked the two bodies and found only billfolds with a little money and driver's licenses that I suspect are forgeries. I'll turn the billfolds over to you, and you can turn them over to the police. However, I hope you can keep us out of it for now."

"Cephid, does this in any way change our plans? I have a meeting scheduled with the President this afternoon."

"My superiors said to proceed as scheduled."

"I'll do that. Are you in any immediate danger?"

"I expect that the danger for me has increased, but that's part of my job and shouldn't be your concern. To give you some peace of mind, David will be resurrected, just as that passerby conjectured. He'll be reconstituted identical to his original state in appearance and intellect. That is one of the wonders of being a bot. We are created and destroyed at the whim of our superiors. David will return to work at Sandia in Albuquerque in a few days. No one there will ever know that he had this mishap. His memory and the work he was doing will be unchanged."

"You guys amaze me. I have to go now. Stay in touch." Both parties disengaged.

"Right this way, sir. The President will see you now."

"Good afternoon, Peter, it's good to see you." George motioned to a chair. "Have a seat. I viewed the video. I had to replay portions of it several times. It was unbelievable—science fiction becoming reality."

"George—you can see that I'm flustered by this whole affair," and Peter looked embarrassed. He still felt uncomfortable sitting in the Oval Office, where so much history had been made.

"I talked to Michael after the meeting, and then I called Cephid about the attack at the airport. Both have further convinced me of the sincerity and seriousness of the Xyrptan commitment to their mission. It now appears that security has been breached, which makes it imperative that we move ahead with some urgency."

The President said, "I think that the next step should be to get the appropriate cabinet members together—State, Defense, you of course, and Ben at NASA. How do you feel about having Cephid present at this first meeting?"

"I think that there will be a lot of doubt, even after they've viewed the video, so I believe it would be important to have him there. He's quite diplomatic. I suggest that Michael be present also, as he's known Cephid for some time, knows about the mission, and would add credibility to Cephid's remarks.

"I agree. I'll see that all participants are briefed and see the video beforehand. I feel we shouldn't release this information to the media yet. I expect there'll be a leak, but let's decide at the cabinet meeting what our next step should be."

"Sounds good to me. Would you like me to contact Michael and Cephid?"

"I'll set up the cabinet meeting and let your office know the date and you can contact the boys— I mean the boy and the bot."

"Just one thing more, sir. What did you think about the attack at the airport? Have you had any follow-up? I talked to Cephid afterwards. He was pretty calm, but then I guess bots don't have emotions. His fellow bot, David, was killed—or rather, I should say destroyed. He vaporized him so there'd be no remains, and walked away. No one followed him and he got away before the police arrived."

"I had my office query the police. They are dumbfounded and have made no sense of the affair so far. The two dead thugs didn't appear to have been shot, but showed signs of having been *electrocuted*, like being hit by lightning. The disappearing body was written off as hysteria. The detectives had no reason to believe otherwise. There are no leads on the perpetrators of the crime. The police contacted Homeland Security because of the strange nature of the crime and the possibility that it was a terrorist attack. They'll keep our office informed."

"One last point of interest—David is to be *resurrected,* so to speak. These bots have something on us humans. He can be replicated in very little time. He'll be back at work at Sandia within a few days. No one will know that he isn't the original." Peter shook his head. "George, I don't believe that the world we lived in a few days ago will ever be the same." Peter sighed and rose to leave.

"Peter, look at it from the standpoint that we'll have lived in two different eras in one life time. That's extraordinary."

That evening Cephid contacted his superiors to see if they had any further information about the attack. He looked on his point of contact as a superior because this was from where his instructions emanated. However, his orders actually came from staff members of the ruling council in Xyrpta who were in daily contact with the compound that served as the Xyrptan headquarters on Earth.

Cephid's construction, particularly his brain, was produced at the highest level, higher than any of the other bots on Earth. He was to be the ambassador to the people on Earth, beginning with the USA. He was instilled with the history of his own planet and the policies of its government. He had extensive knowledge of the sciences and the military. In the time he had been on Earth, he had stored up an amazing amount of information about his new surroundings, receiving a considerable boost from the massive data bank of information already accumulated at their headquarters on Earth. He could regurgitate this information ad infinitum. Much of this latter data had been filtered through an Earthlings brain to give it some interpretation, so it wouldn't be so sterile and less meaningful. The human source was unknown to Cephid.

Little more was known about the attackers. However, Cephid's superiors wondered why someone would want to attack them. They were suspicious that another extra-terrestrial group might also be on Earth. The prime suspect was the nation with who they had been at war several hundred years ago. They would have the technology. If they were the culprits, this would be a serious handicap to their galactic efforts. The highest investigative priority would be given to this problem. Cephid was to be on guard and to inform them immediately of any further contact and of any new suspicions.

The day of the cabinet meeting arrived. Cephid had contacted Peter after their last meeting to suggest that David be invited to attend as well. He would be invaluable in answering scientific questions that were sure to arise. Peter had referred this recommendation to the President's office, and they had replied in the affirmative.

The bots had been instructed to enter the White House by a back entrance so as to not attract attention. They were met by security, and after a check for weapons —they were wise enough on this occasion to not bring anything questionable with them— they were escorted to the waiting area outside the room where the cabinet was meeting. The secretary said that the session had started, and they were to wait until called. The wait was a little more than an hour. They assumed that there were a multitude of questions to be answered before they would be invited to participate.

Cephid started updating David on his recent talk with Peter.

The receptionist interrupted and said that they were to follow her. They entered a small conference room in which eight people were seated.

Peter rose and approached them, extending his hand. "It's good to see you both again," and he gave David a quizzical look, not being sure he was seeing the same David as before. "Mr. President and cabinet members, I have the pleasure to present to you the ambassador from Xyrpta, Mr. Cephid Aenid," —he extended his arm toward Cephid— "and his scientific advisor, Mr. David Standid, who presently works as an engineer at Sandia Labs in Albuquerque."

The president rose, strode toward them both with a smile, and extended his hand. "Welcome gentlemen. It's a pleasure to meet you both under this extraordinary circumstance. Let me introduce you to the others present—Ms. Madeline Albrecht, Secretary of State." She did not rise, but smiled and gave a slight nod. "Mr. Herbert Alton is Secretary of Defense, and Mr. Doug Black is head of Homeland Security." Both nodded.

These officials were being quite guarded which Cephid could understand.

"Mr. Ben Walton is head of NASA. I imagine that you and David will want to get together later to compare your respective space programs." Ben rose and came around the table. "Cephid, it's a pleasure to meet you." After releasing Cephid's hand, he clasped David's hand with both of his and gave him a hearty shake, "David, we can't wait to get together with you and glean as much information as we can from you. I'm sure you'll be an *invaluable* source of information." David returned his smile but said nothing.

The president, who had remained standing, continued. "And of course you know Mr. Bradford, our National Security Advisor, and I believe you already know Michael Thornberg." With the introductions completed, the President invited their guests to sit down.

Herbert Alton, rose, as with a last minute thought, and came over to shake hands. This tall man who was on the beefy side had thinning reddish hair to accompany his reddish face and bulbous nose. When he smiled, you received no clue as to what he might be thinking behind his secretive eyes. He gave Cephid a perfunctory handshake, turned to David and clasped both hands over David's. All the while smiling, he squeezed David's hand tighter and tighter.

David was surprised and initially didn't know how to respond. Although David had a thin build, he was, after all, a robot with greater than human strength. Pain was not a sensation he felt, but he could sense pressure. He responded in kind, thinking this was appropriate. He gave more than he received, continuing to increase the hand pressure, all the while realizing that he could crush the hand within his grasp. David observed that the secretary's smile turned to surprise, and then he began to turn pale. David, let up on his grip. Herbert frowned, turned, and returned to his seat without a word.

As the bots sat down, the president began. "Gentlemen, I believe this is an historic meeting. We are on the verge of events that may even be of the same magnitude as the discovery of the New World. The decisions we make in the near future may well determine the course of events for the next *millennium*. As Peter elaborated earlier, it is clear that we are no longer alone in this universe or for that matter even in our own galaxy. We've looked for life outside our planet, and so far have found none. But life has found us. I know you have your doubts, as did I, so Misters Cephid Aenid and David Standid are here to answer your questions. But first, Mr. Aenid, would you please tell us briefly what you told Peter at your meeting the other day? They have already seen the video of your meeting, but I would like them to hear a few words from you."

Cephid had watched the president intently and was impressed by his demeanor, poise, and understanding of the situation. He rose and walked to the head of the table. Part of the training instilled in him was the ability to present before a group in a professional manner—either formally or informally— and in a comfortable style that would ingratiate him to his audience. He hoped that he would be understood as if he were another Earthling speaking to one of their own. The last way he wanted to come across was appearing condescending.

Cephid smiled. "Gentlemen, I bring greetings to you from our President Palid Lindid and our Supreme Council on Xyrpta, a planet some 24 trillion miles from Earth. We've been on Earth for thirty five years. Our reason for secrecy until now was to indoctrinate ourselves with your ways so that, when we did reveal ourselves, we would be more acceptable. We did not want to appear to be a foreign alien aggressor invading your planet. On the contrary, our mission has always been a peaceful one. If anything, we have been overly cautious. I am the ambassador from Xyrpta to your people. As you have been told, and as you have seen from the video, both David and I are robots. The fact that we are here should show you how advanced we are in technology and space exploration." Cephid could see that he had all of their rapt attention. "It took us nine years to make the trip from Xyrpta to Earth. That precluded any living being from our planet making this trip. Fortunately, our robotic development has kept pace with our space program to make all this possible. I am sure that Mr. Walton can appreciate that fact."

"Our early assessment determined that your country would be the one to first contact on Earth. Our headquarters is on your soil—the location, for now, I can't say. As we get to know each other better and come to some agreement, I'm sure that most of our doings in your country, as well as those on Xyrpta, will become transparent to you."

"Our mission here is to further our space program. It makes more sense to move further out into the galaxy from satellite centers that are closer to the next inhabitable planet than to attempt to do so from one central source. To us you present an *ideal* first satellite center. As time goes by, we presume that *together* we can establish other such satellite centers as we find more inhabitable planets."

"You are now aware of other life in the universe. You can't go back. You must move forward. There are likely other alien forces out there that are *not* friendly. Several centuries ago we fought a prolonged war with a group within our solar system, so we know this to be true. Fortunately we won. At your present stage of development you would present no contest against such an enemy. We feel that it's fortunate for you that we are here and willing to join and help you. The benefits versus risks are weighted heavily toward the former. And, yes, we would act to help protect you in the event that alien forces attacked you, providing we can come to some agreement. As we go forward, we are asking you to join us as a partner in this mission."

"I'll answer your questions now."

There seemed to be some confusion, and some loss for words. Everyone looked around as if looking for clarity. The president felt the temporary paralysis and intervened. "Cephid and David, perhaps you could demonstrate your uniqueness to us as you did for Mr. Bradford."

Both bots rose and took off their coats and shirts. Cephid opened David's rear port, and on this occasion, David did the same for Cephid. David explained what they were seeing. There were '*oohs*' and '*ahs*' and a '*My God.*'

Secretary Alton asked, "How do we know that the rest of you is not human?"

David turned Cephid around and opened a panel in his upper abdomen.

"So what?" He raised his eyebrows as if he weren't impressed.

David reached under Cephid's right armpit and appeared to press something. Cephid slowly disappeared. Gasps rose from those present. David was the only one who could still see Cephid. He pressed again. Cephid slowly reappeared. Mr. Alton's jaw dropped. He said nothing further. Cephid and David then closed each other's ports and re-dressed.

Cephid went over to Ben Walton and asked, "Sir, may I use you as a subject for a few moments? No harm will come to you."

Mr. Walton hesitated but then agreed. Cephid placed his fingers on the subject's temples. He looked upward for perhaps a minute, this latter for affect. He then let go and said, "Any fortune teller would give her right arm for this power. I could give you various details of Secretary Walton's background but then you would say that I had prior knowledge. However, only Mr. Walton knows what he and his son discussed last night. Isn't that right, sir?" Ben nodded in the affirmative. "As a senior at Madison High School, he received an A in American History, a B+ in English, an A in Science and a C+ in Advanced Algebra. You asked him about the C+ because he had a B+ the previous semester. He explained that he had missed several critical classes on which they were tested and so didn't know the material. He said that it wouldn't happen again. You were satisfied with his answer and you congratulated him on his effort. Is that true?"

"I can't believe it. It's true in every detail."

Looking worried the president asked, "Can you read all of our minds?"

"Only if I have physical contact with both temples, so that I can detect the brain waves, which are quite weak. I have sensors in my finger pads that pick up impulses from your brain and transmit them to my brain for interpretation. This is a unique feature. I am the *only* robot on Earth with this ability."

David continued answering Secretary Walton's question. "We discovered life on Earth a little over a hundred years ago. Several exploratory missions later we substantiated that life existed here— not far different from our own human beings on Xyrpta. We embarked on a mission to establish a colony on Earth. A freight ship was sent containing a dozen bots to set up an initial outpost. From there we continued to build a compound that is now fairly sizable. Most of our facilities are underground, similar to what we have constructed on Xyrpta. We have about a hundred bots on earth. At our main facility, we are now able to construct bots without having to ship them in from Xyrpta."

"Initially, it took us nine years to make the passage from Xyrpta to Earth, but now we can make it in a little over seven years. Our speed out in space was 300 million miles per hour (mmph) on our initial voyage. Now it's almost a hundred mmph faster. That's about as fast as we'll be able to go, considering that were going about 80% the speed of light."

Walton's eyes bugged out and his jaw dropped. He was realizing how far behind his space program was compared to that of the Xyrptans.

Secretary Black had a question. "Although you say you've come with peaceful intentions, I have to point out that you are *alien transgressors*. You came *without* our permission. You are illegal immigrants. On top of that, I presume that you have *usurped* some of our land, public or private, I don't know."

Michael Thornberg interrupted, "I have known these bots for several years and I can verify their good intentions. They are *not* humans, so I don't believe that you would consider them illegal immigrants. I realize that nothing of this nature has occurred here before, so I imagine that some sort of legislation will have to be passed to make their presence legal. Furthermore, not long after they made a home here, they purchased the land that they now occupy."

Black said, "I'm not trying to be difficult. In fact, I realize the *importance* of this event, but I want to point out that we'll have to make a place for robots of this complexity in our society. This will *obviously* require new legislation—as you mentioned Michael."

Secretary Albrecht took the floor. "Mr. Aenid mentioned that other bots are present in other countries so this is an *international* matter. Rather than each country devising its own rules it might be best to have this matter taken up by the United Nations to first give us some guidance in coming to a global solution."

Walton said, "Since space programs and robots are most closely aligned with our jurisdiction, I suggest that our agency be the contact with the Xyrptans. In that way we'll know where they are and who to contact."

The president took command. "Ben, I think that's a good idea. However, I have done some thinking on the matter, and for now, I would like to have Peter take charge and be our contact with the Xyrptans. Later, I believe we should transfer jurisdiction over to NASA. Is there any disagreement?" The president looked around. He saw Herbert wiggling in his chair with a frown on his face, but he said nothing.

The president looked at Peter for comment.

"Sir, thank you for your trust. Now we need to determine our next step."

"I was just coming to that. The media will most likely have heard rumors of what has occurred, so our next step should be to have a press conference. I don't know whether or not it would be possible, but it would be ideal if we could bring the humans on Xyrpta into the conference." The president looked at Cephid for an answer.

"Sir, it wouldn't be possible to have human Xyrptans here because of the distance involved and the time for such a trip. However, such an endeavor might be possible in the future. Our only means of communication now is via our radio telescopes that can accommodate video."

"Understood Mr. Aenid. Please make the appropriate inquiries of your people and let me know if and when we can begin communications. I believe that this has been a good first meeting, and I want to thank everyone in attendance for their civility and interest in what is an historic event. Until we make an announcement to the media, I ask you to not make this information public, though I expect that you'll be discussing these events with your staffs. Peter, may I see you briefly before you leave?"

The meeting broke up, though some of the participants stayed behind to discuss what had just transpired. The President beckoned to Peter. They would have to create a new organization that could communicate directly with the Xyrptans. As he had said earlier, he wanted Peter to take charge of this organization. He would have direct access to the president at all times and would work closely with NASA. Since Michael was the closest earthling to the bots, he should be an integral part of the team too.

Peter was perplexed, "Sir, wouldn't this be more appropriate for the State Department? Madeline might feel we we're stepping on her toes."

"Right now State has as much on their plate as they can handle. I don't want to upset their apple cart. I foresee this being a big job. It might even require your taking leave from your position for a while. Peter, I believe you're the best man for the job now. I need someone I can trust implicitly."

"I can't see my being able to do this job and being National Security advisor too. I suppose I could beef up my staff and delegate much of what I do. I have some excellent people who can take over many of my duties." Peter was known for his decision-making prowess. "I'll do it. There's urgency in this matter, so I'll get on it right away. I'm sure I can find people who will be excited to be a part of this new team."

Several of the cabinet had gathered around Cephid and David. More friendly now, they were peppering their guests with questions. Peter thought he should rescue them, and see that they got on their way, while they had still made a good impression. Cephid looked relieved as Peter approached, "Gentlemen, I'm afraid I have to get these two on the way to their next appointment."

As they exited the room, David asked if he and Cephid could talk with him privately for a few minutes. Peter said they could use a small room just down the hall. After they were seated, Peter said that the president had just put him in charge of organizing a division that would deal with the Xyrptan issue exclusively, and that they would be closely associated with NASA.

Cephid and David nodded approval.

David said, "Our superiors have entrusted to me a task that involves you, Cephid. You'll understand in a moment. This information was *just* downloaded to me last night." David stopped for a few seconds.

"As you know, since we have been on Earth, we have made contact with certain humans over the years whom we felt could be of benefit to us and whom we felt we could trust to keep our presence secret. One such individual became so enamored with much of what we were doing—particularly within his field of astrophysics— that he said he would do anything to have access to our astrophysicists' knowledge. At this time we were interested in delving into the intricacies of the earthling mind and how it differed from our own. Our Xyrptan humans came up with the idea of exchanging information—if the human would allow us to download some of his memory and thought processes we would upload some astrophysical knowledge to him. He agreed and the transfer was carried out four years ago. We gave him enough information to make some good advances in his own area. We have since analyzed his mental function and have detected significant differences in how we and earthlings process information. It recently was decided that it would be advantageous to upload some of his mental functions into a bot's brain on Earth to compare the two. A bot would process information using his normal mental functions and then process the same information through his human thinking for comparison. Thus, we could better determine the rationale of the earthling mind. In your position, Cephid, you have more contact with earthlings than anyone else. As ambassador, it would be advantageous for you to be able to assess their reasoning. You were chosen to be the recipient of a portion of this human's thought processes. This transfer was done within the past year, but without your knowledge."

"This individual is an American with a genius IQ. In addition to his field—in which he is recognized as one of the top researchers— he has broad knowledge in many areas. It's expected that in the near future you'll meet each other."

Cephid smiled and with a little chortle said, "I've realized that I had something foreign instilled in my brain, but I have never been able to quite put my finger on it."

David said, "That network has never been turned on, but our superiors plan on doing so tonight. The idea is that you'll have the best understanding of the Earthling's mindset, and that'll help us in dealing with them in the future. You'll have, so to speak, half an Earthling's and half a Xyrptan bot's brain." David smiled while Cephid looked somewhat dazed.

"David, I understand your position. I thank you for your thoughtfulness in explaining my new heritage."

"And Mr. Bradford," David continued, "It's our feeling that this individual, as well as Cephid, should become members of your team. Both he and Cephid should be able to provide valuable insight into bridging the gap between our two civilizations."

Peter stood. "That certainly sounds like a good idea. However, I want to meet this person before including him on the team. Cephid, please contact your people as soon as possible about our holding a joint press conference." With that, they parted ways.

A week passed. Peter formed a skeleton team, and he was starting to flesh out the rest of the group. They were to be called the Xyrpta Commission or XCOM for short.

The press conference was in the works. Cephid had consulted with his superiors, and he had replied to Peter that the Xyrptan Supreme Council asked that a series of questions be submitted to them so they could respond via a video. This was necessitated by the great distance between the two planets, which ruled out any two-way conversation. The US government could then view the video and respond with further questions. The Supreme Council would add these questions and their answers to the original video. The video would show the Xyrptan Supreme Council answering these queries. The Xyrptans requested permission to show this video to their countrymen too.

Alien Sacrifice

This was the day that Cephid was to meet his human counterpart. Leaving his new quarters— that had been provided by the US government—he took a taxi to a small government building. Going in the side entrance, he walked down a hall to a door that was numbered. He knocked. The door opened. A young, stocky individual with blue eyes, sandy hair and an engaging smile stood there. Cephid was immediately drawn to him. He grabbed Cephid's hand and began shaking it vigorously. "I'm Eric Russell and you must be Cephid Aenid."

Taken a little aback, Cephid acknowledged this reception with a nod and a smile. Placing his hand on Cephid's back, Eric gently guided him into the room and to a chair. Sitting across the table was an attractive female—dark brown shoulder-length hair and soft brown eyes above glasses that were perched almost on the tip of her nose. She had a pleasant smile. Eric introduced her. "This is Robin Armstrong, a robotic engineer from NASA."

Cephid extended his hand across the table to Robin who grasped it firmly.

Eric sat at the end of the table facing both Cephid and Robin. "May I call you Cephid?" Not waiting for a reply. "I've wanted to meet you ever since I heard that you had received some of my mental functions. In return, I believe you're aware that I received some advanced information from Xyrpta on my area in Astrophysics."

"Eric, just last night I was downloaded with some of your memory. It's a lot for me to process, and I can't say I've been able to accomplish much so far. Perhaps you could relate some of your memory and we can see if it corresponds to what I have."

Eric smiled, and a litany of information came forth: where he attended school, his family, and experiences.

This all seemed familiar to Cephid, and he expressed this fact to Eric. They both smiled, realizing that there was a bond developing between the two of them already.

Robin interrupted, "Cephid, I feel I should explain why I'm here. As Eric mentioned, I'm a robotic engineer at NASA. I've known Eric for quite a while, but it was only this week that he told me about you and the existence of extraterrestrial life on your planet. I asked Eric if I could tag along to meet you. I find it hard to believe that you're a robot. You certainly are far ahead of us in robotic development and space technology. Could you give us some details about your robot program?"

What followed was a rather detailed explanation of robotic engineering over the past few centuries on Xyrpta. Cephid was a first level—the highest order of robot— with the ability to think and make judgments and decisions. The lowest orders were non-speaking robots that did menial tasks.

"Bots are used for housekeeping duties, waiters in restaurants and for many other service tasks. We can be made very strong, agile and fast. One of our specially constructed robots could easily out pace and outdistance any of your world class runners. Our most remarkable feature is the mental capacity that can be instilled in us, and that can be at a number of different levels." Cephid let all this information sink in. Robin seemed astounded by this level of sophistication.

Eric mentioned that he had just met Peter. He felt that he had made a good impression on him because he had been asked to join his new team. Taking a leave of absence from work would allow him to work closely with Cephid and help him in the many meetings that were to come. To have someone of Eric's stature to help him was very welcome.

Eric stood abruptly, "I have to go, got another meeting scheduled. Cephid, why don't we get together for dinner this evening? We can get to know each other better." Bending over the table, Eric wrote down the address of a restaurant on a slip of paper.

Cephid was a little taken-aback. Eric was abrupt, loud and very self-assured. He could accept this manner. Dinner was fine even though food was not a necessity for a bot. The ability to eat had been built into his innards, just a holding tank, which could be cleansed as needed, sort of like flushing the toilet.

As he entered the restaurant, Cephid saw Eric and Robin conversing and enjoying cocktails. He had thought that it would be just him and Eric meeting to get to know each other better. Standing and watching them for a few moments, he wondered if they were romantically involved as they appeared to be intimately enjoying each other's company.

Eric stood up to greet him, and Robin extended her hand. "Cephid, can I order you a drink?"

"A Vodka Martini, dry, would be fine." He could act as humanoid as they, and he gave them a big smile. He thought that they might be role-playing, ingratiating themselves to him for whatever reason. He felt they were trying to force a friendship a little too fast instead of letting it grow with time, but then time was of the essence. He did not believe that they were aware that he had no feelings. Instead he had been given thirty or so signs that would reveal a human's feelings and emotions; facial expressions, body and extremity positions, and movements that would signify mood and attitude. He, in turn, could then respond appropriately.

After passing a few pleasantries, they ordered. Cephid requested his usual Caesar salad and as an entrée, a New York strip steak, rare, with baked potato and veggies. He kept it simple, trying to appear sufficiently sophisticated but not overdoing it. He could not appreciate the food but he had to partake as a sign of friendliness.

Robin appeared particularly interested in Cephid's order, "Can you digest food?"

"I can eat just as you can, but I have no digestive system. My eating is just a formality. I'm afraid that the food will leave me in the same state it entered." He did not go any further, feeling it would be embarrassing to them. Robin nodded, accepting his explanation.

Eric cleared his throat. "My meeting this afternoon was with Peter Bradford and some others who will become members of the team he is forming. Robin, this is confidential so don't repeat any of this." He looked intently at Cephid. "Shortly, the President will hold a press conference to inform the media and public of the existence of extraterrestrial life and of the presence of aliens on Earth. Two days later he'll address both houses of Congress, at which time he'll explain how we became aware of Xyrpta, and he'll show the video from your Supreme Council on both occasions. He'll then explain the position of the US government and the tentative plans for the near future."

"The President would then like to introduce you as the ambassador from Xyrpta and would like to have you say a few words. Then he'll let the press ask questions. How does that sound to you?"

"It seems everything is coming to a climax very fast, but then that doesn't appear to be something that can be avoided. I'll check with my superiors for their approval and guidance. Remember, it takes forty eight hours to send and receive a message back from Xyrpta."

"Do that and let me know ASAP. Here's my number." Eric handed Cephid a business card. "Word has already leaked out about your presence here. There's already unrest apparent in the populace, which is the reason for expediting the announcement."

"One thing that we're deficient on is knowledge of your planet, and your people. Can you fill me in? I believe that I have some of this information instilled in my brain from the transfer, but I'm not sure how accurate it is. I have never had any of it verified."

"Perhaps the most startling difference is that our humans' skin color is light green. This is due to the presence of chlorophyll which allows for photosynthesis as an extra energy source. Our atmosphere is similar to yours— principally nitrogen and oxygen— and we use the latter, as you do, as a staple of life."

"Our people are shorter than yours, averaging about five feet tall. This may be due to our planet being larger than Earth—with the higher force of gravity you might expect less stature. Our bodies are lithe with virtually no obesity. We're quite strong and agile. We're a very active people and engage in sports as much as you do. Compared to your people, our humans' have larger ears which are pointed. Their facial features— such as their cheek bones and chin—are sharper while their nose is flatter. Our hands and feet have four phalanges—our ancient ancestors did have five digits, but the small finger and toe disappeared with evolution."

Cephid paused to let this information sink in. Both Eric and Robin had paid rapt attention.

"Our planet is not unlike yours. We have abundant water, a large part of which is salt water. We have tall mountain ranges and abundant vegetation that is quite different from yours. We have forests and wild animals—the latter you would find fascinating as compared to yours. Your biologists would have a heyday on our planet and so would ours on yours." Cephid grinned and gave out a little human-like chortle.

Robin was fascinated as she watched Cephid talking and eating at the same time. He just swallowed his food—the teeth were just for appearance.

A commotion was occurring toward the front of the restaurant. A man came running down the aisle toward their table. He dropped a package at Cephid's side. The runner turned into another aisle and ran out the way he had come in. Cephid jumped up, retrieved the package, and while curled up over the parcel, ran toward the kitchen where there were no people. A muffled explosion occurred. Bits of metal, plastic and clothing went flying throughout the restaurant. Scattered cries came from the patrons as they crowded the exit. Luckily, the restaurant had only been partially full, so there was little danger of one getting trampled. A few curious individuals remained at some distance. The couple closest to the explosion had been blown off their chairs. The woman staggered to her feet still dazed while the man remained splayed out on the floor.

Eric jumped up. "Robin, you stay here." He ran to where the remains of Cephid lay amid a scattering cloud of smoke. Clearly he had given his '*life*' to save them all. Body parts were scattered around the restaurant. His torso was gone. Portions of his extremities remained.

Turning to the couple nearby, Eric could see that the man on the floor was stirring. The woman gestured toward the floor. "Please help my husband."

Eric bent over him. Gasping, the man sputtered, "My chest hurts. I think I'm having a heart attack." Acting quickly, Eric called 911 on his cell, explained the situation, and requested an ambulance and the police.

He then returned to check on Robin. She was all right. "Let me do the talking when the police come." He turned and looked around the restaurant to see if anyone else needed help. Several people were standing around talking and observing the goings-on. None appeared to be in distress. Eric could see that a few had been hit by flying debris from the explosion— some minor cuts and bruises. One man came over to offer help, but Eric assured him that they were OK, and that he should remain to inform the police of what had happened. He explained that the individual that had saved them all was a robot, and not human, so no life had been lost.

Sirens stopped abruptly outside the restaurant. EMTs rushed in and over to the man who was lying on the floor. After checking his vitals, they placed him on a gurney and took him out of the restaurant accompanied by his wife. The man gave a feeble wave of his hand toward Eric as he was wheeled out. Eric gave a little wave back. Another EMT checked with the other patrons to make sure none needed attention. Shortly after, the ambulance siren began blaring as they took off.

The police had entered and were talking to the owner who had raced out of the kitchen on hearing the explosion. Eric went over to help. The officer shifted his attention to him. "So, what happened here? It looks like a bomb went off." Sticking out his hand to shake, as he was wont to do, the officer looked at Eric and ignored the hand.

"Someone dropped a package on the floor by our table. My friend"— he pointed to Robin— "is a robotic engineer, and we were having dinner with one of her advanced robots. Sensing that the package was dangerous, he picked it up and ran with it toward the kitchen where no people were sitting. Within seconds there was an explosion. He sacrificed himself for our safety. It's lucky we had him with us."

They walked over to check out what was left of Cephid. The officer appeared skeptical of Eric's explanation of the events that had just transpired, but on seeing what was left of Cephid he said, "Well I'll be damned." Bending over, he picked up a piece, put it down, and repeated this maneuver several times. He looked up, "How long did it take you to make this thing?"

"Years" Eric wanted to say the least possible so as not to incriminate himself with too many lies. He couldn't tell the truth about aliens coming from Xyrpta before the news was officially released to the public. "Officer, I presume that you'll collect all the pieces of the robot for your investigation. Treat them carefully. We'll want them back to study ourselves." The Xyrptans, themselves, would surely want the remains back, particularly the head. He knew that they would not want any of their advanced technology to get out in this way.

"Where's the head," asked the officer?

In the moment that he had checked on Cephid, Eric hadn't noticed that the head was missing. He now looked around the scene; then he looked over at Robin. With a hand to her stomach, she was on the verge of throwing up. At her feet was Cephid's head which must have separated from his body and either flew or rolled to their table. He rushed over. "So sorry Robin." He bent over to pick up the head.

"Ah, ah, don't touch! This is a crime scene." The officer further admonished Eric by raising the open palm of his hand toward him.

Eric thought it best if he and Robin left the scene as soon as possible. He didn't want to answer any more questions. He asked the officer for his name and how he could be reached. In turn, the officer called over another policeman and asked him to get the same information from Eric and Robin.

The formalities being over, Eric beckoned Robin to exit the restaurant. Before doing so, he reminded the officer to be careful of the remains of Cephid. It was imperative that they get the body parts back for their *own* investigation.

Their car was parked nearby. Once inside, Eric pulled out his cell phone and clicked Peter's number. Fortunately, he was able to reach his office and explain to Peter what had just occurred.

"Eric, you did well. Your little lie about Cephid was brilliant. That should keep the press quiet until we hold our press conference. Unfortunately, that might have to be postponed because of Cephid. I'll take it from here."

Before they drove away, Eric noticed that several policemen were interrogating people in the crowd that had gathered outside the restaurant.

After hanging up, Peter sat for a while, pondering what his next move should be. He needed to contact the Xyrptans to apprise them of what had just happened. The only other alien, besides Cephid, with whom he had contact, was David Standid. He recalled that he worked for Sandia Labs in Albuquerque, so he had his secretary track him down. He was surprised that David did not seem upset by the demise of Cephid. Also, he needed the name and number of someone in authority whom he could always contact, someone at their Center who was aware of their activities and negotiations. David said he would make the appropriate call immediately.

Next he contacted the President's office to alert them of the situation. He thought that the FBI should be informed and should get involved in the investigation. They would be the best source for damage control. He called an old friend high in their hierarchy, filled him in on the attack at the restaurant and requested that they give this matter their immediate attention at the highest level of secrecy. The remains of Cephid were to be impounded and to be examined by no one.

No sooner had he hung up than the red light on his phone began blinking. His secretary said that a Mr. Maxid was on the phone. The call was urgent.

"Hello, Mr. Maxid, what can I do for you?"

A voice with authority replied. "David just called and informed me of the events concerning Cephid. I am the CEO of our Center for Earth Affairs—C-E-A-F." He pronounced it *seef*. "It's most urgent that we obtain the remains of Cephid as soon as possible. It would be catastrophic for us, and for you too, if his technology were to leak out, especially to sources that are unfriendly to you and us. And please, just call me Maxid."

"Maxid, I contacted the FBI and asked them to impound the remains and to leave them untouched. Can we send the remains to you?"

"I would rather pick them up. If you'll give us permission and the location, we'll pick them up tomorrow. Every minute that those pieces are out of our hands is a considerable danger."

"I'll get right on it and get the information to you as soon as possible. This situation now poses a quandary for us, as we had planned to hold a press conference to announce your presence on Earth. Cephid was to participate as you probably know."

"The ambassador being a robot helps. We can reconstruct Cephid at our Center, so you'll not recognize any difference, just as we reconstructed David. From what you said, his head is still intact. That will help. We can restore all his brain functions up to the day of his demise using the information that we download each evening. If we're lucky, we can retrieve his activities for the day of the attack from his head. This will take several days after we get the pieces back. We'll start immediately to rebuild him using the templates from his original construct. If you can postpone the press conference for a few days, he should be ready to go again."

Peter gave a sigh of relief. A few days postponement would be acceptable, particularly in view of what had just happened. "That sounds excellent. I'll get to work on my end. I believe that we should be in touch *daily* until everything's done."

"Mr. Bradford, I'll give you my number. You can reach me at any time, 24/7. It's a pleasure talking to you. We've heard many good things about you from Cephid, and I'm looking forward to meeting you in the near future. We'd like to have you and some members of your team visit our facility. I'm sure you'll be fascinated to see what we do." There was a click ending the call.

No sooner had he hung up than his secretary told him that the president's office had called, and would he call back as soon as possible. He did just that and waited several minutes.

"Peter, I see you've been busy. What is this affair about Cephid getting *blown up*?"

Peter smiled at his description, and related the events of the past 24 hours. "This puts a crimp in our plans. Maxid said that he could have a facsimile of Cephid made within a few days, but perhaps, we should go ahead without him. What do you think?"

"I was just having the same thought. This most recent incident will be in all the papers. If the media should connect this with the attack at the airport, or rumors of aliens on Earth, we could be in trouble. Let's go ahead with the press conference and do it, say, the day after tomorrow. You make the arrangements."

After hanging up, Peter allowed himself a big sigh. It looked like things would work out. If by some miracle Cephid could make it too, they could inject him into the program at the last minute. He then had one of his staff arrange with the FBI the packaging and pickup of Cephid's remains.

Later the president's office called to say that the press conference, to avoid being on a weekend, would be moved two days, to a Monday. That might make it possible for Cephid to participate in the conference.

The next day Maxid called to say that the new Cephid was under construction, and they anticipated that he would be activated and on his way to Washington by Sunday. Anticipating when Cephid would be home, Peter called his apartment and left a message that he would like to talk to him Sunday evening to confirm his presence at the news conference on Monday. That left a lot of arrangements to be made between now and then.

By Sunday, Peter was mired in details relating to the conference, so he asked Michael to meet with Cephid. He felt that a face-to-face meeting would be best to confirm that they were dealing with a good facsimile of the original Cephid.

A call Sunday evening indicated that Cephid was home, so Michael took a cab to his apartment. Cephid greeted him as if nothing had happened. "Ceph, I can't believe it. You look the same, talk the same— identical in every respect to the original blonde, blue-eyed bot I knew."

"I'm the same. I even remember the explosion in the restaurant, but I still have a stomach ache." Cephid smiled.

Michael look startled. Then he realized that Cephid was joking so he gave a little laugh in return. "My head was decapitated, but my brain was intact, so they were able to rescue the memory from the day of the explosion and incorporate it into my new brain."

Cephid's apartment was sparsely furnished. There was nothing of a personal nature in view.

They went over the part Cephid would play in the news conference the next day. The bot had been prepared by his superiors for the event already. He briefly summarized his remarks to Michael's satisfaction.

"Eric sent us a report of your conversation at the restaurant before the explosion. You were telling him about the people on Xyrpta. Can we continue that conversation, and I'll forward the information on to the other members of the team?"

"Certainly, I told them about the characteristics of our people and was beginning to tell them about the physical layout of Xyrpta. We have a solar system similar to yours—one sun and ten planets. We have two moons. We mine minerals from two of the planets."

"I believe that I related previously about our 30 year's war. More than 50,000 years ago, our people evolved from two evolutionary groups similar to your Neanderthal and Cro-Magnon man. One group, the Praetor, is our enemy. They have a green skin, like us, but they are taller, have a longer head, but a short forehead, and much more body hair. They are very aggressive and war-like. We had many skirmishes with them before the big war. They are very intelligent and *almost* as advanced as we. The war could have destroyed our entire population. As it was, we lost almost half of our people as did they. After *we* won the war, and after much deliberation, it was decided that the entire Praetor population should be banished to another planet. That was a major undertaking and it took 10 years to accomplish. Although their planet has a harsher environment than ours, they have survived and flourished. They are still our enemy, and we watch them very closely.

Many of our cities were destroyed. As a consequence, our cities are now largely subterranean. We have no skyscrapers. Transportation in the cities is public and virtually no private vehicles are allowed. We have rapid transportation both within and outside the cities. We have gardens both on the surface as well as subterranean. Our manufacturing centers are all well outside the city limits. This keeps our cities clean. As you might expect, our defenses are quite strong and should protect us from any attack from the Praetor." Cephid stopped, thinking that he had given Michael an adequate beginning to understanding his people and how and where they lived. He looked at Michael expectantly.

As he rose, Michael smiled and gave Cephid a little pat on the shoulder. "That's a good start. I can't believe I'm seeing you as you were before. I wish we humans could be reincarnated. That was a heroic thing you did in the restaurant, and we all greatly appreciate your sacrifice. I'll see you tomorrow at the press conference." He said goodbye and left.

Press Conference

Michael rose early the next morning. He had to be present for the preparation of the conference. Peter had asked him to manage this task. He was surprised to see Cephid present so early. Cephid had brought several bot techs with him to help in their end of the setup. He was impressed by the fact that the bots worked very well with our human techs and knew what they were doing.

An hour before the conference, Eric and Robin had arrived. David joined Cephid in setting up, and Maxid had arrived to observe the proceedings. The president was said to have arrived also. They were set to go.

The huge conference room was packed with standing room only in the back. The fire standards for occupancy were being ignored.

The president strode in from the back and proceeded down the aisle, stopping occasionally to shake hands with a few of his acquaintances. As he stood at the lectern, he smiled and looked over the sea of faces. He took a sip of water and smiled, thinking of the importance of the speech he was about to give.

"Members of the press corps and guests, this is an historic occasion that we will all remember for the rest of our lives. You have recently heard rumors of aliens being on earth— unconfirmed reports that have recurred every few years since World War II. Well, it's no longer a rumor. *It's a fact.*" The president paused.

A swelling of voices erupted, many in dismay.

"I am both happy and *relieved* to announce that they are friendly, and they are with us today." He nodded toward Cephid, who sat on stage with Peter and his team. Cameras flashed en masse, momentarily blinding those on stage. There was a rustling in the crowd, and one could sense a general uneasiness.

The president went on to explain from where they had come, how they had arrived, and how they had made themselves known to him and his staff. He said little else, leaving this for Cephid and the video for elaboration. He mentioned that the earlier sightings of *UFOs* could have been those of these aliens, and that the stories that had emanated from Roswell, New Mexico and environs now showed *some* truth.

It flashed into Michael's thoughts that, if this were true, then the Xyrptan headquarters was likely in that area.

After making a few closing remarks, the president introduced Cephid as the ambassador from Xyrpta.

Cephid strode confidently to the podium, smiled and began. "I bring you greetings from our President, Palid Lindid, our Supreme Council, and the people of Xyrpta. We have been among you now for some 35 years, preparing for just this moment. You may ask why we took so long to announce our presence. The reasons are several. The great distance between our planets consumed much time for travel, it taking us some nine years to make our first trip here. Thereafter, we brought in freighters of equipment and materials regularly to establish our first colony. After obtaining some basic information about Earth and its people, we conveyed this information back to our leaders—humans who look slightly different than you—who gave us direction for our next steps forward. It was determined that it would be best, if we first appeared to you *less* alien and more like you, so you would find us more acceptable. Thus the 35 years to accomplish this feat and arrive at this day. Our leaders have prepared a video to show you what we are like, and particularly, to explain why we have come here to seek your help in accomplishing our mission." Cephid spoke slowly and convincingly. The restlessness in the crowd had largely dissipated.

"Before we start the video, I need to make clear to you who I am. Yes, I am the ambassador to you from our planet, Xyrpta. You see me appearing the same as you, both in body and clothes. Thus you see me as one of you. But you must know. I am not human. I am a robot." Now there was a loud murmuring of discontent. "You find that hard to believe, I'm sure. However, our civilization is a thousand years more advanced than yours. The most remarkable feature of our robots is their artificial intelligence, which closely mimics the earthling brain and allows me to speak and think *almost* as well as you do."

There was a further stirring in the crowd— a mixed reaction of believers, non-believers, and worriers.

"The video that you are about to see was produced just a few days ago by our government. Your leaders submitted a list of questions to our Supreme Council, which they have endeavored to answer. In turn, our leaders submitted a list of questions to your administration which we expect you'll answer and make a video of your people and land to show *our* populace. This video shows you our people, the cities we live in, and some of the characteristics of our land. It ends with an explanation of why we have come to Earth, and the mission we hope to accomplish with your help. Lastly, I would like to assure you of our *peaceful* intentions." With that Cephid turned to sit down. There was a smattering of applause; the crowd seeming to still be largely in a state of shock.

The video began. During the showing, there were 'oohs,' 'ahs,' a *'God help us,'* and an assortment of remarks showing surprise and disbelief. It wasn't so much the words as the appearance of the Xyrptans that seemed to unsettle the audience.

The presentation ended with the Xyrptan president explaining their mission to seek the help of Earthlings in extending their space exploration program.

After the showing, the President rose and returned to the podium. "I'm sure there will be a few questions," and he smiled. Virtually every hand in the audience went up. He chose a news reporter from CNN whom he knew. "John, you start."

"Mr. President, how could aliens be present in our country for 35 years without our knowing it?"

"We heard the rumors, as did you all. We checked them out and didn't find any convincing evidence of their presence. Could we have done a better job of discovery? Probably! Next question, Paul?"

"Should we require some further proof of the intent of the Xyrptans besides their word?"

"We've only been aware of aliens on Earth for less than two weeks. There are many questions to be answered. I don't have an answer for you now. Spencer?"

"Sir, what'll happen if we decide to not participate in the mission with the Xyrptans? Will they go away?"

"The Xyrptan ambassador has told us that, if we decline their invitation, they are prepared to present their mission to other countries. Also, their request was not only to us, the US, but, if we go forward, the next step would be to go before the UN to request their help in seeking the support of *all* the countries on earth. The return for us, and especially for the poorer countries, could be enormous in the form of technical and other help to further our economies. Jim?"

"How many robots are there in our country? And should they be allowed to *roam freely*? And, a second question, if I may, how are we to distinguish a robot from a human?"

"Good questions, Jim. To my knowledge there are about sixty robots in the U.S. and a fewer number in other countries around the world. As to their roaming freely, that's a question that we have yet to answer. How we're to distinguish them from humans, I don't know. However, it seems logical that some distinction should be made? Tom?"

"Sir, if we were to join them in their mission, what would be the expense to us?"

"I can't answer that question at this time, as we have no details of what might be expected of us, but I believe that many countries would participate to share the burden. Mary?"

"Mr. President, are there women robots and, if so, what purpose do they serve?"

The President turned to Cephid and asked if he would answer that question. "Miss, we don't have female robots on Earth, as it seemed unnecessary up to this point, but if we did, they would serve in communications and diplomatic appointments as I do. On Xyrpta we have many women in government positions. We have female robots that do about the same tasks as men, though I have to admit that for home duties the preponderance is female. For serving in the military, robotic soldiers are asexual as are policemen and fire fighters. There's no need to dress these robots up as humanoid, so they are easily recognized as bots."

The President pointed. "Samantha, one last question."

"Sir, will Xyrptans be coming to Earth, and will we be sending astronauts to their planet?"

"I don't see that happening in the near future, but if and when the time to travel between our two planets shortens, I can envision it." The President held up his hand, signaling that the press conference was over. "One last thing ladies and gentlemen, I believe we are beginning an historic journey never before seen in our world. We have much yet to learn about our new and distant neighbor. Be assured that we will keep you informed with the utmost *transparency* as we go forward."

As the President turned and began his retreat, an aide stopped him and gave him a note. He unfolded it and read it with consternation showing on his face. He looked into the audience. The room was clearing rapidly as the newsmen clamored to leave to use their cell phones and get the news to their respective outlets. One individual stood alone in front. As the President looked down, the man gave a slight wave of his arm. The President jerked his head toward the stage. He looked and saw that Peter had not left and was still talking to some of his new staff. "Peter, come over here," he called out.

As the two men approached, the stranger held out his hand to the president, "I am Maxid, the CEO of the Center for Earth Affairs from Xyrpta." He turned to shake hands with Peter, too. "I'm very sorry to intrude like this, but it's a matter of the utmost urgency for both our nations but more so for you. If we could meet in private for a few moments ...."

The President signaled to one of his security guards standing nearby and asked that he find a room close by where they could meet; immediately. The guard consulted with another member of his team and shortly they found a room down the hall.

After they sat down in what was someone's office, the President began, "OK, Maxid, your note said that a major terrorist threat was imminent," He looked intently at Maxid and wondered if he could trust this robot.

"Sir, one of our bots in Beijing stumbled upon an alien *unknown* to us. Ever since the two events involving Cephid and David, and then the explosion involving Cephid, we've been looking for an explanation. It was clear that these occurrences were aimed at us and *not* at you. That narrowed our investigation and made us suspicious that we may have been followed to Earth by our neighbors, the Praetorians. Because we have heat built into our framework, when our man in Beijing came upon an individual *not* emanating heat, he immediately became suspicious that the person was a bot. Our man followed him to his dwelling, and he was put under surveillance. We have a device that can deactivate a bot. When he went to an area where no one else was around, we immobilized him, and now have him in our possession. He is being shipped here, and we should have him at CEAF in a couple days. From his brain, as well as from his assembled parts, we should be able to tell if he's Praetorian. If our suspicions are correct, and he's Praetorian, then we have to presume that they are here for a *hostile* purpose. Just as they tried to destroy us on Xyrpta several hundred years ago, they may have a similar intent here."

Both the President and Peter appeared appalled and at a loss for words.

Maxid continued, "Mr. Bradford, I suggest that you send some of your team to our Center for the interrogation. Depending on what we find, we can then plot a course of action. I have to warn you, if our suspicions are correct, and the Praetor are truly here, then an attack is likely to occur for which you are ill prepared. I'll contact our Supreme Council to alert them of this occurrence and get their input. That's about all I can say for now."

The president cleared his throat, "This is devastating news. I hope your suspicions aren't correct. Let us know as soon as you have an answer. Is there any way that we can talk directly to your leaders?"

"I believe so. I'll check on that, too, and let you know."

The president rose. He and Peter left, followed by Maxid. Peter and George were in earnest conversation as they walked away.

Alien Threat

Peter's burgeoning team had taken residence in a new, as yet unnamed, government building. Some of his employees had been transferred here. Cephid had been given an office, so that they would have contact with the Xyrptans at all times. A morning meeting was scheduled to make plans for the future and to inform team members of the future threat.

Introducing his team to the members of his staff who would be join-ing them was the first order of business. Brandy, a young lady endowed with a long neck, high cheek bones, and a sensuous figure, wore her bru-nette hair in a doughnut-type bun which went quite well with her large, round glasses, her plain white blouse and black slacks, as if she were trying to down-play her beauty. "Max" (short for Maxine) appeared the opposite—plain looking, short, and stocky. She was Peter's secretary, known to be extremely smart and quite efficient. She was devoted to Peter and had become indispensable. Cephid, Michael, and Eric were present. Eric had made a strong argument to Peter about adding a robotic expert to the team and had suggested his friend Robin for this position. Peter met with her, was impressed, and had added her to the team.

Peter looked up but said nothing until he had their rapt attention. "Since we've met the bots on our planet, events have been occurring rapidly. The latest is a *possible* terrorist threat from another alien force on Earth." He went on to explain what Maxid had told him the day before. Then he outlined the possible consequences.

Michael was shaking his head in disbelief while Eric stared intently at Peter.

"Michael has agreed to be my second in command. We have been asked to send a representative to CEAF, the Xyrptan Center, to observe the interrogation of the foreign bot. This is the bot that was discovered by the Xyrptans in China. This will be a great opportunity to see their Center and how it functions. Eric, I would like to have both you *and* Robin take on this job.

This will be a good chance for you, Robin, to get a heads up on how their bots are constructed and how they work."

A big grin broke out on Eric's face while Robin's jaw dropped in disbelief at being given this opportunity.

"You have to be on your way first thing in the morning. They plan to start interrogation of the foreign bot as soon as you get there." More mundane office policy completed the day's meeting after which they broke up.

Robin strode over and gave Eric a poke in the arm, "I can't believe it. This is the chance of a life time." Her grin was about as wide as her face could handle.

Eric patted her arm "Calm down girl! I'm as excited as you. We better get a good night's sleep. I'll see you at the airport in the morning.

Their eyes met as she sighed.

Eric was at the airport at 5 a.m. Robin showed up shortly thereafter having the same grin as the day before. Two men met them whom they assumed were bots. Little was said as they were led out of the airport to a waiting car. They were whisked a short distance to a waiting plane— a two engine jet, that was already revved up and waiting to fly. Climbing aboard, they took seats and buckled up as the plane began its taxi down the runway. A bot closed the door and took a seat across from them.

The window shades were down so Eric began to raise his to watch their takeoff.

The bot reacted, "Leave the shade down. You are not to know where we are going. Our flight should be about six hours."

Eric pulled the shade back down.

Eric and Robin were discussing the events that had brought them to the team. Eric called it, '*The Xyrptan Adventure.*'

"Eric, don't you wonder if the Xyrptans are *truly* our friends? I mean, can we really trust them? They may have an ulterior motive in befriending us. It could be just a ploy to catch us off guard," Robin said, glancing at the bot.

"I look at it as a probability—an eighty percent chance that they are being truthful and a twenty percent chance that your fears are correct."

"So, how do we verify their true intentions? Our only association has been with bots with no human-to-human contact. That gives me chills running up and down my spine."

"That's a good question. Let's look at what we know and then at what further we *need* to know to answer your question. Their mission—looking for partners to help them explore space— sounds plausible. Sending bots here and then waiting 35 years before contacting us, presumably to get to know us better, sounds a little strange, but doesn't sound like an aggressor. I understand that Michael has known them for a good amount of time, and as far as I know, he has seen nothing to make him distrustful. Then they found and informed us of the Praetor. We'll have to find a way to verify what they've been telling us. So far, our only contact has been with bots. We'll need to have contact with their humans, as well, before we can verify their true intentions."

Robin smiled as she looked into Eric's blue eyes, "What if the Praetor are friendly and the Xyrptans are the real enemy? How can we tell?"

"We know nothing about the Praetor, so we can't say. Perhaps we'll get an answer to that question when we get to CEAF and watch the interrogation. From what we've been told, the bots are able to communicate with their home base on Xyrpta. That's something we should be able to do as well. I think I'll raise my odds to ninety percent friendly and ten percent enemy."

"You're reassuring. I think I'll take a nap. It looks like a long flight." She turned her head, confirming that she wanted some quiet time, if not to sleep, then a time to think alone.

About two hours into the flight, the bot asked if they would like something to drink. Eric nudged Robin and repeated the question. "Water, please."

"I'll have coffee, black, if you have it." The bot nodded.

Robin stretched and looked at Eric. "That felt good, I feel refreshed. Do you think the bot heard what we were talking about?"

"I thought of that when we were talking and decided that it might be good if he did hear and voiced our concerns to his superiors." Undoing his seat belt and reaching into his trouser pocket, Eric withdrew a key ring, looked at it, and put it back in his pocket. "We're heading due west. With six hours traveling time I think we're headed for the Arizona/New Mexico/Colorado area."

Robin raised her eyebrows.

"I have a small compass on my key chain." Eric gave Robin a little smirk of satisfaction.

The bot brought their drinks and asked if there was anything else he could do to make them comfortable. Both said no.

Then looking at him quizzically, Robin wondered, "Eric, what do you expect to see when we get there?"

"Your guess is as good as mine, but I'm sure we're in for many surprises. They must have brought a level of sophistication with them that is far beyond what we could do. We need to be especially alert. I brought my digital recorder along to register what I hear and see along with my thoughts. I'll let you borrow it so you can do the same."

"Don't bother, I brought mine too. I even brought my Flip video recorder, but I can't imagine they'll let us take pictures. We should get together at the end of each day to compare notes. How long do you think we'll be there?"

"I don't know. I would think several days at the most. We all have a lot of work to do back home."

Finally, they could feel the thrust of the plane begin to descend.

On disembarking from the plane, they saw a crude runway carved out of a wooded area. After a short drive in the jeep that had picked them up, the bot carried their bags and led them into a large ranch house, very nice, but nothing out of the ordinary. They entered a small lobby which led to a rather large dining area, but otherwise there was nothing to suggest that this was a Center of any kind. They were given adjoining suites, which were well adorned, more than what the two of them had been expecting. After saying someone would be calling, the bot left.

Not long after he had finished unpacking Eric heard a knock on his door. Maxid introduced himself, and they proceeded to pick up Robin who was ready and waiting. "I want to show you our facility, but the Praetorian alien is here and I think that takes precedence, so we'll proceed to the interrogation."

They were led out to a waiting jeep. As they took off, Eric wondered about the bot driver's ability to negotiate the rough dirt road ahead. But his doubts were soon put to rest, as they expertly sped along the curving, rutted road. Twenty minutes out they came to a large barn-like structure. Though it looked weathered on the outside, once inside they were met by a modern-looking interior with offices surrounding a central pod. Maxid led them to an elevator that had no floor designations. On descending what felt like several floors, Maxid uttered instructions in a foreign tongue and the elevator stopped.

On exiting the lift, both Eric and Robin were startled to see a large room full of machinery manned by bots that were not covered by human-like skin but rather consisted of their bare essentials, rods and bars for extremities with hinged joints.

"This is our bot room where we assemble our people. There's no need to disguise the bots here as humans so we leave them *nude*." Maxid smiled at them, thinking that his last remark was funny. "We work 24 hours a day with no need for shifts. No one gets paid nor do we need to give them food or health or pension benefits; just a charge every month to keep them going. We are virtually a world unto ourselves." Maxid smiled at his guests open mouths and wide eyes. "Let's go over to the lab." He led them to a room off to the side.

On entering, they saw a body lying on a gurney with wires fastened to its head. His eyes were closed. He seemed unconscious or inoperative. He had been unclothed and he appeared almost humanoid, similar to the Xyrptan bots.

Maxid said, "We were able to disable him before he was aware of us in China, so we're expecting that we we'll be able to access his thoughts right up to the time he was zapped. So far, we've determined that he *is* from Praetoria. They are a formidable enemy, but at least we know with whom we're dealing and what to expect. An unknown alien would be more difficult to evaluate."

The technician looked at Maxid, who nodded, indicating that further interrogation was to continue. "If you have any questions, ask *me*. Don't interfere with the debriefing."

A lot of electronic equipment surrounded them. Eric presumed that everything was being recorded for later analysis.

The interrogator asked a question in a language that was foreign to both Eric and Robin. The Praetorian answered in the same language. He had awakened, although his eyes remained closed. Sidling up closer, Maxid whispered to Eric and Brandy that they could actually download the answers without vocalization, but they were doing so for their benefit.

The tech looked at Maxid, "Would you like a simultaneous translation into English?" Maxid nodded in the affirmative.

"What is your name and from where do you come?"

In a deep voice, "*I am Rastor and I am from the planet Praetor.*"

"What is your purpose on earth?"

"*We are here to befriend the earthlings.*"

"Why did you contact the dissident Chinese and not the US government?"

"*I don't have that information.*"

"What is your job here on earth?"

"*I am a cultural attaché*"

"How long have your people known of life on Earth, and how long have your people been here?"

"*I do not know the answer to the first question. We have been on earth for seven years.*"

"How long did it take you to travel from Praetor to Earth?"

"*Seven years.*"

"How many of you robots are on earth now?"

"*There are three dozen.*"

"When did you arrive?"

"*I arrived seven years ago.*"

"Then you were among the first to arrive?"

"*Yes, I was on the first spaceship.*"

"What are the intentions of your people here on earth other than to befriend the earthlings?"

"*I do not have the answer to that question.*"

The tech threw a switch that put the bot into a holding pattern. He turned to Maxid, "I think he's holding back some information. What do you think?"

"Look in your download and see if there's any evidence of encryption. If he was among the first group to arrive, I suspect that he's *not* a cultural attaché. I think we need to dig deeper." Maxid signaled that Eric and Robin should follow him, and they exited the room. "The interrogation will be going on for quite a few hours. There's no need for us to witness it all. I'll inform you of any further findings."

"What will happen to him once you've finished the questioning?"

"We'll send him back close to where we found him in a disabled state so his people will think that their lost contact was due to a malfunction. On occasion bots go haywire, and hopefully his cohorts will assume that's what happened to him. In addition, we'll insert our own device into his brain to monitor his activities, conversations, and thinking. Hopefully, his people won't discover it. He'll have no recollection of being here. His last thought will be that of just before we zapped him."

At this point the tech came out, beckoned Maxid to one side, and spoke to him quietly in what appeared to be their native tongue. Maxid nodded and the tech departed. Maxid smiled. "Apparently they found an encrypted area in the records, and they're going to try and break the code."

On returning to the lobby of their residence, Maxid left, saying that he would contact them later in the day. Robin and Eric agreed to meet in his suite shortly to go over and record what they had just experienced.

Robin knocked on the door adjoining their two suites, opened it, and without waiting rushed into the room—and into Eric's arms. She blushed. "Sorry, I'm a bit excited. Eric, do you think they would let me get a closer look at a robot to see how it really works?"

"I don't see why not. Ask Maxid when we see him. If we're going to work together, they have to let us in on some of their secrets. Otherwise, I believe, we would be very suspicious of them. I'm going to try and get some more information on my area of expertise too. That's the main reason I'm here. I see that's your motivation, too. But for now let's get down to business and compare notes on what we just observed." They exchanged views on their recent experience. Then they both recorded their observations and their interpretations.

Maxid called and asked that they meet him for a late lunch in the dining room.

After being seated by the waiter, Maxid asked what they thought about the interrogation.

Eric said, "It was interesting, but I hope they're able to get more helpful information out of him. I still can't believe how advanced your robotic technology is."

"It took us a thousand years beyond where you are to achieve this level of sophistication. I expect that with our help you'll make that transition *much* more rapidly."

Looking inquisitive, Eric said, "Maxid, perhaps you're not the one to ask, but I like to get answers from both sides of the equation. Being so human-like, don't your humans worry that the bots will try to take over from them? You have some major advantages—perfect memory, you can think, you can work tirelessly for indefinite periods, you don't need meals, you don't get sick, and your upkeep is minimal."

Maxid frowned. "That's a good question. As you've noted, we can think so we are aware of that possibility. However, our humans have put in several safe guards to prevent any insurrection. They have given us a service mentality, and like your soldiers, we are trained to be loyal and obedient. There are occasional insubordinations, but these are handled immediately, usually by death, which for us is disabling all our functions, such as you saw with the foreign alien. One advantage for humans is that they can *completely* wipe out the mental status of a bot, and then re-establish a new virgin one so the bot becomes usable again. An advantage for us is that we can be resurrected whereas you *cannot*." He smiled. "At home we have a bot museum where famous bots from the past are memorialized. Their 'brains' have been kept intact, so you can ask them questions and obtain an answer. For the most part, these are bots built with older designs that are now obsolete. It's a popular destination for our human populace."

Robin jumped in. "I was mesmerized by your bot shop this morning. Would it be possible for me to observe close up one of your bots being assembled?"

"I think that's likely. The Supreme Council has instructed us on what information we can release to you, and that is one area that is available.

I'll speak to the manager of the bot shop to arrange a viewing. The tech bots have only a limited mental capacity, so I'll have one of our IT bots sit in with you to answer any questions you might have. Perhaps we can do it in the morning. For the rest of the afternoon I want to show you our campus."

"While talking about your operation, Maxid, as you may know I'm an astrophysicist and my area of interest is string theory, particularly M-theory. I was downloaded with some information in this area a few years ago. I'm interested in extending that information. I'd be interested in talking to one of your experts about that."

"That's a possibility, but there may be a problem. I know *little* about M-theory, but I do know that our mathematics is far more advanced than yours, and you would have to become familiar with it to get an understanding of what progress has been made in the last thousand years. I'll check back home to see what they say about your interest."

At first Eric felt insulted that his mathematical skills were being questioned. But then he realized that a millennium separated them, and he might be offered help in bridging this gap. "Thank you. I'd appreciate any help you can give me. I'm sure Robin feels the same way."

Robin nodded vigorously in agreement.

"Well then, let's get started on our tour. Few outsiders have seen our facility though Michael saw our Center several years ago." Before leaving the building, Maxid stopped at the front desk and asked the clerk to page Torbid, one of their space pilots, and ask him to join them at what he called the Big Barn. They exited the building, climbed into a waiting jeep, and drove through a lightly wooded area until they arrived at a clearing that held a rustic, over-sized barn. On entering the building, they met Torbid who would take them on a tour of the building. A modern hanger lay before them and in the center sat two space vehicles.

The larger-appearing vehicle was disc-shaped, about 50 feet in diameter, while the other was cylindrical and more typical of what was used by NASA. Torbid explained that these ships were convertible from one shape to the other, even in space flight. The vehicles were composed of movable plates controlled by micro-motors, which allowed for change in position of the sections to alter the configuration. This might be compared to the movement of the tectonic plates in the Earth's surface. The rocket-type shape is used for take-off while the disc-shape is used in outer space. On entering the Earth's atmosphere the disc shape is maintained and used for landing.

Eric asked how the interior could be maintained during the transition from one shape to the other and how this would affect the humans or bots on-board. Torbid explained that the design allowed for the movement of walls within the vehicle, and as long as the flight personnel were strapped into designated seats, they were safe during the transition. This conversion could only be accomplished on the ground or out in space, but not in atmosphere where the force of gravity would preclude this change, causing free-fall of the vehicle, if such were attempted. Both Eric and Robin looked at each other in disbelief. Torbid saw their expressions and assured them that this did work, and that he had triggered this change on several occasions without mishap. He said that this type of "tectonic" engineering was common on Xyrpta and perhaps they would participate in a flight in the future where they could experience the transition. Torbid led them over to take a look inside the disc-shaped ship.

The vehicle rested on four struts. They climbed up a step-way to enter the ship. Torbid explained, "This is a freighter and not a transport or warship. It was first used to ship bots until we could construct them on Earth. Now it's used primarily to move equipment and materials."

The outer surface appeared smooth and uniform throughout with no apparent windows. On entering, however, Eric saw the windows. They were transparent and meshed seamlessly with the walls. Torbid explained. "The surface material is unique. In designated areas, the molecules in the material are aligned directionally to yield the transparency. The windows can be made larger or smaller by toggling a switch on the panel board. This material also gives the pilot the ability to zoom out for a panoramic view or zero in on an object resulting in a more rapid way of assessing and reacting to any external situation.

The control room was filled with panels showing a myriad of switches. Eric remarked that this appeared to be something out of a Star Trek movie. Being more practical, Robin asked about their power source.

"I can't give you any details. It's a process that we have been working on for almost a hundred years back on Xyrpta. I can tell you that it is the latest technology and allows us now to travel from Xyrpta to Earth in about seven years. You may have heard that it took us nine years to come here 35 years ago."

Robin wasn't about to give up. "But Torbid, we were told that we'd have access to *all* information relating to your space program and robots."

Torbid seemed at a loss for words momentarily. "All I'll say is that we now have an unlimited source of fuel that allows us to travel extremely long distances. *Running out of fuel* is no longer a worry." Torbid gave them a big smile.

It was, as if a light had just turned on in Robin's brain, "There's only one source that could fit that situation and yet I can't believe it—dark energy."

Torbid's face was expressionless. "Let's move on." It was clear that Torbid wasn't going to say anything further on the subject.

Robin gave Eric a quizzical look and he responded by saying softly, "We'll talk about it later."

Torbid went on to explain that they destroyed the freighters after arrival, since there would be no return trip. It was actually cheaper and quicker to build and send a new ship each time than to take seven years to return the ship for reuse. They had kept these two ships to be available for show. They had added some features to indicate how the ship could be adapted for human use.

They were shown a rudimentary galley containing a microwave, a sink, a refrigerator and a storage area for food. A small table and chair were hinged to the wall. There was a small closed off area for bathroom needs. A cot was hinged to a wall for sleep. It was obvious that these were bare-bone furnishings necessitated by the limited space available.

The last tiny area to view was a shop with tools. One had to assume that the ship, and even the bots might be in need of repairs.

Robin pointed out that there was room for only one human. Torbid explained that the humans could take turns. If each worked an eight-hour shift, one could sleep on his off time and another could read. They could actually accommodate three humans. Robin wrinkled her nose. Torbid smiled, "Of course, we bots need none of these facilities. That's what makes us *superior* for extended space travel." Robin saw his point.

They took a brief tour of the other, cylindrical, spaceship to show that the same rooms were present but in a different configuration.

Having completed their examination of the spaceships, they continued the tour. They were shown another building that contained a machine and carpentry shop.

The afternoon tour finally ended and the guests returned to their suites. Maxid left a message indicating that he would see them in the morning. Eric and Robin decided to meet for a late dinner. Right now both felt the need to record, think, and talk about what they had just seen.

"Dark energy falls into your area of expertise, Eric, so what do you think of Torbid's remarks about their power source?"

"He didn't say it was dark energy, but your guess might have been on the mark in view of his lack of a denial. But that's so far *beyond* what we know about dark energy that I'm at a loss to say anything. If it isn't the answer, whatever their energy source, it's far beyond anything that we have. Thinking realistically, though, their energy source most likely is some type of fusion process, but then their being a millennium ahead of us, perhaps that's archaic thinking on my part. It's obvious that we have a lot to learn from them. That's exciting."

The food at dinner that evening was surprisingly good. They began with cocktails and an appetizer followed by an entrée of Filet Mignon with assorted vegetables and scalloped potatoes accompanied by a marvelous Cabernet Sauvignon. They finished with Bananas Foster. Neither had talked about their experiences at the Center during dinner, feeling the need for a break. However, while indulging in after dinner drinks, their talk reverted to their day's experiences. The engineer in Robin showed as she talked about the bots and the spaceships. Eric was more concerned about the immediate future, especially the discovery of the foreign bot.

"I can't help but have a foreboding about their being *two* sets of aliens on earth, Robin, one supposedly friendly, and the other is said to be their enemy. The fact that the Xyrptans have been here for some time and are now befriending us makes it likely that they are sincere and truthful. Their presence here and their mission are believable. The Praetorians, on the other hand, are unknown and have been here for a shorter time *without* announcing their presence. It's unlikely that they have the same explanation for their secrecy as the Xyrptans, and it wouldn't be believable that they are here, too, to invite us to participate in space exploration with them. So, why their secrecy? If we accept that the Xyrptans are our friends, then they are presumably being truthful about the Praetorians. I'm hoping that the interrogation comes up with some useful information."

"I still feel apprehensive too. I think that, whatever the outcome of the interrogation, we need to get back and meet with our team to make some decisions about our course of action. If the Praetorians are here for nefarious purposes, we need to prepare for the worst. We'd have little chance of success fighting a foe that's a thousand years more advanced than we. Of course, I think that it would be difficult to fight a war from trillions of miles away. If this is the case, our best chance would be to enlist the help of the Xyrptans. I don't know if they would help us, but they could strike the Praetorians at home. I wonder if they feel any guilt for leading the Praetorians her?"

They continued to discuss the situation for a while longer until Robin tried, unsuccessfully, to suppress a yawn. She smiled ruefully. "I guess I've had it. It's been a long day. Let's get some sleep. Tomorrow will be another big day."

Both rose but Robin stumbled. "Need some help?" She put her arm around Eric's waist and he did likewise around her waist. They walked out and down the hall to their suites.

Having settled into bed, Eric was just starting to doze off when he heard someone jiggle the door handle. Then he heard a knock. He rose and was on his way to the entrance door when he heard the knock again. The knock was coming from the door adjoining his and Robin's suites. He unlocked the door and opened it to find Robin standing there in a black negligee with a coy expression on her face. "Can I come in? I feel restless and thought perhaps we could talk a little longer."

Eric bowed to her and extended his arm. "Your wish is my command."

She sashayed into the room, over to Eric's bed, and climbed in. "I'm ready to talk," she said, as she placed the pillow behind her back.

Not being sure of her intentions, Eric was reticent to act, but he crawled into bed beside her. "So, what do you want to talk about?"

"Oh, I don't know. What do you do when you've been under a lot of stress and strain and can't sleep? How do you relax?"

"I don't notice much stress. I look forward to challenges, and I try to meet them head on. Otherwise I take a long, hot shower and go to bed. I sleep like a log. What do you do?"

Robin turned on her side and snuggled up to Eric. She put her arm across his chest and turned her face upward in anticipation. She wasn't disappointed as Eric kissed her. There wasn't much pillow talk thereafter.

Formulating a Defense

Eric and Robin talked quietly as they ate breakfast. The new warmth between them was evident even to the bots who served them.

As they were finishing breakfast, Maxid came in and sat down. "I have good news and bad news. First the good—we were able to break into the Praetorian bots encryption and get much of the information we were looking for. Now the bad, he is not a cultural attaché, but rather a military officer. The Praetorian's intention is to make Earth a satellite by any means possible. He said that their bots are to make a proposal to the governments on earth to set up their nation to supersede the UN and take control of *all* government functions—a world-wide totalitarian regime. If their demands are not met, they intend to accomplish this transition by forceful means. When asked how, the bot became evasive. He may not have exact knowledge of their plans, but he thought that it might be by an attack from outer space via missiles. It's their intention to *colonize* Earth. Their planet's climate is very harsh, so I imagine they are looking for a friendlier habitat. If their spaceships are as up-to-date as ours, they could make the trip in seven years. Also, I am afraid that they realize that the population on earth is large and likely uncontrollable, which means that their intentions by force would end in genocide. They might use neutron missiles to preserve structures while killing the population. I told you that these are a cruel people."

"Oh my God, oh my God," Robin was beside herself.

Eric looked stern. "This means that we have to get going immediately. We need to get back with our team and plan for this eventuality. Robin and I discussed this possibility last night. We're woefully unprepared for any attack from outer space. We would be sitting ducks with no adequate defense. Our only salvation would be for you Xyrptans to help us. Would that be possible?"

"I've already talked to Peter Bradford this morning, so he is apprised of the situation. He wants you two to return to Washington immediately. Also, I have sent this information home and I'm sure that our Supreme Council will be considering what action they can take from both here and there. As soon as I hear anything, I'll inform your leaders. I can't imagine that we wouldn't take some action. The Praetorians would be destroying our mission here *while* increasing their threat to us on Xyrpta."

"When can we get a flight back to Washington?" Eric was anxious to get going.

"Our plane is out right now, but we can arrange a flight by noon. I think that we should adhere to our original plan. Robin, an IT person will be waiting down in the bot room to show you the intricacies of our bots. You better take advantage of this while you can. I presume that, once you return to Washington, you are going to be very busy for some time. Eric, you remain here. I'll return shortly. I can fill you in on a lot of information that you are going to need about us as we plan for the future. Have another cup of coffee. Robin, you had better get going." Both Maxid and Robin departed while Eric signaled the waiter for more coffee.

Maxid returned shortly. "Eric, I want to give you a heads-up on what you may be facing, a worst case scenario. In our war, both we and the Praetorians were well equipped with modern weaponry. Our offensive equipment has not changed much since then. The big difference today is in our *defense*. Then we were both on the same planet. After we won the war, the Praetorians were relegated to another planet. Our defenses had to change at that time to include an attack from space. That was a whole new ballgame. We have built a system that is almost foolproof.

No system is one hundred percent effective, particularly from a massive deployment of missiles from space."

Eric was listening intently. He had the capacity to absorb information rapidly and work out a solution if a problem existed. "We do have a National Missile Defense partially in place, but I'm sure it would be dreadfully ineffective against any such challenge from space. If you have such a defense system on Xyrpta, would you help us deploy such a system here?"

"I haven't heard back from our Supreme Council, but I'm sure they are discussing that possibility right now. I have several points that I want you to take back to your team. I'll be talking to Peter Bradford about this as well. First, you'll have to determine if such a threat really exists. Remember that it takes years for a spaceship to arrive here from our solar system. If the Praetorians have plans to attack, those plans would have been made years ago and the missiles could well be on their way now. That's something we'll have to determine. The fact that a small group of Praetorians are already on earth makes this all a distinct possibility."

"Maxid, you didn't answer my question. Would you help us?"

"As I mentioned before, I believe we would help you but that's not for me to say. We could advise you on what to do, but first we would have to determine how long before those missiles will arrive here, their number, the type, and how much damage they could do. Based on that information we could help you prepare a defense. If this is the case, the crucial point would be to determine how much time you have to prepare a defense."

Eric looked glum. "Thanks Maxid. That *'tin heart'* of yours is in the right place. Is there any reason why I can't use my cell phone here? I'd like to call Peter to find out what's in store for us when we get back."

"Go right ahead. There's no problem calling out from here as long as you use one of our phones. We don't have cell reception here."

"We're going to beef up our security here at the Center, anticipating that our privacy will soon be threatened by the media. And Eric, I know that you'll not be a *'cowardly lion'*." He grinned.

Peter answered on the first ring. "Eric we need you and Robin back here as soon as possible. Things are happening at warp speed. When can you make it?"

"We can't get a plane until noon, so I estimate we'll get in about six. Have you talked to Maxid today?"

"Yes, we talked earlier this morning. He brought me up to speed. I briefed the president and he wants us to come up with an initial plan post haste—one that he can present to Defense as soon as possible. Come to headquarters directly as soon as you get in. We'll be working tonight. He disconnected.

Eric went back to his suite to pack. Shortly, Robin showed up, enthused about her session with the bots.

"You better get packed. Peter wants us back pronto and our plane leaves soon. You can tell me about your bot experience on the plane."

Not long after, their plane took off. Relaxing with his seat back and a bottle of water in hand, Eric said, "OK, Robin, tell me about the bots."

"First, the IT guy told me that anything pertaining to the space program is to be made available to us. On the other hand, he had been told that many unrelated areas of new knowledge would be dealt with over an extended period of time. They fear that too much knowledge all at once might lead to confusion and 'brain freeze'—their term for malfunction in thinking. They've seen this happen when they've overloaded a bot's brain. This has occurred rarely on uploading to a human's brain as well."

Eric was dubious. "That's interesting. I can see that happening in a brain that's disorganized but not likely where there's a more orderly assemblage of information."

Robin said, "There are no wires and no cables—it's all done with nano-motors at each joint and wirelessly. The IT guy, Idid,"—she pronounced it I´-did,—"diagramed and explained the nano-motors which was a little dense for me, but I got the gist of their workings. If the bot is to have a human appearance, a foam-like material fills in the extremities and torso. Then a thin soft plastic skin covers the body. Idid felt that, once bots were accepted here on Earth, they would most likely drop a lot of the humanoid features, so they would be *easily* recognized. He felt that this would help differentiate them from us, and satisfy some of the critics who don't want to see any confusion between humans and bots. He suggested that bots here might be best represented by looking like their humans at home—green skin and all. I *think* he was kidding."

"That's all pretty amazing. What are you going to do with your new knowledge?"

"I've been thinking about that. The defensive planning that the team will be doing now is beyond my scope of expertise. I might serve best by sticking to my area. I'd like to go back to Houston, tell my colleagues of my experiences, and help develop more advanced robots. I didn't have time to get an idea of how their 'brain' functions. Idid invited me back, so I'll be returning to CEAF soon. I can't express how excited I am. This is a dream come true."

"I know what you mean, Robin. I'm excited *for* you. The whole reason I joined the team was to be able to obtain information from the Xyrptans on my field. For now it looks like I'll be involved in the herculean task of helping to defend Earth against a formidable enemy. It's unbelievable. I think we should both get some rest. Peter wants us to join the team as soon as we get back. We're probably in for an all-night session." Eric turned his head in the opposite direction and closed his eyes. Robin frowned, but after a moment smiled again. She closed her eyes and drifted off as well.

They landed on schedule. A car and driver were waiting for them, and they were whisked off to their new headquarters.

They rushed into the conference room and were met by a dozen faces turned their way.

"Sorry, we didn't mean to barge in. You said to hurry back, so here we are." Eric gave a half-hearted smile as it looked like they had just interrupted an intense discussion.

Peter smiled. "Glad to see you guys back. Have a seat. I've brought everyone up-to-date including my talk with Maxid this morning. So, I believe that brings us all to the question of what should we do now. Of course, we won't know whether or not there's a real threat to us from the Praetorians until we get *furthe*r information, but knowing that they are on Earth and from what the Xyrptans have told us about them, we need to at least make some preliminary plans. Eric you've just returned from CEAF. You may have gleaned more information from Maxid than I did from our recent conversation. What do you say?"

"Maxid and I discussed what we might expect if our worst fears unfold. If I'm being repetitious, please stop me. First, we don't know what's transpired on Praetoria or on Xyrpta, and, until we do, this is mostly speculative. For better or worse, it appears that a lot depends on how much help we can expect from the Xyrptans. I would pressure them, as much as possible, to help us. In that regard, we need to have direct contact with the Xyrptans. Working through the bots here on Earth, isn't good enough and *could* be dangerous. They aren't human and, although they have excellent thinking skills, we can't trust that their intelligence and judgment will be equal to that of a living being. So, direct communication with the Xyrptans has to be a top priority."

"Trying to discover missiles in trillions of miles of space is virtually impossible. I believe our best chance for discovery is for the Xyrptans to infiltrate the Praetorian planet with their bots, if not their humans, to get answers. They must have agencies like our CIA, the KGB and the like to serve that purpose. In fact ... I wonder why they haven't discovered this Praetorian plot before. It had to be a rather massive effort I would think."

"That's good thinking, Eric. How would you propose advancing that idea?"

"Our President should contact the head of their Supreme Council."

"I talked to the president this morning to apprise him of the situation." Peter couldn't have looked more serious. "Our UN delegate is doing the same with members of the Security Council. I'm afraid we have no choice now but to wait for a response from the Xyrptans. According to Maxid, they have been meeting and should give a response in a day or two. Do you have anything else to say?"

"If and when we discover the presence of missiles, we'll have to determine their location, what type, their distance from Earth and how long before they would arrive here. Hopefully the Xyrptans can help us with a missile defense. Lastly, we would have to prepare the populace for such an attack."

"Very good, Eric. Before you returned, we meted out several tasks. We're asking you to be our liaison with NASA. Michael will hold the same position with the Defense Department as well as being second in command here. Robin, we would like you to have you work not only on developing new robots, but on understanding our new friendly bots. Maxid expects you to return to the Center for more briefings. This'll be very important for us going forward."

"Sir, I was going to make the same suggestion. I'm happy to comply."

Eric cleared his throat to draw everyone's attention, "Sir, what you're asking me to do is outside of my area of expertise. I realize that we're facing a catastrophic situation and I want to do my part. I just want my background to be clear to you."

Peter's brows drew together. "I'm familiar with your work. You are outgoing, speak well, and make a good impression, but above all you are brilliant and creative. Those are important qualities for the job I'm asking you to do. Your job will be that of communicating our thoughts and plans to the head of NASA. I realize your work is important to you and to your colleagues in your area, but I want your help until this affair is over. I can't guarantee you a reward. I know you want to obtain more information from the Xyrptans about your field of research. I'll help you in that regard, and I think it's likely that you'll get your wish. If we should be on the wrong end in this affair, it won't make any difference."

"Sir, that's very gracious of you. I accept the appointment."

Seeming to recollect a thought, Peter gestured toward Eric and Robin, "Before you arrived, I mentioned to the team that we had further information about the attack in the restaurant. The police interviewed bystanders outside the place, after the attack, and several mentioned seeing a black car parked across the street along with a driver who appeared to be Chinese. It looks like it may be the same Chinese man that Cephid and Torbid saw in the attack at the airport. Cephid is here,"—nodding toward him, —"and he feels that the person who dropped the explosive at his side in the restaurant was a bot. That makes it likely that the bots in China have teamed up with some unsavory humans over there. This could explain the thugs at the airport. The 'Chinese Mafia' has connections over here, which just adds to the evidence we are accumulating that shows that the Praetorians do *not* have friendly intentions toward us."

The meeting went on far into the night, sketching out tentative plans for a defense against the possible attack on Earth from outer space.

War a Reality

Peter was in his office early the next morning when his phone lit up. "Sir, you have a call from Mr. Maxid of CEAF."

"Good morning Mr. Maxid. I was hoping to hear from you."

"Just call me Maxid. We have just one name and we don't need a prefix. Cephid Aenid and David Standid have a last name to conform to your customs."

"I've heard back from the Supreme Council. They have agreed to help you in *any* way they can. They consider a strike on Earth a strike against them. However, they would like to avoid an intra-galactic conflagration if possible. That would be devastating for all parties. They don't have any information yet on whether or not the Praetorians have launched missiles. They feel their best source of information will be directly from the Praetorians via agents they have secreted within their government. Unfortunately, they haven't picked up any indication of this action so far. The Praetorians set up a separate, secretive organization some years back and that may be the origin of this venture. We haven't been able to penetrate that group, but we'll make a more concerted effort now."

"You asked for direct communication with the Xyrptan government and that can be arranged. You'll have the same access that I do. You can provide them with a set of questions and information, and they will answer and vice versa. It takes about a day for a message to get to them from here and the same back to us. Hopefully, in the not too distant future, we can speed up that process."

"That sounds good. I guess that's about as much as we can expect right now. Keep us posted. You can reach us here at the office anytime."

The Defense Department was reviewing the defensive ideas submitted by Peter and the team. The National Missile Defense System was the basis for their thinking, but this was woefully inadequate if there were a sophisticated attack from outer space. A few intercontinental ballistic missiles (ICBMs) would have a negligible effect in stopping a massive missile attack. It had to be assumed, until proven otherwise, that the Praetorians would not send just a few missiles on a multi-trillion mile trip over a period of years without having planned for it to be a devastating blow. The worstcase scenario would be an overwhelming number of missiles. This is what they would have to prepare for. Prior planning had considered a satellite-based system using laser beams or a similar device to intercept Earth-borne missiles, but to create such a system and deploy it would take years and the cost would be exorbitant so that plan had been shelved.

Some within the State Department and Homeland Security were considering the consequences of complying with the Praetorian's demands if they should insist on surrender. However, the Xyrptans statements that the Praetorians were a cruel people with the desire to make this their new homeland spoke loudly. But who should make this decision? Should there be a national or world-wide vote? Would the voters be sufficiently knowledgeable to make a rational, unemotional decision? Perhaps a vote by governments would be more logical. A dilemma of this magnitude had never before occurred.

The President's office called Peter to indicate that there would be a cabinet meeting the next day and they wanted him, Michael and Cephid to attend. They would be discussing the Praetorian threat and possible responses.

The President called his cabinet to order. "I believe that all of you have been brought up-to-date on the crisis that we are now facing. This meeting is to obtain your thoughts and recommendations, and also to answer any questions that you might have."

Madeline Albrecht, from State was first. "I understand that all our information is second hand via the robots from CEAF. I think that we must have *direct* contact with the leaders in Xyrpta."

The president asked Peter to respond. "I broached this subject to the head of CEAF several days ago. He asked the Supreme Council on Xyrpta about this, and he obtained an immediate response. They have agreed to establish a communication system similar to what they have with CEAF. The equipment for this communication can be set up by them on short notice. It takes almost 24 hours for a transmission going in either direction so we are talking about 48 hours to get a response to any query. For now I think that all communication with them should go through *one* source to avoid confusion. I suggest that we be that source. Funnel the questions to us and we'll filter them and send them on to Xyrpta."

Herbert Alton furrowed his brow. "I hate to continue beating a dead horse, but I still have doubts as to the veracity of the bot's statements. I would like to see some proof to back up what they're saying."

"So, what would you look for? What would convince you of their truthfulness," asked the president?

"I would like a face-to-face meeting. I know that can't be done, but if each communication was accompanied by a video that would help. I'd like to see their facial expressions and body language that accompany their words. I'd like to get to know these people better. As for communication with the Xyrptans, I feel that we should have a direct line without Peter's filtering our transmissions. We *undoubtedly* will have the greatest amount of traffic, since we'll be setting up the defensive network. I'm sure we'll be communicating with them every day for quite a while, and I think the same goes for NASA."

Ben stood up for emphasis. "As Herbert said, NASA should have a direct transmission line, as well. I can see the other departments going through Peter's office, so there isn't a plethora of communications, but Defense and NASA need their separate lines."

The president smiled. "Herbert and Ben, when communications are established, Defense and NASA will get direct transmissions but Homeland Security, State and the Pentagon should go through Peter's office. I know that all of you would like to have direct communication, but unless you are going to be directly involved in negotiations, it would be simpler and less confusing to do it this way."

Later that day. "Peter, Maxid here. I've heard back from our Supreme Council. They indicate that they will give you all the help they can. Most important, they will help you with a missile defense system. On Xyrpta we have an *extensive* defense system against intra-solar and intra-galactic missiles that you might duplicate. The big question is how much *time* you have to prepare. They want to know what defenses you have in place. I sent them the information I had on your National Missile Defense System. I faxed it to you, too. Please review it and fill in any gaps and get it back to me ASAP. And lastly, they reaffirmed their willingness to establish the communication system as soon as possible."

"Thanks Maxid!" Peter continued, "I'd appreciate it if we could set up the communication system stat. We need direct transmission sites at XCOM, Defense and NASA because of the heavy volume we expect to receive. XCOM will then transmit information indirectly to the others, such as State, Homeland Security, etc.

"That sounds fine. I'll get to work on it immediately. I estimate that we can be out there in a few days to do the job. It should take a couple days to set up the three transmission lines."

"We'll be ready and waiting. Nice talking to you Maxid." Peter hung up.

True to their word, the bots came two days later and installed the equipment.

Anxious to try out their new communication system with the Xyrptans, Peter asked his people to prepare questions for him to ask. He would review and condense them to a reasonable number and send them along with a greeting from him and his team. It was understood that communications would be via video, so they would be able to see the Xyrptans for the first time since their appearance at the press conference.

A few days later the questions had been sent, and a response from Xyrpta had been received. The team collected in the conference room to view it. Excitement was rampant. Peter had to quiet them down before turning on the communication.

The Xyrptans appearance again raised exclamations. The Supreme Council members wore black robes. They had produced simultaneous translation into English. For the most part, the questions and responses were what had gone on before except for one.

"Is there any further information on possible missiles heading our way?" The Xyrptan answer was disappointing. No further information was forthcoming. They were still investigating and would let Earthlings know as soon as they discovered anything. There was some rustling about as the session ended with evident disappointment. Peter was just happy that the transmission had 'gone off without a hitch.'

In the ensuing several weeks it was hard for the team members to subdue their restlessness, waiting for further information from the Xyrptans. Peter and Michael kept in touch with the various bureaus. The Defense Department had prepared a detailed history of the National Missile Defense System which had been forwarded to the Xyrptans. Defense was also investigating how they might construct an intra-galactic defense. This was producing a lot of controversy, as they were unable to come up with a practical, realistic system that would protect Earth from a massive missile attack. Their hope was that their alien neighbor would be able to help them plan a defense. However, it was *their* job to *produce* a defense, and they had to be prepared to do it alone if the Xyrptans didn't come through with significant help.

Homeland Security and State busied themselves with deciding whether or not the bots should be considered illegal immigrants, and if so, what should be done about it. Then there was the question of deciding how to distinguish bots from humans.

On a Sunday morning Maxid called Peter to let him know that an important transmission would be coming in that afternoon, and he might want to have his entire staff present. Bots don't have a great range of tone in their voice, but Maxid's attitude was foreboding. Also, it sounded like Maxid had received important information *before* Peter—so much for direct communication. Peter felt that he should be the first to hear from the Supreme Council, particularly when it concerned Earth matters. He was *very* unhappy. He would have to make this clear in his next transmission to Xyrpta.

77

The staff was all on tenterhooks, having been warned that the news might be bad.

As the video came in, it was noted that the entire Supreme Council were present—nine in all. By this time the team members were getting used to seeing the Xyrptans as they really were—short, green, and with skewed head-shape and facial features; not ugly, just different.

Palid Lindid stood at the podium. "Greetings to Mister President, bureau chiefs, Peter Bradford, and his team from the Supreme Council on Xyrpta. By finally penetrating the Praetorian intelligence organization, we have been able to obtain detailed facts that appear to be above reproach. The news is not good. As we now know, they did follow us to Earth, but how they discovered our plans is still unknown. However, ours was a large project, involving multiple bureaus, so it was not hidden very well. Their intention is to make earth a satellite for inhabitation by their people in the near future. For this purpose, they intend to decimate the majority of the population on earth but leave a small portion intended for *servitude*. As you were told before, these are a cruel, ruthless people. I don't doubt their intentions."

"We have determined that three flights of missiles were sent out five year ago with the expectation of a seven year trip. This leaves you two years to prepare a defense. To our knowledge, there are about a thousand missiles in each batch and each group is being shepherded by a gunship to guide and protect them along the way. The groups may be separated by a few days depending upon whether the space ships are following identical routes. Once in space, the small missile engines need little fuel. They are not much larger than the size of your ICBMs. We have not yet been able to discover where these missiles are in space, but we have started to look. I expect that we'll find them well before they pose any immediate threat to you. Transmissions between the gunships and their home center on Praetoria should help us locate them."

"For our part, we will aid you in your defense. We have a very secure system in place against intra-galactic missiles and I think that would work for your purpose too. We have been in contact with your Defense Department, and we'll expedite our efforts to help with your protection."

The video ended and everyone in the room fidgeted nervously. Now they knew that the threat was real. Peter could not hold back. "Damn," he said followed by a sigh, "We now know that the worst has come to pass. I'll respond to President Lindid immediately. If we introduce their defense system here on Earth, we need to know what the estimated time is for completion. *Hopefully* it'll be less than two years. I'll ask for cursory details about their own defensive plan, so we can see what to anticipate." Peter called Max, his secretary, over and gave her notes on what he wanted to say in the transmission. "Call me when it's ready. I'll come in and review it and then we can send it."

"Cephid, would you call CEAF, and ask Maxid if he received this transmission. If so, does he have any thoughts? Michael, call your counterpart at Defense for the same." The meeting ended shortly thereafter, Peter explaining that he needed to call the president about this latest news.

"George, this is Peter. Did you see the latest transmission from Xyrpta and their Supreme Council?" The President indicated that he hadn't "I'm afraid that our worst fears have come true. Missiles were actually launched toward us five years ago. It's expected that they'll reach Earth in two years. That gives us a little time to prepare, but I'm not sure how long it will take us to get ready and whether or not we can mount a defense that'll be adequate."

"That's a nightmare, Peter. I was hoping that this wouldn't happen. Will the Xyrptans help us prepare a defense?"

"They will. I presume that Herbert will be in charge. I only hope that we'll have the wherewithal to produce the defensive equipment. With their advanced technology, can we jump a millennium in two years? God help us."

"I trust Herbert to do a good job. As an alternative, Peter, do you think it would be worthwhile to contact the Praetorians to see if we can negotiate some sort of peace settlement? I think we have to make the attempt whether or not the Xyrptans approve."

The president was searching. "I believe that Maxid said that they felt that an attack on us would be an attack on them. So, would they consider this an act of *war* on them? Would they attack the Praetorians on their home ground? Even the *threat* of doing so might halt the Praetorian attack on us. The Xyrptans would be in a better position to negotiate with them than we are. Perhaps *together* we can negotiate with the Praetor. What do you think?"

"I hadn't thought of those options. I'll get Maxid's input. In any case, I'll pass your thoughts on to the Supreme Council. I'll get your approval of the document before submitting it to them."

"There's also the question of *halting* the attack. We were told that the missiles are accompanied by Shepherd spaceships to guide them, so it might be possible to destroy or at least *divert* them. First we'd have to find them, and at this point it appears that we'd have to depend on the Xyrptans for that task. I wonder if the spaceships the Xyrptans have on Earth would be up to fighting the Shepherd spaceships. We have a lot of unanswered questions."

"Yes, but you're doing a good job, Peter," the president said before he hung up.

Discovery

A few days later Maxid called Peter. "I have some news and felt you should be the first to know. We returned the Praetorian bot to China in a dysfunctional state and placed him in an area where his cohorts would find him. They found him and took him to their headquarters. We were able to track them and find out *where* they're quartered. We're not sure of the next step, but we're thinking of *destroying* their facility. It might be best if we eliminate them from Earth."

"Maxid, I wouldn't do that right now. I had a talk with the President, and he feels that we should consider trying to open *negotiations* with the Praetor. That might be successful, particularly if they understand that an attack on us would constitute an attack on the Xyrptans and mean war. I believe you said that an attack on us would be interpreted as an attack on Xyrpta. Does that still hold?"

"Only the Supreme Council can make that decision"

"Well, I'm preparing a video for your president with that in mind. If we do try and make contact, do you have an opinion as to whether it would be better to try and contact the Praetor bots here on Earth, or would it be better to contact their humans on Praetoria?"

"I don't have permission to make that decision. You should put that question to our Council. Offhand though, contacting the people who can make the decision, and *not* the underlings, seems like the *obvious* choice."

"I'll get my query off to the Council. Is there anything else going on at CEAF?"

"No. We have Robin coming back for another session with our bots."

"One last question. Why have the Praetorians not contacted us yet? Their missiles have been on the way for five years now."

"I would have to guess that they're waiting until their missiles are closer, so you'll have insufficient time to prepare a defense. Perhaps that would be another year or year and a half from now. When they find out that we are aware of their plans, that may change, so now would be as good a time as any to contact them."

The next day Peter sent his questions to the Supreme Council. He knew that considering an act of war would take some time to decide, so he would be patient. He also mentioned that any business pertaining to Earth matters should be sent first to XCOM and not to CEAF.

In the meantime, he would check to see how the world was handling the news of alien bots being on earth. So far there had been mixed reactions—some in disbelief, some considered them enemies to be dealt with as such, and others accepted what they had expected to happen sooner or later. The UN Security Council was debating what action to take. One decision had been made—to have the Xyrptan ambassador appear before the UN to answer questions. Cephid was preparing to handle this task.

Other countries were asking the US for more information. One positive was that bots in other countries were making contact with the governments where they resided to put them at ease and to bring them up-to-date. No information on the missiles heading toward Earth was being released yet.

Only a few cabinet members had been informed of the missile attack—Defense, State, Homeland Security, the Pentagon and NASA. A decision had to be made on how to inform the public before word leaked out. For now, it had been decided to hold off any release until they had contacted the Praetorians. Defense was communicating with the defense minister on the Supreme Council about whether an *adequate* protection of earth could be mounted within a two year time frame. The expense would be enormous, but a proposal to bring the matter before the UN was being considered so that the cost could be distributed worldwide.

It took only a few days for a communiqué to be returned from the Supreme Council. It said that, since the war between the Xyrptans and the Praetorians several hundred years ago, formal relations had not been re-established with them. However, they did have several informal contacts and they could use these to communicate with the Praetor. The Supreme Leader proposed being up front with them. Tell them that we are aware of their presence on earth, that we know about the missiles headed toward this planet, and their intent to colonize earth and subjugate the natives to their will. The Supreme Council would not go so far as to declare war on them, but they would indicate to the Praetorians that an attack on Earth *would* be considered an attack on them. He proposed that his people meet with the Praetor to discuss the situation before the matter got further out of control. For now, he would not disturb the Praetorian bots on Earth. However, they should be kept under surveillance.

A defense against the missiles hurtling toward earth now became Peter's top priority. He had called a meeting with Herbert, Ben, and Michael. Herbert stated that he was developing a good relationship with his counterpart on Xyrpta, and they had made progress in coming up with a plan that they believed would be effective against a missile attack, but there were two reservations. "It won't be possible to establish a defense as sophisticated and advanced as the one on Xyrpta. The limited time for producing the materials, the construction time, and the launching of satellites in a two-year time frame make this impossible. They recommended that a system of satellites be put in place in a network surrounding Earth. Lasers would be placed on the satellites. These would send out beams, like spokes on a wheel. Beams from nearby satellites would overlap each other to provide a solid barrier. With their advanced technology, the Xyrptans can strengthen the lasers so that they would be effective over a greater distance. The second reservation is a time constraint—it might not be possible to place an impenetrable shield around the globe, so it was recommended that the tightest net be placed over heavily populated areas and a looser network over less populated regions. The estimate of effectiveness was 99.9% for the more concentrated network and 95% for the looser network. If 3000 missiles were incoming, 99.9% effectiveness would mean that three missiles would get through. For 95% effectiveness, 150 missiles would get through. These numbers could be reduced somewhat by using existing land and sea based ICBMs."

Ben came up with another possible solution. "This idea wouldn't preclude the satellite defense as my idea might be a total failure. Two spaceships exist on Earth. They could be armed and launched to intercept the shepherd spaceships. They might be able to destroy those ships and change the course of the missiles or even destroy them. Realistically this is an unlikely possibility, because of the number of enemy ships being faced and the likelihood that these are gunships. Alternatively, it might be possible to change the course of the missiles without *challenging* them by jamming or otherwise interfering with their missile guidance systems."

"The risk here is that there are three sets of Shepherd spaceships and missiles that have to be nullified which increases their chance for success and increases our chance for failure. It would be nice, if an armada of space ships could be launched from Xyrpta, but it would take seven years for them to arrive—too late to be useful."

Herbert said, "Our best chance right now is to have the attack aborted by the Praetorians, themselves. That might require the Xyrptans threatening to declare war on them. However, to avoid that possibility, while still exerting pressure, they might gradually *escalate* a confrontation. Their war lasted years and was devastating to both populations, so the implication is that this has to be avoided *at all costs*. The Xyrptan defense minister implied that they ultimately would not go so far as declaring war if it came down to that decision."

Herbert finished on a down note, as he realized that there were a lot of ifs and buts in this conjecture. Hopefully, these would be reduced as time passed. He looked at the others for their input.

Trying to be more optimistic, Peter said, "Herbert, I believe you've made good progress in the short time that's been available. I wouldn't be so discouraged. At least we have a number of viable options. Is it possible to incorporate some of the Xyrptans more sophisticated defensive techniques into our plans? Is their reticence to give us more help due to not wanting to give away secret technology for fear that the Praetorians might get their hands on it? Or are we too far behind them technically?"

Choosing his words carefully, Herbert said, "I don't know the answer to your questions, but I'll ask the Xyrptans to get a better insight into their reasoning. Although I'm thinking somewhat more favorably about the Xyrptans, I still have my doubts. I just hope that they're not playing some elaborate, devious game with us."

A reassuring smile came from Ben. "I believe we all have doubts, that's natural under the present circumstance. After all, we are seeing science fiction becoming reality. That has to be a strain on all our imaginations."

Looking at Herbert while nodding, Ben said, "We at NASA will coordinate with Defense on the responsibility of getting the satellites built. We'll have to figure out the logistics, including the expense. The latter will be astronomical I'm sure. We better bring State and our UN representative into these discussions as soon as possible. It'll be necessary to bring the defensive plan and cost before the UN. Our plight is so egregious that it hardly seems likely that we wouldn't get approval, but you can never tell with that body."

Peter had been making notes. He looked up. "Michael, do have anything to say?"

"I'd like to touch base with Cephid and get his input. He must have the ear of the Supreme Council, and as such, be privy to information not available to us. I've known him for years and we have a good rapport. He's been totally honest with me in the past and I trust him." Michael ended with a curious expression on his face. He hadn't thought of it previously. Cephid's allegiance was first to his people and not to any earthling. So that trust had to be put into question now. Still, talking to Cephid could be useful, and he is one of the team.

A few other minor matters were discussed and then they broke up. Peter collared Michael before he left. "Talking to Cephid is a good idea. It might give us a different perspective. However, I suspect that their Supreme Council is going to be very careful about giving Cephid information that they're withholding from us but you can never tell. Go for it."

Michael walked over to ambassador Cephid's office. After shaking hands and sitting down. "Cephid, we've been good friends for years. I trust and respect you. I realize that it's to your government that you owe your allegiance. So, what I'm going to ask you may put you in a difficult position. Other than me, the team has known you and about bots for a very short time. In our dire circumstance, they have some doubts about the information we're getting from your Supreme Council. Are we getting the full picture, or only what they want us to know? Is there anything else we should know or you can tell us?"

"Michael, I feel the same as you do about our friendship. You have to realize, too, that I'm bound by my people, and as you said, my first allegiance is to them. I believe that we've been honest with you and have kept you up-to-date on the thinking going on in the Supreme Council. We have related to you various options. The last one—declaring war on the Praetorians—is a grave step. I don't think I am betraying any confidence, when I say that it is very unlikely that we would declare war. Would it be worthwhile for us to take that risk for a planet that is trillions of miles away from us? I'm being very blunt, but realistic too. We feel responsible for leading the Praetorians here, and as a result, we feel that it is our duty to help you with everything that is in our power short of declaring war. I have discussed the situation in detail with a member of our Council. I hope that you'll keep this information within the team. Otherwise I could be in trouble"

"I appreciate your candor. One last question; Herbert indicated that in one of his conversations with the defense minister on Xyrpta, it was mentioned that they were contemplating sending a number of spaceships to circle the planet Praetoria as a show of force; hoping that this would be intimidating. Might not *this* trigger a response from the Praetorians that would amount to war?"

"First, this would not be done until *after* we have communicated with the Praetorians and obtained an unfavorable response. We are much stronger now than during the prior war. The Praetorians had to rebuild from scratch. It's assumed that they are still a good way behind us in technology and strength. However, the fact that they are on Earth shows us that they can't be too far behind. We're going to have to reassess their capabilities"

Michael stood up and held out his hand, "Thanks Cephid, I appreciate your openness. I don't know that it makes me feel any better, but it solidifies my feeling that we are on the right track even if it fails." Michael left.

Michael was on his way back to his office when he saw Peter sitting at his desk talking on the phone. He decided to tell him about his talk with Cephid. He walked in, sat down, and waited for Peter's telephone conversation to end. It was obvious he was talking to Maxid, and it didn't appear that he liked what he was hearing.

Peter hung up shortly, a frown on his face. He looked at Michael, "Maxid had no news and nothing *at all* encouraging to say. I hope we aren't being blindsided by the Xyrptans. I sometimes think that Herbert might be right in not trusting them."

"Sir, I just finished talking to Cephid. The Xyrptans are *trillions* of miles from us. Why should they endanger their population and way of life for us? It's *very* unlikely that they are going to war against the Praetorians, or for that matter, going to take the chance that the Praetorians might attack them in retaliation for being aggravated by their solar neighbor. So that leaves us no choice but to depend upon *ourselves* for a defense. Cephid assured me that his people would help us, and I think, from what we know so far, that we can depend on them. I believe we need to put all our efforts into our defense and push ahead as rapidly as we can."

"That makes good sense. Why don't you take another trip out to CEAF, and stay on top of Maxid until things are clearer? I'd like to know if their spaceships can be rigged for battle and whether they could be used to intercept the missiles and Shepherd spaceships. That and our satellite defense are about the only things going for us now."

"Sir, I had one other thought. I don't believe that the Praetorian bots are any use to us, and are likely spying on us. I think we should destroy their center of operations in China and as many of them as possible. They're not alive. That would take away a source of communication for the Praetorians and leave them in the dark. It might make them abort their attack if they don't know what to expect on their arrival. They would know that they're coming into a hostile environment with *no* one to greet them. But ... I don't know if that would be *much* of a deterrent. Their Center is our only source of communication with the Praetorians presently, but it looks like we should be able to reach them through the Xyrptans, and that would likely carry much more weight than our rather feeble effort directly from here. I think there's *little* risk in getting rid of their Center and a lot to be gained."

"That's an interesting idea. I'll give it some thought and pass it by the team. Take Brandy with you out to CEAF. She's a brilliant strategist and should be a great asset. And ... thanks, Michael. You're showing why I picked you to be on the team."

New Dilemma

Michael had not been to CEAF in a few years. He was looking forward to seeing what changes had occurred.

On the flight out he wanted to get to know Brandy better. He found that she was a graduate of Harvard and had served an internship at the White House. She then had sought a position in government and had been hired by Peter. She looked on him as a father figure.

After taking off and getting comfortable in their seats, Michael asked. "Brandy, why do you wear your hair in a bun and why do you always wear large glasses, why not contacts?"

She looked at him quizzically for a moment, then slowly undid her bun and let her hair fall down to her mid-back. Shiny, brunette spirals spread over her shoulders. She took off her glasses and gave Michael a big smile. He was wide-eyed.

"Brandy, you could be a model. You're a gorgeous woman."

"Why do men always think that a woman's *primary* goal is to be good looking and glamorous? I know I'm beautiful, and I get my share of attention—which I don't mind—but my interest in life is intellectual. I *yearn* to be of service to mankind and to my country. That may sound trite, especially in this age, but it's true. I wear my hair up and use glasses to send a message." With that Brandy put her glasses back on and put her hair back up into a bun.

Michael hadn't expected such a strong reply. "One more question if you don't mind. Your name; why don't you use a middle name or change it to something less suggestive?"

"It's a family name. I don't look on it as a burden."

"I didn't mean to be intrusive. I'm just trying to get to know you better. I'm impressed with your background and your goals. Just so you know, I'm a happily married man and I have two kids. Right now, I don't know how happy my wife is with all this work, but she understands what's at stake." Michael took out his billfold and showed Brandy pictures of his wife and kids. In turn, she was complementary and remarked on how cute the children were.

"No offense taken. I'm glad we got the matter of my appearance out of the way. It's hard to explain to men sometimes. They often think that I'm just being coy and playing hard to get, that I'm not serious."

"What about family. Any plans for marriage and children?"

"I've thought of that, but not for the near future." They then settled down, passing back and forth further information about each other for the rest of the flight.

Maxid was at the field waiting as they taxied in. As they exited the plane, he clasped them both by the arm and said that he had something of immediate importance to discuss with them. He led them to a small conference room, and asked if they would like coffee or tea. Michael chose coffee and Brandy deferred.

"The Praetorian bot that we captured and interrogated has been decommissioned. We suspect that they discovered the device we inserted in his brain. Almost immediately afterward they captured one of our spy bots. We were lucky enough to detect this early, so I don't think they were able to download any significant information before we zapped him. Zapping a bot doesn't erase his memory; but we *can* do that, if we so choose at the time of zapping, which is what we did in this case. Spy bots are at a lower level so they don't carry a lot of information with them. They're mainly expected to detect and retain information. But this tells them that we know that they are here, and I expect some sort of response."

Michael smiled. This played right into his recent ideas. "Sir, I was discussing this with Peter just before leaving Washington. For us, they are an enemy that serves no purpose. They are no longer our only source of communication with the Praetorians, which now can be best done through your people. They're likely spying on us too. They're the Praetorians only contact with Earth. Without that communication they'll be in the dark and won't know what our defenses are or what type of hostility they will face when they come here. To my way of thinking, they should be eradicated. We won't be taking lives, just removing spyware"

Brandy jumped in. "I agree entirely. The longer they're allowed to remain here, you can be sure that they'll "procreate" and spread, making it more difficult to track them down and eliminate them. As you said, Maxid, you expect some sort of response from them now that they've been discovered. I would attack before they do."

Maxid had sat expressionless. "My two Earthlings, there's a lot of sense in what you say. I've been thinking along the same line, and in fact, voiced these concerns to my superiors in Xyrpta. Since you've voiced your concerns to Peter, I'll give him a call to give him my input. Why don't you two think of ways we might rid ourselves of the enemy bots here on Earth." Maxid pushed back his chair, and continued, "I have to leave, but I'll see you sometime tomorrow. Incidentally, two of your cohorts are here, Robin and Eric. You might want to tell them of your concerns." Maxid rose and left the room.

Brandy said, "Wow, this is some start to our trip. Right now I could use a little rest. I'll see you at dinner. Do you suppose that Eric and Robin will join us?"

"I'll take care of that. See you at dinner." Michael called Peter and updated him on Maxid's thoughts.

Dinner at seven found four of the team together, but their demeanor was far from happy.

"Gang, let's have a nice dinner." Michael was trying to lighten up the atmosphere. "Afterwards we can do some serious brainstorming on how we might handle the enemy bots. Peter will be talking to the other team members in Washington, and I'm sure, the president as well, but there seems to be little doubt but that we should go ahead and destroy these bots."

In spite of Michael's efforts, a rather somber meal followed. Eric tried to liven things up. "Have you heard the joke about the minister, priest and rabbi?" The women both gave him a stone-faced expression. It was obvious that they were already brainstorming—silently.

Perhaps it was because they were the only ones in the dining room. The waiter always stood, expressionless, just a table away, awaiting their next order. A nice gesture, but Michael wondered if he was listening in on their conversation. This was un-nerving, so Michael called him over. "I'd appreciate it if you would wait over by the serving door and not next to our table." With a stoic expression the waiter nodded and moved as requested. The others at the table gave Michael an approving look.

"I want to say one thing before we get started," Michael began, "The Xyrptans have said the Praetorians are inferior to them, but we have to remember that *both* are a millennium ahead of us. So, who wants to go first?"

Everyone hesitated, but then Brandy began. "Someone needs to state the *obvious*. Assuming that we're going to attack their head-quarters, a frontal assault seems senseless. I'd assume that they have defenses in place to alert them—guards, cameras, and they might even have laid down mines. My thought is that we need to get the input of our friendly bots. Being almost kin, they would be the ones most likely to *think* like them, and they would be up-to-date on what we might expect defensively and offensively. I assume that we can disable them just as was done to the enemy bot we captured. That would take away their offensive capability and prevent them from alerting their home base in Praetoria and their other bots spread around the world. I'm assuming that the attack would be by our bots and not involve humans." The others nodded in agreement.

Eric cleared his throat, indicating he wanted to go next. "I first considered dropping a bomb on them, but that would destroy all their records of communication with Praetoria and with their fellow bots here on earth. That information would be too valuable to lose. Therefore, Brandy's idea of sudden decommissioning of the bots sounds good."

Michael nodded at Robin. "Well, you know that I've been working with the bots here at the Center. I've learned a lot, but really have only *touched* their trove of information. I've learned that decommissioning bots is not as simple as it sounds. Before doing that, I believe that you'd have to insure that they couldn't get a message off to their superiors in Praetoria and their fellow bots here. It would be best if their Center just disappeared with no sign as to what had happened. That would make us *look* stronger. Destroying their radio tower should be the first order of business. Secondly, not all bots are made the same. Both the Xyrptans and the Praetorians know they are vulnerable to decommissioning. I've learned that their *soldier* bots have *two* sources of power. They have a separate battery pack that isn't vulnerable to zapping their brain. If their main source of energy is interrupted, they're automatically transferred to the other system. We could decommission their non-soldiers in the usual way, but we would still need human soldiers or soldier bots to handle their military. So, I see destroying their radio tower first, then decommissioning their regular bots, and then having our own bot soldiers fight their troops. I would preface *all* this by saying that we're probably using outmoded thinking by Xyrptan and Praetorian standards. I think we shouldn't go too far in this planning without getting Maxid's input."

Michael complimented them all. "I appreciate all your input. Robin's remarks were good ones to end on. Let's get Maxid's advice before we go further. I'll see if I can set up an early morning meeting with him."

Their meeting was scheduled for seven the next morning. Maxid was the first to arrive. He greeted each as they entered. To Michael he seemed more formal and distant than usual. Maxid took charge and opened the meeting. "Michael has brought me up-to-date on your discussion. Your thinking and conclusions were quite good. Robin was correct in her construction of a plan to rid the Earth of the enemy bots. However, there was one omission. The Praetorians are *exceptionally* good at spying and copying what others have created. Much of what we see, as advances on their part, are copies of what we Xyrptans have accomplished. That's very discouraging for us. It shows us that we're not good at protecting our own developments. But in your case it's fortunate. As Robin noted, the soldier bots can operate independently of a central control so jamming the circuits of these bots won't stop them. What you don't know is that we would never be so careless as to allow a renegade soldier loose to wreak havoc without having some ready way to stop him. A laser beam to the body, as well as to the head, will incapacitate these soldier bots. That would best be accomplished by our own soldier bots. I think it likely that the location of their extra battery pack and circuitry is in the same location as it is on our soldiers, their right upper abdomen, so we'll know where to aim."

The four guests were smiling. Maxid was just continuing from where they had left off the night before. Michael felt that his initial impression of Maxid, seemingly aloof, when they first came in, was wrong. "That's really good news. Do you think that Robin's plan is feasible, considering we now have a way of handling the rogue bots?"

"It's a good plan. I recommend using our soldier bots which I believe are superior to theirs. If a battle ensued, I feel certain that we could defeat them. We feel that there are, at most, 36 total personnel. My other contribution is that you should *not* blow up the radio tower. I think that we can decommission their radio crew before they can alert anyone, including their superiors in Praetoria. After we've gained control, we'd like to take over their communication system. I think that we could re-commission their radio operators, so that the Praetorians would think that they were continuing to communicate with their original staff. I think that would work at least for a while. That might allow us to obtain valuable information—their plans for conquering Earth, the location of the missiles, their arrival date, and their thoughts about Xyrpta acting against them."

Hardly able to contain his exuberance, Eric said, "Maxid, I think you've come up with a brilliant idea. What do your superiors think about attacking the enemy bots?"

"My superiors don't know of this plan yet, but they have agreed that we *should* eliminate them. I think it likely that they would go along with our ideas. I talked to Peter last night, and I relayed your ideas to him, and he was in general agreement. He wants to talk to the President and Defense, before giving his *full* approval. Michael, you might want to give him a call and inform him of our latest thinking."

"I'll do that." Michael started to rise but Maxid held up his hand indicating that he wasn't finished.

'Oh, oh, here it comes,' thought Michael.

"Our Supreme Council has been debating what they should do because of the impending attack on Earth. Should it be war, or nothing, or something in between? Their decision is to inform the Praetorians that they're aware of their plans. They are going to make a formal request to begin negotiations to establish diplomatic relations between the two nations. At the same time, they now will follow through on what they told you before, to send an armada of spaceships to circle the Praetorian planet to *emphasize* their displeasure with their actions toward earth. We are extending a hand in friendship while being assertive. That's as far as Xyrpta is willing to go to force Praetoria to withdraw their attack on Earth. This is their final decision, and I believe, this demonstrates to your people how serious this matter is for us. I think that this is the *most* that you can expect, and I'm happy to relay this information to you." All four of the humans started to speak at once. Maxid held up his hand again to stop them.

"They also stand behind you in your decision to exterminate the enemy here on Earth and take over their base. It was *their* idea to *covertly* take over the Chinese Center, not mine, and to maintain communication with Praetoria as if no change had occurred. When it's been determined that we have obtained all the useful information available, we should destroy the Center. That would tell them that you aren't to be trifled with."

"So, we're left with the defense, which we've already discussed. Before going further, we'll have to await the approval of your government. I think that brings us up-to-date. So now, Eric, why don't you check out our spaceship for its suitability as an interceptor of the Shepherd spaceships? Torbid, whom you met before, will show you around. Brandy, why don't you tag along with Robin and get to know our bots better?"

Brandy frowned. "I'd rather tag along with Eric and check out your spaceship."

"Do as you please."

Perhaps the way these bots treated human females reflected on how Xyrptans thought of females in their world, contemplated Brandy.

Eric wanted to check out the spaceship for its use as a gunship to intercept the Praetorian Shepherd ships. Torbid took Eric and Brandy on a brief tour of the disc spaceship for Brandy's benefit, since she hadn't seen the ship before. It had a basic crew of two—pilot and copilot. "In our solar system," he explained, "There's always a potential threat from the Praetorians, so our ships are always armed, particularly when in the

environs of Praetoria. Several of our spaceships have mysteriously disappeared, and we're suspicious of our planetary neighbor, but nothing
has ever been proved." He'd heard of several run-ins with Praetorian
spaceships in which there was no conflict.

Eric was interested in adding guns to the freighter they were exam-
ining. Torbid pointed out that this was not a warship, and as such, would
stand up poorly against a real gunship. "It might be like a flying fortress
during your World War II that had guns, but was slower, more cum-
bersome, and less maneuverable and thus the need for accompanying
fighter planes."

Eric persisted, not wanting to give up what might be their only
chance to eliminate the Shepherd ships and missiles.

"We have guns in storage that could be fitted to this ship." Torbid
said, then he appeared hesitant, as if he had blurted out something he
shouldn't have. Maybe it was because he felt the need to cover. "We
expect that, after the United States and the other countries on Earth sign
an agreement with Xyrpta regarding space exploration, we'll send an
armada of ships of various types to Earth to begin the satellite program.
This will include gunships and other types of warships which would be
used for defensive purposes." Torbid appeared discombobulated, glancing about in an almost-human nervous mannerism.

Eric and Robin looked at each other. This suggested that the
Xyrptans might have plans beyond what they had revealed. It raised a
whole new series of questions. Eric quickly changed his face to a stoic
expression. He was puzzled by this information, but he wasn't going
to let on that he was surprised. "So, Torbid, how would you add the
guns to this ship?"

"We could modify the ship and put in four guns, ninety degrees
apart. You'd be hampered by the relatively slow speed of the ship.
Moreover, you wouldn't have the protection of a warship, which is covered in a protective skin that can deflect most beams. You would be a
sitting duck for a *modern* gunship. As I understand the situation, there
are three Shepherd ships, and if you had to take on all three at the same
time, you would stand zero chance of success." Torbid now appeared
more comfortable.

He explained that they used rays—like laser beams—which were
more effective than bullets or shells. Torbid had never been under

enemy fire, but he had training in battle techniques that were practiced regularly. Both he and his fellow bot had worked together on simulated attacks to perfect their skills. This had all been done at CEAF in their spaceship simulator.

That increased Eric's uneasiness. *Why would the bots be practicing simulated attacks while on Earth?*

Brandy asked Torbid about the operation of the ship, the speed it could attain, and particularly their fuel source for such a long journey. Eric recalled the answer to the power source from before but he didn't interrupt. Torbid was prepared this time. He said that they had a power source that provided them with the ability to travel prolong distances without worrying about running out of fuel, but he was not allowed to give out further details. Brandy pursed her lips and looked at Eric. Eric shrugged his shoulders.

"Torbid, would you take us up for a little spin?" asked Brandy with a seductive smile.

In turn, a smile appeared on the robots face "Not today, maybe some time in the future."

A pouty look showed on Brandy's face as she wrinkled her nose.

Recalling, too, Maxid's negative comments about the ability of the freighter, even when armed, to compete with a gunship, Eric tried to force a better answer. This time Torbid was emphatic. "You would stand no chance for success, even if you took both freighters." Eric got the message, loud and clear. They both thanked Torbid for the tour and information and departed.

That afternoon the four team members met in Michael's suite. Eric remained standing. He appeared distraught. "Guys, our tour of the freighter with Torbid was a total bust. Sending one, or even two, armed freighters against the Shepherd gunships would be suicide—they'd have negligible chance for success."

Robin piped up. "Perhaps we should at least try. Negligible chance is better than no chance."

Eric, still downcast, "We have to come up with something better. It's too bad we don't have three freighters. We could pack them with TNT, and each could ram a gunship. With only bots on board there would be no loss of life."

"Geez, Eric," Robin exclaimed, "Maybe even two Kamikaze ships would help—but then the remaining gunship could maneuver the missiles and finish the job." Robin looked almost as dejected as Eric.

"I know things look hopeless." Michael noted the somber mood of his team-mates. "Remember, a lot of people, including our country, are counting on us. We need to keep moving forward. I truly believe that we'll find a solution; that we'll weather this storm." Michael tried to smile. In turn, his friends responded with feigned smiles.

"Moving on, I talked to Peter this morning, and he said that Cephid had spoken before the UN and had been well received." Michael was trying to make his words sound more upbeat.

"Also, the news of the missile crisis was released yesterday. People appear stunned. For the most part, nations appear to be welding together. The UN Security Council held an emergency meeting and voted that their five nations should have equal footing in deciding what our response should be. Peter immediately saw a problem and met with the President. He designated Peter to talk to members of the Council to establish a hierarchy of control with the US being the leader."

"Lastly, Peter said that the team had met, and he had been in touch with the President and Defense. All agreed that the Praetorian Center should be destroyed. The next step was to get Chinese approval since the Center was on their soil. Secretary Albrecht was to undertake this task."

After the meeting, Eric cornered Michael and asked if they could go for a walk. "Michael, I don't know quite how to begin ... Brandy and I heard some information this afternoon that was *very* disturbing, so much so that I thought I should tell it to you in private. I don't know if the bots would eavesdrop, but I don't want to risk it."

Michael's forehead crinkled and his lips turned down. He nodded as they walked away from any possible prying ears and eyes.

Eric then related the information that Torbid let slip that afternoon about the Xyrptan plans to send an armada of spaceships—including warships—to Earth after a space exploration agreement was signed.

Michael thought for a few moments. "How would a *pilot* bot have that information? It's unlikely that he would get that type of news from home, so he must have overheard someone at CEAF, most likely Maxid talking to one of his staff, or maybe he saw a transmission. It's very disturbing, particularly seeing they gave us *no* prior indication of such. You're right in feeling that we should keep this secret. I'll think about it further, but off hand, I think we should get back to Washington ASAP. I don't want to tell Peter about this over the phone, so let's keep it among the three of us until we get back. Tell Brandy to keep quiet for now."

Eric nodded.

The bots had been no slouches when it came to providing creature comforts for the humans visiting them. They had provided hors d'oeuvres along with before dinner cocktails, Michael chose a dry Martini, a taste he had acquired from his uncle Peter. Eric was a teetotaler while the women preferred white wine. The entrée was a salmon, goat cheese combination with assorted vegetables. For dessert they had Cherries Jubilee. There were no other diners. In all the time they had spent at the Center, they had seen no other humans.

Michael thought that this would eventually come to an end with all the publicity the bots were receiving. He could see where the bots might even open up their Center for tours, but of course, this could only happen *after* they had dealt with the missile crisis.

Shortly after starting their entrée, Robin took a sip of water and cleared her throat. "I had a remarkable thought today. It took over 200,000 years for us humans to evolve to our present status. In a little over a millennium, these robots have progressed to a level that, in many respects, exceeds our evolution. Of course, living beings developed them, but just think: we have "soft wires"—nerves that connect the various parts of our body to the brain—and they do it wirelessly. They have *perfect* memory for text and pictures. They don't have to eat or sleep. All they need is get a charge every so often. I wonder if we humans will evolve to this remarkable level in another 100,000 years. Don't you find that fascinating?"

Brandy furrowed her brow and hesitated before she spoke. "I don't know that I'd want to give up eating and sleeping—two of the joys I have in life. The disabled would certainly benefit from some of their gadgetry, like using nano-motors and wireless controls to operate nerve-impaired extremities. I think that the advances in neuroscience today suggest that *someday* we'll have artificial intelligence interactions via an implanted chip connected to the brain which will give us better memory, and maybe even clearer thought. So, I think that we'll evolve sooner than you think, and it'll be with the aid of the advances in robotics. I don't think that we'll ever evolve to a robot status though. At least, I *hope* not. But you never know, perhaps we could be genetically engineered to produce a *more* perfect brain. I'm not sure that would be a good thing either, though. While we're brainstorming along this line, I wonder if the Xyrptans could transfer all mental functions from an elderly brain into a child, or even a baby, so that one could live two or more lifetimes? Thinking further out, maybe they could clone a life and make a brain transfer. One might be able to live forever. Robin, this is crazy. Let's get back to some serious talk. "

Michael said, "I believe that we, as humans, will follow a *different* path in evolution though I'm not sure what that'll be. In another 100,000 years we might be looked at as we look at the Cro-Magnons now."

"Brandy, do you have anything further to add to the conversation?"

Brandy's thinking had reverted momentarily to Maxid's earlier implication that women should stick together and let men do the work. She perked up when Michael asked her opinion.

"We were very disappointed by their spaceship not being battle-worthy. However, there might *still* be a way to use it to stop the missile crisis. I want to think about it further. I'm not sure that the robots have a good *creative* thinking ability. One thought is to have our spaceship crash into one of their Shepherd ships, but that would still leave two ships functional. Too bad the Xyrptans didn't send more spaceships here, or better still, several of their gunships."

Her implied jab toward the Xyrptans was met with nods of approval from around the table.

Brandy mused, "With their technology and help, I wonder if it would be possible for us to *build* gunships in the two year timespan we have left. I think we should look into that possibility."

"Robin's eyes popped open and Eric leaned forward with interest. Michael said, "Brandy, that's a brilliant bit of thinking. I'll pass it on to Peter right away."

With soft music playing in the background an air of joviality became apparent in spite of the black cloud hanging over all their heads. In the midst of this scene, Cephid walked in to everyone's surprise. He grabbed a Martini to seem sociable.

Michael congratulated him on his appearance before the UN. He accepted these complements graciously. He had been with them since the team had formed, and for the most part, he acted as human as any of them.

Eric looked around and asked, "Brandy, are you a vegetarian?"

"I'm a vegan and a Buddhist. Is there anything else you'd like to know?"

"I didn't mean to pry. I was just curious." He smiled and shrugged.

"No offense taken." A hint of a smile tugged at her lips.

Eric liked Brandy. He'd been trying to form a closer relationship with her, but whatever he said, always seemed to rub her the wrong way. He didn't feel he was being too aggressive. He wondered if she felt he had a sexual interest, and she was trying to squelch that feeling.

Robin and Brandy sat at one end of the table whispering to each other. They stopped, both with broad smiles, as if they had just indulged in a secret.

They were acting like two school girls.

Brandy said, "Cephid, how do male robots react to females? Are you attracted to one another?" Brandy fluttered her eyelashes—her glasses on the table—with an ingratiating smile. Robin also smiled, but in a demure way.

Cephid at first appeared to be at a loss for words. "Girls, you caught me completely off guard. However, I'm sterile. I can't show real affection, though I suppose I could fake it. However, that doesn't mean that I can't form *friendships* that are real. On Xyrpta we have both male and female robots that are built to show affection. I suppose, you would have to consider this fake, too, since it's artificial. You might call these *sex slaves*. A small portion of our population prefers to have a robot rather than a human partner."

Brandy was not satisfied and persisted. "So, if I flirted with you, I couldn't expect a response in kind? You're a blonde, blue-eyed, *handsome* man. I can understand that in your culture some humans might *prefer* a bot as a partner rather than a human. I might feel likewise if I lived on your planet."

Brandy's brazen comment caused Eric and Michael to stare openly at her. Cephid had recovered his usual stoic demeanor. "As I mentioned,

I could fake it, and I believe that I could do a good job of it. However, I would do that only if I felt it was necessary as part of my job. I'm built to perform as I'm instructed. When we're not in use, we are more or less inert—no dreaming and no thoughts other than those related to the task we've been assigned. I hope this doesn't disappoint you."

Brandy looked down. She had no smile. She replaced her glasses and was once again guarded. Robin had a smile on her face, as if this were the answer she'd expected. Michael wondered if the two girls had made a bet on what Cephid's answer would be.

Eric looked crestfallen. He felt jealous that Brandy could act so flirtatious with Cephid, though put on, when his own feeble attempts produced no such reaction.

The conversation then reverted to their progress in preparing a defense against the incoming missiles including what should be the next step, but nothing new was forthcoming.

Chinese Center Under Siege

The team members returned to Washington except for Cephid who remained at CEAF for a routine checkup. The immediate goal was now focused on the impending attack on the Chinese Center and neutralizing their activities without alerting their home base in Praetoria of the change in command. The former was routine, while the latter was a sensitive undertaking that would require, not only thorough planning, but meticulous performance as well. The Defense Department, XCOM, the Xyrptans on their home planet, and the bots at CEAF were the planners of this action. The Chinese were participating as well.

Meanwhile, Homeland Security and the State Department were focusing on the position robots should have in our society. Their first step was to contact the Supreme Council in Xyrpta. They were referred on to the Department of Robotics. On their planet the bots had long been accepted as a part of society.

The majority of bots on Xyrpta had a protective covering, but not like human skin. Their dress was determined by their job. Their facial features were fixed, making it obvious that they were bots. However, when one was willing to pay for a bot as a sexual partner, they were constructed to appear as human as the real thing.

From this information a committee had been established. The consensus so far was that bots should be dressed distinctively along with a skin-like covering, but not be humanoid in appearance. The largest disagreement was related to their mental function and how close this should be allowed to mimic humans. It was unanimously decided that no changes to the bots were to occur until the missile crisis was solved. The committee had plenty of time to come up with a plan for categorizing bots.

On their return from CEAF, Michael set up a private meeting with Peter to include Eric and Brandy. The utmost secrecy was required.

"So, why all the secrecy?" Peter scowled, annoyed to have this added to his already busy schedule.

Because Eric had the best memory, Michael deferred to him to relate what they had heard at CEAF. Brandy then added her impressions as well.

Peter, perplexed, remained in thought for a while before he said anything. "You might be building a mountain out of a mole hill. You're implying that the Xyrptans might be planning their *own* invasion of Earth, correct?"

Michael said, "I have my doubts—as did we all—as to the significance of Torbid's remarks, but we felt that we couldn't disregard them."

"Where do we go from here," Peter asked.

Brandy couldn't have looked more serious. "We're presuming that Torbid's slip of the tongue was *exactly* that, and that the Xyrptans have plans of which we haven't been told. I've mentioned previously that I had doubts about the extent of the bot's thinking processes. They obviously live in a more advanced civilization than we do, but I'm not sure about their ability to assess information and come to a logical conclusion—I'm questioning their decision-making prowess and their judgment. I know that isn't what we're talking about here, but I wanted to insert my thoughts about their thinking ability in general. Torbid's awareness that he had made a mistake was clear. That should have been picked up by his A.I. before he blurted out the information. We're dealing with *robots*, not humans. I think it would be worthwhile to obtain an expert opinion of the extent of the bots' artificial intelligence. We have our own experts, and I think we should bring them into the ball game."

Eric cleared his throat. "I recall now that David Standid mentioned to Cephid and me—that when they placed some of my thinking processes into Cephid's brain—they determined that the thinking process of the Xyrptans was different from ours. He didn't indicate what the difference was though."

Peter spoke slowly, as if he were thinking while he talked. "You're bringing to the forefront something that we've been remiss in doing. We've assumed that the Xyrptans, because they are a millennium ahead of us, are superior to us in *every* respect. And maybe they are, but perhaps they aren't. They may not think the same way we do, and that may play into their coming to different conclusions. It's worried me that they always insist on *destroying* anything Praetorian. Brandy, your idea of bringing on board some of our own experts on artificial intelligence is an excellent idea. I'm embarrassed that I didn't think of this before. I believe that we need to establish a separate group, one whose purpose will include determining the truthfulness and worthiness of anything Xyrptan, whether from a human or a bot. We need to know whether or not our thinking processes are aligned. I think that one of us needs to be on that team, and I'm ruling out Michael and myself, because we have as much on our platter now as we can handle. I think this is true for Eric as well. Robin is already working on understanding the bots, so I think she is the logical choice."

Michael didn't want the meeting to go too far astray from its original purpose. "We need to determine what the Xyrptans have in mind for the part that we are to play in their space exploration program. We shouldn't let that go until we've finished our present crisis. Maybe it's premature, but I believe that we should get some idea of their intent, particularly in view of our new information. That should be the main purpose of this new group, and at the same time, they can assess the quality and trustworthiness of the Xyrptans' mind."

"When you first mentioned the purpose for this meeting, Michael, I was dubious that it was a worthwhile endeavor. I didn't think it would evolve into something this *big*. So, thank you all. I'll contact Robin to sketch out the new committee." Peter closed his notebook and left.

Several weeks went by. The military, with Chinese consent, set a firm date for two weeks hence, for the attack on the Chinese Center.

XCOM had been kept apprised of the planning which led to ardent discussions of the various aspects of the attack. One such debate was over the use of bots versus humans.

The Xyrptans were vehemently opposed to using anything but bots. They said the soldier bots were made to perform exactly as directed, but still with the ability to alter their actions based on their assessment of the current situation. They had no fear. The humans finally acquiesced to the Xyrptan demand for total control and the use of their bots. In the evaluation it was conceded that their soldier bots were the equal of our forces, and for us that meant no risk of loss of life.

The bot's plan included two platoons, each composed of several squads. Surveillance of the Chinese Center had revealed no more than fifty bots, half of which were soldiers. The number indicated that they were still importing bots from Praetoria. We would have the advantage of surprise. They were to silently eliminate the bots guarding the communications building, break into the structure, and quickly decommission the bots at the radio transmitters before they could alert Praetoria. Our soldier bots would then take on the enemy bots. There would be minimal human supervision. The lead field bot, who had been trained in Xyrpta, would be in constant contact with the head bot, and at his side would be one of our Special Forces personnel—the only human involved in the whole operation.

The Chinese Center was located in northeast China in a remote, wooded area with rolling hills. Observers were to watch the proceedings from hidden sites on the surrounding hills. Their number was to be limited so as to not endanger the operation. Videotaping would be done from several sites.

The two weeks went by rapidly and everyone was rushing to meet the deadline. The number of observers was kept at a minimum—Eric, a UN representative, two from the Pentagon, and a couple Chinese observers.

Forty eight hours before onset of action, an army transport plane filled with soldier bots along with Maxid, Eric, and the pentagon observers had arrived in China. Maxid introduced Eric to the head soldier who bore the markings of what appeared to be a Captain in their forces. He also met the lieutenants in charge of each platoon and the sergeants leading each squad. Maxid was trying to impress Eric with the quality of his bots. He was successful.

Two hours before the attack was to begin, a Chinese soldier led Eric and the others to a wooded knoll overlooking the Center. They were about two hundred yards away, where with binoculars, they had a good view. Fortunately the communications Center was at one end and not centrally located, which made it more vulnerable.

After everyone was in place, the waiting began. There would be another hour before dawn. Maxid came up behind them silently, and nodded to his lead bot, and Eric.

Eric began reviewing in his mind the various decisions that had been made along the way. Would it not have been better to just blow up the tower initially to avoid any communication going out before they had secured the building? On the other hand, being able to remain in touch with the Praetorians without them being aware of a change in personnel would be a huge advantage—if they could pull it off. Eric wondered if the reward would be worth the risk. The remaining question for him was how they planned to mimic the enemy bots in communicating with Praetoria.

Using their night vision binoculars, Eric and the others began to familiarize themselves with the terrain where the conflagration would occur. There were five buildings arranged in a pentagon formation with entrances all facing one another. They could look down and see three entrances, one of which was to the communications building. The captain pointed toward soldiers standing at the entrances and pointed his index finger at his head and then his stomach, signifying that they would soon be zapped and then shot in the abdomen.

The captain said something quietly into his headset in Xyrptan.

Eric could see one of our soldier bots crouch and move slowly toward the front of the communications building where there was a guard. The Xyrptan bot raised his gun, and without a sound the guard bot fell to his knees, remained there a few seconds, and then pitched forward on to his face. From prior surveillance they knew that there were two other guards on duty. They presumed that the other bots had succumbed to a similar fate. They could now see the one enemy bot being dragged to the side of the building to take him out of sight.

Two Xyrptan bots had donned Praetorian uniforms and were approaching the communications building entrance in the light of the lit compound. They didn't hesitate and disappeared behind the door. Other soldiers now entered three of the buildings, all except for the barracks. Here the soldiers were planting something at the sides of the building.

The captain had a direct link to his soldiers. He recounted what was happening inside for the humans present.

Inside the communications building, our soldiers encountered two bots sitting calmly in chairs before their radio equipment oblivious to what was going on outside. Silently our bots raised their weapons, drew aim and fired. One radio transmitter slumped backwards in his chair, while the other pitched head first onto his keyboard. One of the bots then went to check for other enemy within the building. It was only fifteen minutes before our bots were again outside and signaled that all was accomplished.

The captain was now engaged in conversation about the beginning of the next phase of the operation. Maxid gave Eric a thumb's up and smiled. Dawn was approaching, the sky appeared lighter, but as yet there was no sign of any enemy activity. Extending one finger at a time, the captain appeared to be counting into his microphone. At five there was an explosion that rocked the area. The barracks was literally raised into the air, torn apart, then it fell back to earth, just a pile of wood and metal debris. There was smoke but no fire. The captain then turned to Maxid, smiled and they shook hands. In English he said, "Sir, I believe the enemy Center is now ours, and the only remaining intact bots are the two in the communications room who are decommissioned and ready for your attention."

Maxid motioned to Eric that he should follow. They hiked down to the compound where two other bots accompanied them into the communications building.

Suddenly, they heard a vehicle approaching at a high speed. The captain was prepared for any eventuality. He signaled his men to hide behind the roadside trees. A van braked to a sudden stop in the center of the compound, and five soldier bots bolted out. They stood, dazed looking at the smoldering remains of the barracks. Because Maxid and his group had gone into the communications building, they weren't visible. At a signal from their leader, a dozen Xyrptan bots rushed to encircle the van with raised guns. A battle ensued.

Surprise decided the conflagration, with four of the enemy bots falling within seconds. The fifth bot ran into one of our bots and began a hand-to-hand fight. The others gathered around to watch. It turned into an old fashioned wrestling match. Where had bots learned to wrestle? The enemy bot wasn't going to play fair, and began trying to gouge the eyes out of our bot. Not wanting to lose anyone, the captain went up and shot the enemy in the head and then the abdomen. This was not very humane, but then these were not humans.

Maxid, who had been watching through a window, came out. The captain said that all was under control, so Maxid returned inside to complete his work.

Maxid was communicating with someone on his cell. Then he hung up. He told Eric, "We have a helicopter coming in. We'll transport these two bots to a local airport, then fly them to CEAF in the States, to *orient* them to our way of thinking. They'll then be slave bots and return here to do our bidding. We'll have them radio the Praetorians that there was a breakdown in equipment to explain the brief lack of communication. We'll get the incoming messages and respond accordingly. Hopefully the Praetorians won't know the difference. The first several communiqués will be vital."

Eric was excited. "You pulled this off like clockwork, Maxid. I didn't really think that your bots could perform as well as our Navy Seals, but they didn't miss a beat. I couldn't be more impressed."

Just then the captain rushed in. "Maxid, come with me. I have a surprise for you." He had a big smile on his face. They followed the captain over to a building that was some distance away from the compound that appeared to be a hanger.

Eric's jaw dropped. Then he shook his head in disbelief. There stood a sleek-looking spaceship. Looking at Maxid, "Is that what I think it is?"

"It's a Praetorian gunship. We are very fortunate. The first thing we'll do is check it out to see if we can use it. I'll have two of our pilots come here and fly it back to CEAF. Now we may have something to work with. Rather than having just an armed freighter, we may now have a gunship that can go up against the shepherd ships. I believe the odds of a successful missile defense are turning in our favor." Maxid walked around the ship counting. There were four gun ports. "This looks similar to our own gunships. Those Praetorians are wonderful thieves. I'll bet that the inside is like our ships as well. This may be one time that we are thankful that our secrets were stolen."

An enthused Eric said, "I'm calling Peter right now. He won't believe our good fortune. How soon will we know whether or not we can use this ship?"

"I'd give it a week. By then we should have most of the answers. And Eric, I think it would be a good idea for you to come out to CEAF, since you're familiar with our freighter ship. Right now you're the resident Earth expert on our spaceships. We might even be able to take you up for a spin. Bring Brandy along. She's the one who wanted to fly in a space ship."

Brief Interlude—Intra-galactic Exchange

A team meeting was held the day after Eric's return to hear his account of the attack on the enemy bot headquarters.

"Ladies and gents, you would've been proud of our bots. Their precision and swiftness was a marvel to behold. In an hours' time they took over the Center and eliminated all the enemy bots. I believe we accomplished our goal of not alerting the Praetorians, and hopefully we'll now be able to communicate with them. Our Navy Seals couldn't have done better." Eric then went into detail and ended with the news that they had discovered a Praetorian gunship that they hoped could be used to intercept the Shepherd gunships.

"Good job Eric," said Peter. "Fighting wars using humans, I believe, will soon be a thing of the past."

"I agree, sir. Their strength, speed, and fearlessness would be hard to match by us, and their thinking ability appears as good as ours. I'm afraid, however, that bot wars might proliferate as there's no human sacrifice. I'd be interested in hearing from Cephid about bot skirmishes on Xyrpta."

Cephid said "You're correct that it makes fighting easier. On our planet we have just one nation, so an incursion of one state on another would make no sense, and in any case, would be suppressed by our nation's soldiers. Our soldiers are bots, but the higher officers are human."

Eric said that he and Brandy had been invited to visit the Center in a week to see the Praetorian spaceship and to help assess its battle worthiness in their missile defense.

Everyone looked at Brandy. She blushed. "I'm good with technical matters and in math, too." Brandy now thought that she had been too hasty in feeling that the Xyrptans thought of women as second class citizens. She was thrilled to be included with Eric in evaluating the gunship. For his part, Eric was happy to have Brandy's company. That she was math savvy, too, was a plus. He hoped that he might now have a topic that they could both converse in comfortably.

Peter interrupted the banter, "You guys pay attention out there. This ship could be an important cog in our missile defense."

A few days later, Robin met with Peter to begin planning the new committee that was to be called QCOM—the query committee. This would be a subcommittee under the jurisdiction of XCOM. Robin had already contacted several AI investigators at the various universities around the country and came up with Dr. Ed Ackerman at Johns Hopkins—a highly respected neuroscientist—as her choice to join the new group. He had the advantage of being close to Washington and thus should be more readily available for meetings. She felt that they should make contact with the human neuro- and AI scientists on Xyrpta to begin an exchange of information between the two planets. She wanted to confine the group to just the two of them initially, until they had a better idea of where they wanted the committee to go. Peter agreed with these recommendations and urged Robin to get the committee working as soon as possible. He would attend their first meeting and help them establish a mission statement to guide them in their work.

On the flight out to CEAF Eric had a chance to try out his new approach on Brandy. "As you probably know, I am a theoretical astrophysicist. My main goal is to incorporate gravity into a Grand Unification Theory with the other three forces."

"Interesting! My introduction to the subject was via the English astrophysicist Stephen Hawking's books. My father is an engineer—which I think explains my technical aptitude—but my mother's social consciousness and her work in this area always dominated our household. She's been the driving force in my life."

Eric felt somewhat deflated. He had been thinking that Brandy had more background in his area of interest. "My experience was just the opposite. Dad was a physicist and he worked in the nuclear area, so we weren't far apart in our interests. I followed his lead while my mother was primarily a housewife and mother. Was there something in particular in Stephen's books that attracted your attention?"

She rolled her eyes. "Is this leading somewhere? My interest now is solely on the missile crisis, and I'm not going to be deterred by any *tangential* relationship. Where are you going?"

"I like your directness. In a roundabout way I was trying to make our budding friendship something *more*. You're a beautiful, intelligent woman. I guess I was trying to push our relationship too fast. Sorry! My apologies. "

"Don't get me wrong. I want to be friends, too, but that's it. Now let's change the subject."

For the remainder of the flight there was small talk, but neither said much of any consequence. Eric decided that he would just work on their friendship.

After landing and getting settled in their quarters, they both met for lunch where a surprise was in store for them. Sitting with one of the bots and in earnest discussion was Robin. With a startled look she got up, rushed over, and gave them both a hug. "What a surprise. I didn't expect to see you guys here."

Eric smiled, "We're here to check out the new gunship that they've flown in from China. What are you doing?"

"I'm working with the bots. Have you met Idid? He's in charge of the bot lab." She turned toward her table and introduced her lunch-mate.

Just then Maxid came in and walked over to the group. "Glad to see the team made it out here OK." He nodded to Idid. Maxid said, "I have something to say, so let's have lunch and get down to business."

Robin said goodbye to Idid and joined the others. After they had ordered and begun their meal, Maxid exclaimed, "I have something for you and I think you'll all be happy. First, we've brought in the gunship from China. It appears to be similar to our own gunships on Xyrpta. I'll be very surprised if we aren't able to use it to intercept the missile shepherd ships. That's our goal."

Eric couldn't hold back. "Fantastic, that's the best news we've had since this whole missile crisis began."

Maxid raised his hand. "There's more. This pertains to you two women. Brandy, I may have misled you when you were last here. I have another task for you that, I believe, is better suited to your training and your interests. You'll not be disappointed. But first, Robin, I want *you* to accompany Eric in evaluating the spaceship."

Robin sat wide-eyed. "I don't know what to say, except that I'm *overwhelmed,* and I'll do my best."

"I know you will, Robin. We want to take advantage of your engineering background, which should help Eric too."

While Robin was all smiles, Brandy had a bewildered look on her face. Maxid seemed two-faced, first supporting her interest in space flight and then taking it away from her.

"After your meal, let's meet in the conference room next door, and I'll show you what Brandy's new job will be. All of you come. Brandy, don't look so *unhappy.* I guarantee that you'll not be disappointed." Maxid rose and left the lunchroom. They hurried to finish their meal.

Eric led the girls next door. On opening the door and walking in, Eric quickly stepped back, bumping into the girls.

Standing before them was a short woman with green skin, pointed ears, and a big smile on her face. She stepped forward with her hand out. "I'm Ingrid and I know that you are Eric, Robin and Brandy. I'm *so* glad to meet you."

Maxid was standing to the side with a big grin on his face, "I told you I'd have a surprise for you. Ingrid is a bot, but made in the *image* of a female on Xyrpta. Even though we are in the midst of the missile crisis, we should be able to handle some of the other important issues we are going to face in the near future. Ingrid is an intelligent, educated journalist. She is replicating an actual human at home, and has the same mental capacity, thoughts, and ideas as the *real* Ingrid. I think that you and she, Brandy, have a lot in common. The idea is for the two of you to exchange information about your lives, homes, and culture. Ingrid will forward her new information back to Xyrpta, where the real Ingrid will report the news in national newspapers. I'm sure she'll have many offers to be interviewed on TV as well. Brandy, your job is to do the same here on Earth. You'll interview Ingrid and write up and report on life on Xyrpta. Peter is trying to line up a spot for you with The *New York Times* and The *Guardian* in London. Once you get started I expect that many other papers will want you on their by-line as well.

Brandy's eyes were wide and her mouth a tight line. She hated the idea of being beaten out for the space job with Eric, but on the other hand, she saw also saw a great opportunity. "Ingrid, I'm very glad to meet you, and I'm looking forward to working with you."

Maxid, standing in the background, had a big smile on his face. This would be a step forward in fostering a good relationship between the two planets.

The team engaged Ingrid in conversation. She showed that she was not only intelligent, but that she was charismatic also.

As they broke up, Brandy invited Ingrid to join them for dinner that evening. Ingrid graciously accepted.

Now, with something to celebrate, they had a cocktail hour before dinner with Ingrid joining in. The overwhelming fear they had about the impending missile crisis receded into the background for the moment.

During dinner, Brandy asked Ingrid what she knew about Earth and its people. "You would be surprised. Maxid's staff has been sending back information about you for *several* years. Ingrid back home has been writing about Earth for this duration. Our people know much more about you than you know about us. I'm here to change that. The other thing is that we have been through *many* of the crises that you are now experiencing, and we can advise you on how we handled these same situations—such as your drug problem."

Eric perked up. "Just how would you handle our drug problem here in the United States?"

"We did two things—the last being the most effective. But first, I have to say that we do not understand why the Mexicans seem so passive and are not *demanding* more help. They are virtually at war on your doorstep. Isn't this as important, if not more so, than your two wars overseas? They are the conduit for the drugs traveling from South America to the United States. If you did not have an enormous number of drug users, the cartels would dry up and Mexico would not be in the dire straits they're in now."

"But, more to the point, we started doing tests via urine samples where people worked, and if it tested positive, we knew that one or more persons were responsible. When a toilet is flushed, a sample is taken. By law, the restrooms at businesses are locked, and you have to know the code to get in. With a positive test, we went to that group and asked for urine samples from each individual that they had to provide. That usually pinpointed the culprit. The name of that drug user is added to a list that is published each week. There are criminal penalties as well. This affected the user's work status, and more often than not, that individual was ostracized. "

Robin chimed in. "What about the privacy issues? Did that cause a problem?"

"Not at all. We have a different form of government than you, which we can talk about later. It has evolved to become quite paternalistic. That brings us to the most *effective* means of controlling drugs. Every human on Xyrpta has a chip in his or her body. The original purpose was for identification, but other purposes were later added. These chips are built to detect various drugs and medicines a person might be taking. They can be scanned from a short distance. Scanners are in stores and in public places. One can hardly go anywhere without being scanned. If their chip detects a tagged drug, it will be picked up along with the person's ID. The police take it from there. It took several generations, but we have virtually *no* drug problem now. I can't tell you everything now, but our police tactics are humane. Drug dealers *can't* go undetected. They get picked up within days of dealing. This may seem to be too much an invasion of a person's privacy, but this is balanced against eliminating a problem that was a menace to society."

"That's remarkable. I hope that we can solve our problem within a generation. With your people's help perhaps we can." Eric was impressed by how clearly Ingrid expressed herself.

The conversation lightened up after Ingrid's discourse. Eric was the first to stand. "Tomorrow's going to be a busy day so I'm going to retire early. Robin, I'll see you at breakfast. From there we can take on the spaceship. Brandy, I think we all want to hear a lot more about Xyrpta. Ingrid, are you in communication with your namesake on Xyrpta?"

"Yes, I'll be getting some transmission time almost every day. Let Brandy know of any questions you have, and I'll get you answers shortly."

The night passed uneventfully. Eric thought that perhaps Robin would knock on his door again, but that didn't happen, and he wasn't inclined to take the initiative.

The Tide Begins to Turn

Breakfast was a brief affair the next morning as everyone was anxious to get started on the day. Robin and Eric went to Maxid's office as they had been instructed. There, Maxid met them with two bots who wore one-piece work-suits with XASA insignias on their chests—Xyrpta Aeronautic Space Administration, similar to our NASA. Torbid they knew, and the other was Rubid, his copilot.

Maxid began. "Before we start, I'd like to make clear what each of you'll be doing. Eric, you and Robin will learn how to pilot a spaceship. We have plenty of time; perhaps eighteen months, before the missiles will be threatening Earth. We anticipate that we will send up one or perhaps two spaceships to intercept the enemy gunships six months before their arrival date. It'll be a long trip, about three months out to engage them and then three months back. One of you will be onboard the gunship, whoever demonstrates the greatest proficiency during the training period. Torbid and Rubid will also be on board."

"Make no mistake, this will be a dangerous mission, and you certainly have the right to turn us down, but if so, we would like to know early on. We won't have room for two, so only one of you can go. I expect you'll want to discuss with each other the implications of going on this assignment. You may be asking *why* you should participate. I've talked with Peter and the officials at NASA, and they want a human being engaged in this part of the defense. NASA wanted to use one of their astronauts, but one of your Cabinet officials requested that a human be on board, one about whom he had some knowledge. Any questions?"

Both looked stunned. Eric said, "Not right now, but I'm sure we will later."

"Fine, let's get started. He led them out to the gunship. It was in its disc shape. Walking around it, Maxid had Torbid point out its features.

"There are four gun turrets, each on an edge ninety degrees apart. These are beam guns that have an effective range of about a mile. Thereafter their strength wanes rapidly. Once the beam is within a quarter mile, it can it can zero in on the object it's seeking. The maneuverability of these ships is fantastic, particularly the smaller ships like this one. First, you want to be the smallest target possible, so you face your enemy edgewise. When you want to evade him, you can make every possible motion, such as a flip forward, backward or to the side. We have certain programmed evasive maneuvers that are random, so that the enemy can't predict where you'll move. In turn, the program is aware of where the enemy is and makes a calculated guess as to his next move." Torbid explained that he and Rubid had been trained in these maneuvers in a simulation module before performing them in space.

Maxid interrupted. "That's enough for now. Let's go inside."

Picking up a paddle, Torbid pressed a button, and a hatch just below the edge of the ship opened. The two pilots then pushed a stairway on wheels up to the ship while Maxid explained that no step-way is built into the vehicle to save space. After climbing up, they entered the control room. Torbid showed them the control panels that operated the ship, and explained generally how the ship operated. Robin had been in the training module for astronauts at NASA. She was glad to see that the orientation was somewhat similar—a thousand years had not made that much difference. Torbid explained that no living quarters were needed, no restroom facilities, and no food galley. Bots remained at the controls 24 hours a day for the duration of a trip.

"With humans on board," Maxid said, "we'll put in the basic necessities for you. We have a person from NASA coming over to help us.

It will be cramped, but it should be livable. Torbid and Rubid will be involved in training you. We want you to be familiar with the gunnery, so you'll get training in that area too. We'll give you a course in galactic navigation, so you can fill in as navigator. All on board have to be able to step in and take over from a person or bot if that becomes necessary. This is a small ship, but it's very suitable for the job at hand. Any questions?" Both Eric and Robin shook their heads. "Then I'll leave you so you can get started. Torbid, why don't you start Eric on the operation of the ship, and Rubid can start Robin on the gunnery."

The morning training session went well. They broke at noon. The bots made it clear that they had exactly one hour. They were quite precise in their use of time.

Lunch gave Eric and Robin a chance to talk about participating in this phase of the defense program.

"This is out of my area of expertise, and I'm not sure I want to jeopardize my career," Eric said, worried. "On the other hand, I realize this is a crisis, and I want to help in any way I can. I wonder why they aren't bringing in astronauts from NASA."

Robin frowned. "I feel *exactly* the same. I think we should bring this up with Peter. I want to talk to my boss at NASA, too He may have some inside information. It would be a lifetime experience, and it might end up changing our careers. I'm going to have to think about this. And what about my new job heading up QCOM? Obviously, Maxid isn't aware of that."

"I have no interest in changing careers. The time I've spent away from my work is troubling enough. It'll take me months to catch up on what I've lost so far. I think that QCOM and your work with the bot program at NASA are about all you can handle, Robin, but let's think about it. Maxid said we have to make up our minds quickly, so I think we should give ourselves a deadline. Say, three days? Can you do that? "

"I can if I'm able to contact everyone in that time frame."

The afternoon session was a continuation of the morning's activities. Eric asked Torbid, "You guys don't breathe. We need oxygen, and what about lighting?"

"We'll have to put in oxygen for you. We don't use much lighting unless we have a problem to fix. Then, we can light up the ship, but we'll have to add more lighting for you."

"One other question—how do I spend my time when I have no assigned task? Six months is a long time to remain inactive."

"You'll have to bring something along to occupy your time. The person coming over from NASA should be able to answer most of these questions."

Rubid, working with Robin, was explaining how the guns worked. "Warships have a shield that protects them from a beam by deflecting it when it hits at an angle. Only a beam that is vertical, or almost so, to the target is damaging. All the maneuvering is to get into just the right position to get a shot. When the beam hits, it usually blows a hole in the vehicle. This may not be catastrophic if nothing vital is hit. There's no gas in the plane so exposure to the outside is inconsequential. However, in your case it would be important unless you have a mask with oxygen."

Having humans on board required a lot of additional equipment, supplies, and room. Robin wondered if it wouldn't be better to just let the bots fight it out. It didn't really seem necessary to have humans on board, and she couldn't see that they would add anything to the success of the mission. She decided that would be one of the questions she would ask Maxid.

With the afternoon session completed, both trainees took a rest before meeting with Brandy for dinner. No one seemed happy.

Dinner was a work session. Eric and Robin began debating whether or not they should accept Maxid's offer to go on the space mission.

"I'll do whatever my country asks in a crisis … if I can see that my help is really necessary." Eric was debating within his own mind. "I can't see that I can do as good a job as one of our astronauts. *That's* what bothers me the most, and *that's* what I have to clarify with Peter and Maxid."

Robin said, "I agree. More so in my case—I'm already playing a vital role in working on developing our robotic program, plus the added responsibility of QCOM. Let's set up a meeting with Maxid first thing in the morning. Brandy, you are the lucky one. We're in a quandary while you're set for the indefinite future with a wonderful position."

Brandy shook her head, a slight smile on her face. "To tell the truth, I *was* a little jealous of you two, but now I'm happy to be where I am. Ingrid is a wonderful person, er, bot. It's getting difficult for me to differentiate between the two, even though she's short, green and has pointed ears." She gave a little laugh.

"You should stick to your bot work, Robin. I think you're better off helping in your area of expertise. On the other hand, I can see Eric staying with the space program, but I would trade tit for tat. If you're willing to give your life, you should have the right to get something in return, particularly if it doesn't cost anyone anything. Eric, you want information on your area of interest, and the Xyrptans can provide that in spades. Plus, if you're going to spend six months in space, use the time to advance your own theories. That's what I would do."

"You gals are good at giving advice, but traveling in a spaceship to engage in battle isn't exactly the type of atmosphere conducive to pondering about M theory. But you make a good point. I agree about Robin being more useful sticking with robotics. And I'm not saying that just to get rid of my competition, Robin, I really mean it. That's where you can serve your country best. For me, I'll have to think further about what I should do. I still don't understand why an astronaut wouldn't do better."

First thing the next day, Eric and Robin confronted Maxid in his office. Both indicated that they thought that an astronaut would do a better job than either of them.

"I wasn't being entirely clear before. We first thought of using astronauts, but your superiors wanted one of you to go along. We would rather have an astronaut. Talk to Peter and see what he says."

Eric responded quickly. "Give us time to call Peter before we go any further." Maxid assented to the request and the two of them returned to Eric's room to make the call.

They had some difficulty in getting Peter, as he was in a meeting, but Eric said it was critical to speak to him right away. Peter finally came on. He sounded brusque and irritated. "What's going on that *necessitated* taking me out of my meeting?"

"Sir," said Eric rather hesitantly. "Sorry to disturb you, but we have a problem here that needs solving right away." Eric related the events of the past two days and indicated that neither he nor Robin felt qualified for the job. Why not use astronauts who are trained for this type of work"

"We've been having trouble with Herbert, in Defense." Peter sighed as if he were embarrassed. "He neither likes nor trusts the bots. If something should go wrong and the missile attack is successful, he said that he would hold me responsible. He had sympathy from other members of the cabinet too. I couldn't dissuade them. I brought up the use of astronauts—the logical choice— but Herbert said he wanted someone he knew and could trust, so that's how the job fell to you or Robin. I'm sorry for not explaining this to you before, but things have been very busy around here."

"Sir, I don't think that Robin should go. She's more valuable working with the bots. If we don't use the astronauts … I'm very reluctant, but if you say so, I'll do it."

"Thank you Eric, I appreciate your attitude. I'll talk to Maxid about sending two astronauts over there for training in case I can get you removed from the mission. But I want you to continue the training. I agree with you about Robin. Tell her to please resume her work with the robots and QCOM."

After hanging up, both Robin and Eric looked at each other with some dismay. They had been on speaker phone. "Thanks Eric for standing up for me. I really appreciate it, but I feel guilty about leaving you on the hook."

"Don't worry. I'm sure it'll work out okay. Now, it's a matter of attitude. I'll get back to my training. Can you go over and tell Maxid what just happened?" They looked at each other. Then Robin gave Eric a heartfelt hug as a tear ran down her cheek.

Eric remained at the Center for further training for several weeks while Robin resumed her old routine of working at NASA, and visiting the Center periodically to gain more information.

Meanwhile, back in Washington, Peter was meeting with the rest of the team, coordinating all the various activities involved in the defense against the missiles, particularly now on the defensive network to be set up in space.

"The UN and all major countries have gone along with our proposed plan to set up a network of satellites with built in lasers that will encircle the globe. You'll recall that the density of satellites will be greatest over the larger cities where the greatest population loss would be expected. Satellites will be less prevalent over the less populated areas and the least over the sparsely or unpopulated areas. The oceans, the Polar Regions and the vast forested areas, such as in Siberia, will have the least protection. This gives us the best chance for minimal loss in population. There will be seven centers around the world that will control the position of the satellites: North and South America, Europe, Africa, two for Asia and one for Australia—which will include Malaysia and environs. Supervision of this network will be left to our Defense Department. Within the next several months we should be ready to start sending satellites up. Questions?"

"What's the density, and what protection does it afford over the best protected areas," asked a new member of the team.

Peter nodded to Michael who stood. "Good question. It should be about 99.9 percent. The weakest link is a missile hitting a satellite, in which case it *could* get through, but most often, the contact would set off the missile. According to the Xyrptans, if we could set up a defense like theirs, we would have virtually 100 percent protection, but that's impossible in our time frame."

"Do we know the type of missiles yet?" asked another team member.

"We don't know for sure at this time. Hopefully the Xyrptans can obtain that information through their spy network on Praetoria. Obviously they'll be nuclear— probably both demolition and neutron."

"What can we expect from our spaceships on intercepting the shepherd ships?"

"Another good question and the answer is, I don't know. We should have more information on that later."

"Will we attempt, and can we build our own spaceships in time? We have almost two years and that would seem to be feasible if we have Xyrptan help." Newer members of the team were now taking a greater part in the activities of the team.

"There has been some thought on that. Let me turn that question over to Cephid."

Cephid was stroking his chin, as if pondering how to answer the question. "Peter raised that question originally and it has been referred to the Supreme Council. As yet, we have no reply. I think the problem is that you are asking us to release *secret* information. The most recent upgrades of these ships are remarkable. They are far better than the Praetorian ships. We would be *very* unhappy if Praetoria got hold of these advancements. That's the main holdup. On the other hand, we know you are desperate. We should have an answer soon. It would take some time to bring everything together—new alloys, designs that are foreign to you, and the use of materials that you have not yet discovered, such as metalo-plastic materials that are very strong. One of your large aerospace companies would have to take on this sizeable undertaking. A plus would be that, after this crisis is over, you would have a good basis for building spaceships for solar and galactic exploration, which was the original premise for our coming here."

Peter wanted to bring them up-to-date on the Chinese Center. "As you know, we captured the transmitter bots in China with little difficulty and *without* them getting a message off to Praetoria. We then took the two of them back to CEAF, debriefed them, and switched their allegiance to us. They were not in contact with Praetoria for three days— the longest downtime previously had been two days. On our first transmission we explained to the Praetorians that there had been a big windstorm that had damaged the radio antenna, which is now repaired. That appeared to satisfy the Praetorian worries. Now we are surreptitiously trying to obtain information about the type of missiles headed our way, their exact location, and if there has been any change in the time they are expected to arrive. Hopefully they will not detect the new ownership of their Center. The bots they have out in the field have been coming in regularly for their periodic charges and checkups. We've been systemically decommissioning them and putting them in storage. Perhaps we'll have some use for them later."

Cephid sat down and looked at Peter, who stood. "Every day looks more hopeful. We should have an adequate shield up in time, and we should have at least two spaceships ready to intercept their shepherd ships. If we can build a few new spaceships in time that would greatly increase the odds. So, let's keep working hard."

Early the next day Peter received a call from Maxid saying that the Chinese Center was under siege, presumably by the remaining Praetorian bots—which he now referred to as p-bots. The remaining p-bots, outside the Center, apparently had banded together to muster this attack. Ten soldier bots had been left to guard the place, but they were being overwhelmed by a superior force. They called their contact in the Chinese government to ask for help and were told that support would be coming.

Maxid said, "They're presently holed up in the communications building, and are able to communicate with us, but have held off on any communication with Praetoria. I hope the Chinese arrive in time to salvage the operation. If the Center were to be captured, it seems likely that the first message sent to Praetoria would be about the initial capture and the false messages being transmitted since that time. If that were the case, then the usefulness of the Center would be negated, and its destruction would have to be considered. Checking with your Defense Department seems to be the first order of business."

Wanting to act on this information immediately, Peter thanked Maxid and told him he would get back to him later to relate what action was underway at our end. He called the President and Defense to relay the news. The only chance for repulsing the attack lay with the Chinese.

Chinese Center — Attack & Defense

Robin had called earlier and left a message for Peter to call her at his convenience. He did so now.

She was very excited. "Peter, I believe I've come up with a great plan. I've been working with Idid on how they build their bots. I believe that we could build our *own* bots at NASA with the help of the Xyrptans. Idid would be more than willing to help, and he has the approval of his superiors at home. We've already incorporated some of their ideas into our program at NASA. First, I think that we could begin building precursor models. We could use them to help in building the satellites for our defense system. They can work 24 hours a day, do flawless work, and the cost for their support would be minimal. If you decide to build spaceships, they could help there as well. Then, in the not too distant future, we could commercialize the program and support building them for industry. I think that the auto and aerospace industries would *jump* at the chance to get in on the ground floor of this idea."

"Robin, that's a great idea. I do wonder about getting started on such a program right now when we have this missile crisis to deal with." Peter's enthusiasm was curbed by reality.

"Sir, why don't you let me work out a detailed plan with my associates at NASA and with the help of some of the bot engineers at CEAF who aren't involved in our defensive plans? Then we'll come back to you and the team for your thoughts?"

Pondering for a while, "Why don't you come up with a *preliminary* plan before you get too involved, and *then* we'll take a look at it?"

"That sounds good to me. I'll get on it as soon as I get back to NASA."

"Have you been talking to Eric? I've been worried. I know that he was discouraged for being away from his work for so long."

"He's fine. Being organized and determined, once he made up his mind, he attacked his new job with enthusiasm. Tomorrow they're taking the gunship up for a trial run, and that has him excited. I don't think that you'll have to worry about him now. Two astronauts arrived and have started training too."

Meanwhile, Brandy was immersed in learning about Xyrpta from Ingrid. Her religious background, having changed multiple times, made her curious about what existed on Xyrpta. "Ingrid, what's the philosophy by which you live? Are you a *religious* people?"

"As we became more technologically advanced, our thinking changed. A milestone occurred when our astrophysicists discovered life on other planets in our galaxy. Discovering that we were not alone in the universe *crushed* the beliefs of some of our religions. What has evolved is a more secular society. We still have small religious groups, but they are not growing and are mainly composed of families passing down their beliefs from one generation to the next. We are a very tolerant people, and we all get along well. Our leaders in the past feared that, with the loss of religious beliefs, humans would become more assertive, more aggressive and we would see an increase in crime. To forestall any movement in this direction, the study of morals and ethics became mandatory and was incorporated into the classroom at both the elementary and secondary levels of education."

"You've seen our bots and the mental function they possess. Their development was preceded by our ability to monitor and record the mental functions occurring in the *human* brain. With this occurrence, we had the ability to decipher a person's thoughts, but more importantly, we could delve into their memory to see what had occurred in their past. It took a while to pass the law, but now we can *legally* examine a suspect's memory. Not only can a person be interrogated, but he can be wired up and his memory examined to see if there's evidence of a crime having been committed. Unlike your lie detector test, our test shows direct factual evidence of a crime. Just as you have recently used DNA evidence to prove innocence or guilt in court, we can use a mental tracing of memory for the same purpose. Over the next half century, our crime rate dropped considerably. Once a crime-prone individual sees that he can be caught and his misdeed revealed without his confessing, he becomes less likely to deviate to this type of behavior. Crimes of passion are what we see most frequently now."

"So, is yours a planet of atheists now? It sounds like you don't believe in a higher being or in an afterlife."

"We look at it as *realism*. After all, it's hard to have faith in something that has been put forth for millennia with still no factual evidence for its existence. It's long been shown that evolution is a *fact* and not a theory. Even in your time, there is so much factual evidence that the original theory has *virtually* been proved. Even your so-called "Big Bang" theory has been *proved* by us and expanded upon but, that's beyond my understanding scientifically. I don't doubt its happening 'tho. When you put *all* this together with life found elsewhere in the Universe, it's hard to support any of these faiths. So, for want of a better term you could call us *Secularists*.

As for an afterlife, we have something real. Our life expectancy now is about 160 years, but in exceptional circumstances, with meticulous medical care, some individuals have lived to be almost 300 years old. We have a retired Supreme Leader who is 280 years old. However, he is now failing rapidly, both physically and mentally, so it's expected that his medical care will be gradually withdrawn over the next year, and he will be allowed to die. We'll have a record of his mental function from the past with *all* his memories like we see in our bots. It's preserved in a computer. It may be hard for you to believe, but we'll still be able to ask him questions and he'll be able to answer synthetically based on his vast past experience. We are in the process now of amalgamating the mental functions of a number of our past leaders and brilliant people into one large 'computer brain.' This will give us the ability to tap multiple generations of minds for answers to difficult problems. So this is our form of existing after death. However, this preservation of memory and thought is not for everyone. Some rich individuals have used this resource to preserve their mental function for their families and future generations. This is not a common occurrence because of the expense. Preservation of minds is largely in the sciences, economics, government, and philosophy."

"We don't believe in a *God* as you do, but we do realize that there are forces beyond our present understanding. We, too, still have many unanswered questions. In the past we have found evidence indicating that there are *multiple* universes, and this is an area that is presently being investigated. Also, we are not pantheistic, but rather feel that there's a physical explanation for creation."

Brandy found this discussion with Ingrid both fascinating and frustrating, the latter because it was counter to her faith. She now had enough material for several articles. Brandy was drawn to Ingrid and felt they would become good friends. She wondered how her parents would feel about this. They would be most accepting she thought. A green bot as a best friend—how fascinating.

That evening Peter received a call from Herbert in Defense to relate the events that had occurred at the Chinese Center that day. Herbert said, "A squadron of eight Chinese helicopters flew to the site. While six of the copters landed in a meadow near the Center with troops, two went on to the Chinese Center and hovered overhead for reconnaissance. This showed p-bots firing at the communications building. Our soldiers were holed up inside and things appeared to be at a stalemate. The Chinese troops surrounded the clearing, and from the protection of the forest began firing at what they thought were p-bots. After they noticed that several of the bodies were bloodied, they realized that they were dealing with humans as well as bots. During the first round of fire, the enemy sought refuge in the buildings, and began firing from the windows and doorways. The Chinese copters were ordered to strike the occupied buildings with rockets while sparing the communications building. The rocket fire from the copters decimated these buildings. The Chinese then scoured the ruins for any remaining p-bots and humans. The latter readily surrendered. Most of the p-bots resisted and were decommissioned. Among the human enemy was a Chinese man who appeared to be their leader along with two 'live' p-bots."

Peter interrupted. "Herbert, you got the Chinese gangster. That's great!"

Herbert resumed, "In the communication building they found that five of our soldier bots had been disabled, while five were in good shape. On checking with the two bot radio operators they found that they were OK, and that there had been no transmission to Praetoria and none had been received. So, the mission was declared a success. The Chinese soldiers are remaining at the Center until arrangements can be made to provide a better, permanent defense."

"Herbert, I'm glad the operation wasn't compromised. I'll call Maxid to inform him of these events. We'll come up with a new plan to protect the Center. I'll get back to you tomorrow."

"Peter, Maxid already knows. I had one of my people call him. I believe he's waiting to talk to you before proceeding."

The next morning Peter called Maxid. "I was very worried, Maxid, but it looks like everything turned out okay. What do you envision as our next step?"

"We'll have to bolster our troops in China. I was thinking of sending twenty soldier bots to reinforce the five remaining bots. We'll have to rebuild at least one of the buildings. I've talked to the Chinese Colonel who's in charge there, and asked if they could remain in place until we get the building built and our bots settled in. He's checking with his superiors, and he'll get back to me as soon as possible. I think we should put an electrified fence around the compound for added protection. The Colonel said that his superiors want to leave some of their men in place *permanently* for our protection. It's their property, so they feel they have a right to participate in what's going on there. I think that's something you'll have to discuss with them. However, I don't see any reason why they can't remain. It would give us added protection."

Peter agreed. "I think we were a little naïve in thinking that we could operate the Center with a minimal defense and expect that we wouldn't be disturbed. I think we need to rethink our initial idea of destroying the Center *after* it's served its purpose. Perhaps we should eventually make it a permanent Center and use it to setup a *real* relationship with the Praetorians."

"Well, that's your job, Peter, and good luck with it, but I think that trying to befriend the Praetorians would be a mistake. They can't be trusted and sooner or later they'll hurt you just as they're trying to do now. It would be better if our two planets worked together in maintaining a *defense* against any invader."

"While we're talking about security, Maxid, how are you coming along with bolstering the defenses at CEAF?" Peter asked.

"We put in an electrified fence, posted '*No Trespassing*' signs outside, and added a guard station at the entrance. Also, we added guard dogs. Oddly, the dogs don't know what to make of us bots yet. I think they are having difficulty differentiating between a human and a bot," and Maxid gave a little laugh.

"There's one other matter." Peter said, "Do you remember the Chinese man who was caught alive, and who appeared to be their leader? I wonder if he is the same person who was involved in the shooting at the airport and was seen at the restaurant attack. We'd like to interrogate him. Can you manage to get him for us?"

"I don't see why not. Where do you want him sent? He's still under guard at the Chinese Center."

"I'll have CIA pick him up, if that's OK."

"Think of it as done. I'll make the arrangements."

Into Space

Eric rose early and had a light breakfast. He was both excited and anxious about his adventure today, being the first earthling to fly outside Earth/moon space.

He wondered about putting his life in the hands of robots. Maybe he was crazy. In the short time he had known them they appeared as competent and responsible as any human he knew. This assured him. He wondered if the bots would feel as comfortable with him as pilot, but then they had no feelings, and he presumed that they never considered that someday they would no longer exist.

In the hanger he put on his gear, which included a helmet for oxygen for the trip. After climbing on board, he felt compelled to check out the facilities. He wasn't depending on the bots assurance to have provided all the necessities he might need, but they had not let him down.

Bots don't waste time. The two pilots were strapping in and prodded Eric to do the same. They didn't need any external help to take off.

Torbid started the engines. A moment later there was a loud swoosh and roar, and Eric was pressed down into his seat. He knew that they were on their way to outer space. The monitors in front of him revealed a receding Earth with all the colors he had seen in photographs of Earth taken from space. It gave him an uncomfortable but surreal feeling.

Torbid said that he wanted to try some maneuvers to see how this ship performed, but first he wanted to convert from their cylindrical shape to the disc shape they would use in space. He knew Eric was wary of this maneuver, so he told him to just stay strapped in and he would be OK. He then toggled a switch and Eric heard a soft machinery sound and could see their shape changing both interiorly by looking around and externally by viewing what was happening on his monitors. Eric marveled at the ease with which this conversion occurred.

Torbid then accelerated upward and then downward. These were all maneuvers done without any lateral movement. Then he did a flip, but that was nothing compared to Torbid's next series of random motions. He felt no G-force—this was all done using the ships four thrusters. Each thruster could rotate, allowing for motion in any direction.

The ship's computer software responded to Torbid's joy stick so that the proper combinations of thrusters and angles were working to produce each maneuver. In space they had no ready point of reference so they just used their prior track to give them a position from which to extrapolate their movements. On a lengthier trip in space they would use the position of known nearby stars to calculate their whereabouts much as sailors do at sea with a sextant. When he took his eyes off the screen, Eric had little sense of movement other than being aware that he would float if he were not strapped into his seat.

The copilot, Rubid, indicated that Eric should unstrap and follow him. They drifted to one of the gun mounts. There was nothing to shoot at, but they wanted to make sure the guns were in working order. The co-pilot showed Eric what he was doing and then held the button (trigger) down. Looking out the window, Eric could see a beam of light that stretched into space, to what seemed oblivion. They followed the same routine for each of the four guns that were mounted on board. They were all in working order.

While he was up, Eric wanted to check out the facilities further that were put in for him. The lavatory was make-shift but private. He wondered why he needed privacy from bots, though. The cot that swung down from the wall, on which he would sleep, while strapped in, was adequate. The kitchen had shelves with room for dry goods, a sink, a few dishes, silverware, and a microwave. There was a table that swung down from the wall with a seat, all adequate but affording minimal comfort. He recognized the need to be efficient in the limited space.

His other need, his studies, had been worked out back home. He would be able to communicate daily with a bot at CEAF who would be conversing intermittently with a human counterpart on Xyrpta—an astrophysicist who would guide Eric through the advances they had made in the millennium that separated the two planets. In turn, Eric would be able to communicate with his team back at Cal Tech to inform them of the new knowledge he had garnered. All conversations would be recorded for future reference. This seemed like a good plan. Eric had made it clear that he wouldn't go on this mission unless he could have access to the astrophysical knowledge base on Xyrpta. This seemed like a small request balanced against putting his life at risk. He had to survive the mission to make this all worthwhile, but at least, his cohorts at Cal Tech would have the benefit of this information even if he didn't survive.

Eric and Rubid returned to their seats. After buckling up, Torbid looked at Eric. "How about taking the controls?" He had not had much training yet, but he was familiar with the panels. He was a fast learner. Eric gave Torbid a wary look. After a minute of no change, Torbid said sarcastically. "OK, you're good at going straight. Let's see something else."

Eric did turns to the right and left. "That seems to work OK, now I have to do something fancier." He rolled the ship over and had a smile of satisfaction his face.

'That's great, Eric, but you made one mistake. Can you tell what it was?"

Eric was mystified. He felt he had done the rollover perfectly. "You went 180 degrees too far. We're flying upside down. Correct our position," and Torbid smiled.

Eric had no sensation of being upside down, but he assumed Torbid was right. He corrected 180 degrees. "You can't expect me to be perfect the first time out," and he gave Torbid a faint smile in return. Torbid took back control.

They returned to Earth, came in, and hovered over their designated landing site. They slowly descended and landed. Torbid gave Eric a thumbs-up indicating that all had gone well. Eric responded in kind.

Maxid met them on their return and indicated that they should follow him into his office for a debriefing. This was routine as everything had gone well. Maxid complemented them all on their achievement.

That evening Eric had dinner with Robin and Brandy, both of whom were ensconced in their work at the Center; Brandy with her interviews with Ingrid, and Robin gaining more understanding on how to construct bots. Both gals were impressed by Eric's feat and enthusiasm; he couldn't stop talking about his first venture into space. Brandy thought him like a little boy with a new toy. Robin kept a half-smile, as if she were a little jealous, but also happy for him.

Half way through dinner Eric realized that he had been doing all the talking. He felt chagrinned so he queried Brandy, "What's been happening with you and Ingrid?"

"I never in my life would have believed that I could be so entranced by a non-human being. To start, we touched base on religion, ethics, morals and crime. Robin, you would be *fascinated* by how bots and humans interact on Xyrpta. I'm going to take Ingrid back to Washington with me tomorrow. It's a two-way street. I have to reciprocate by explaining our culture and society to her, so she can relay that information back to Xyrpta and her journalist counterpart. She's interested in our government and how it works, so what better place to start than Washington. I'll show her our buildings, give her some history, and hopefully introduce her to some congressmen and administrative officials. I'm going to ask Peter if we can have the team meet her. I think she'll have a blast. She'll be staying with me and I plan to introduce her to my parents. Can you imagine the impression that a short green bot with pointed ears will have on everyone?"

Robin frowned, "Don't you think that you might be giving Ingrid too much exposure too soon? Shouldn't you let her get better acquainted with her new surroundings *before* you introduce her to the world?"

"I talked it over with her. She felt that she could handle any situation. She's a bot, so she won't be scared. I'll be with her every moment. I think she's looking forward to it very much. What do think Eric?"

"If she were a human, I think it would be too much too soon, but as a bot, I don't think she'll have any problem, particularly if you're there to handle any awkward situations. I'd avoid crowds though. I'd hate to see her get trampled."

Then Eric turned, "Robin, what's been going on in your neighborhood? I hear rumors from the team that you're going 'gangbusters' on your bot program."

"I talked to Peter about starting to build bots at NASA. They could be used in helping to build the satellites, and even spaceships, if that plan goes through. Then we could expand into industry, especially for autos and planes. Of course, the actual building would be at their sites, but under our direction, at least initially. I do worry, though, about bots actually displacing human workers? Peter said to come up with a preliminary plan."

Brandy and Eric both started to speak at once. Eric then motioned Brandy to go ahead. "Aren't you trying to make a *millennial* jump in too short a time? Don't you think that your plans are a little … *grandiose* right now, what with the missile crisis staring us in the face?"

Robin bristled. "I feel we'll be *helping* our defense. There isn't any reason why we shouldn't go ahead."

"Girls," Eric interrupted, "I don't know the answer, but I think it would be a good question for the team to consider. I'm taking a few days leave from here next week. Why don't we all meet in Washington and set up a meeting with the team. You could spring your plan on them then."

"That's what Peter told me to do. I can have it ready by then." The rest of the evening was spent in light-hearted banter. They ended up by toasting each other with snifters of Brandy for their individual accomplishments for the week—Brandy's choice.

The following week the team met. Ingrid was the sensation of the meeting. There were many questions which Peter had to cut off after an hour, so they could continue with their agenda.

Robin explained her plan to build bots at NASA. Eric was the first to critique the plan. "For now, why don't we just have the bots constructed at CEAF as they are presently? We could help them expand their program. They have the knowledge and the materials. I think that's a no-brainer. For our defense program, speed is of the essence, and we would get the biggest bang for our buck by just expanding their program. At

NASA you'd have to use humans to build the bots, and that would be much less efficient than having the bots do the construction."

Robin was deflated, "At NASA we already have a bot program, albeit quite elementary compared to the one at CEAF. Our engineers are chomping at the *bit* to build these new bots. Perhaps we could do both, have CEAF build bots to help out in the satellite and spaceship programs, and simultaneously expand our program at NASA with the *help* of CEAF's bots."

Peter intervened, "We have to be careful that we don't try and do *too* much. I agree with Eric, we should do what is most expeditious, and that's to have CEAF build our bots for now. Robin, you should continue advancing your program at NASA with CEAF's help, but I wouldn't go so far as to ramp up robot production at NASA. There'll be time for that later. I'll talk to Maxid about increasing his production of bots that can be tailored to our needs."

Robin's face fell in disappointment, but she nodded.

Eric recounted his first space flight experience, which brought forth many questions. Everyone was happy with the excitement Eric showed. They all knew that he was making a big sacrifice by halting his work for the defense of his country.

Michael, who had sat quietly, listening up until now, cleared his throat to gain their attention. "I want to bring you up-to-date on our defense. The satellite program is going unbelievably well. We've put into orbit our first satellites armed with the new laser system. We've contracted with three companies to help us build several gunships. We chose Boeing to head the program. They'll do the final assembly of the ships. Unfortunately, there wasn't enough time to put the work out for bids, so we chose the firms with the most experience, and those we felt could get up to speed most rapidly. Our goal is to have at least two gunships ready for launching before the missiles arrive. Ideally we should launch them six months before the missile arrival in concert with the space ships from CEAF taking off. That's a tall order, but it's what we're aiming for."

The team had been updated previously on the action taken at the Chinese Center. Peter added, "We interrogated the p-bot soldiers we caught when they tried to recapture the Center. They indicated that some of their group had escaped when we initially captured their facility."

"Interrogation of the Chinaman has not been fruitful, he's clammed up. It's too bad that we don't have available to us the ability to monitor a humans brain functions like on Xyrpta. We'll most likely send him back to China, where they've been looking for him for some time. He'll be facing numerous criminal charges."

QCOM Begins Its Mission

Dr. Ed Ackerman joined Robin for the first meeting of QCOM. Peter sat in to indicate the tasks he wanted them to consider: first to assess the capabilities of the bot's AI brain—level of intelligence and capacity to think, judge and create. They had been told by Cephid that there were different levels of intelligence depending on the job the bots were to perform. They also wanted to find out if a filter was in place to screen information coming from bots to prevent them from disclosing restricted information to an outsider. This would be a reflection of what the Xyrptans were capable of constructing but hardly a measure of their own human minds. Perhaps they could decipher some of the latter from the communications they would have with the humans on Xyrpta.

To accomplish their mission they would have to have access to bots and their internal workings at *all* levels of intelligence. The humans on Xyrpta could be of great aid in this endeavor if they would agree to help. However, they might not want to divulge this detailed information, at least not this early in the game. But then, they had been told that they would have access to the knowledge on how to construct bots so asking for this help now seemed appropriate. This was all based on the presumption that the US and other nations on Earth would accept Xyrpta's offer to participate in their space exploration program.

The second part of their mission would be to glean any information they could about the future intentions of the Xyrptans toward Earth, not only relative to space exploration but also relating to dissemination of other information. Would they hold back some information to keep us in a more dependent position, never quite reaching equality, allowing them to maintain control?

Then there was the matter that had instigated this whole inquiry; do the Xyrptans have an armada of space ships prepared to send to Earth? If so, for what purpose?

Ed would concentrate specifically on his area of expertise. He saw the potential for making a quantum leap in AI. His first efforts would be to seek government funding to enlarge his staff at John Hopkins.

Robin would work with Peter to obtain permission to examine the bot mind in those that were already built. When Idid told her that she had carte blanche with respect to information on constructing bots, she now wasn't sure how far this would go. Xyrptans probably thought that it would take years for Earthlings to rise to the level of sophistication of themselves, but now QCOM wanted to thoroughly check out the mind of higher level bots—not later but now.

QCOM was getting off to a good start, so Peter left. He said that he would set up a meeting with Maxid to apprise him of their intentions and to get permission from him to proceed. He wanted Robin and Ed to flesh out their parts in this endeavor and be ready to present it to Maxid in the near future.

Final Preparations for Defense and Offense

Over a period of six months the installation of the satellite defense system made good progress, and it looked like they would make the deadline of having the most populated areas in the world protected, and a looser network over the less populated areas in time. The spaceship program had been slowed, because of difficulty in finding the materials necessary for construction. The design and manufacturing facilities were geared up to start work once these roadblocks were overcome. The bots were in place and ready to help in both programs.

The team met once weekly to bring each other up to date. Eric had finished his basic training on spaceship operation, and had returned to Cal Tech to resume his work. Robin continued her work with bot development at NASA, while Brandy was making a name for herself and Ingrid through their writings and as guests on a variety of TV shows.

Their first appearance on TV was on the Pers Morgan program, which had a tremendous ad buildup running up to the show. One of the largest audiences ever, watched the event. Ingrid didn't disappoint. She charmed everyone with her charismatic personality. Ingrid and Brandy had developed a pleasing banter, playing off against one another. Throughout the show, Ingrid was able to intertwine information about Xyrpta and their people. Pers ended by complementing Ingrid for being a great ambassador, representing her country to Earth. Afterwards, there was evidence that Ingrid fan clubs were starting to form among teenagers.

In another six months all members of the team would be called back to Washington. That would give them a year before the missiles were expected.

In the ensuing months, good progress continued in the satellite program, and the spaceship project had finally gotten underway, after the problem of producing the metallo-plastic material was solved.

The team was now meeting. This was their most important get-together in the past year. All members of the team were present. Peter appeared very serious as he spoke. "Our satellite program is going better than expected. We're ahead of schedule in placing satellites in orbit. We're finally building spaceships, and two should be completed in nine months, *three months earlier* than we originally expected. That brings us to a major decision. Originally, we had planned to send up our captured Chinese gunship and one of our freighter ships six months *before* the missiles are expected to arrive. It would take three months to intercept the shepherd ships, leaving three months before we expect the missiles to arrive here. We have, as yet, not been able to pinpoint the location of the missiles in space. We haven't been able to penetrate the Praetorian military to get this information. We presume that they will follow the shortest trajectory from their planet to ours. Still, that leaves a vast space in which they can hide, and when you're talking about years of travel, the actual error in predicting their arrival time is pretty large. It's now estimated to be plus or *minus* three months." Peter paused for a few seconds wanting this information to sink in."

"We've talked to Defense and have come up with an alternative plan. We're considering sending up two spaceships within the month, a *year* before we expect the missiles to arrive. It would be three months to interception. We stand a much better chance of discovering their location if we are out there closer to them. They'll be in contact with their home base, and we should be able to pick up that transmission if we're in the vicinity.

The second part of the plan is to have the new spaceships ready for takeoff as soon as possible in case they are needed for a last minute interception. This gives us more time and more chances for success. What are your thoughts?"

"Sir, I'm not sure where this places me in all of these changes." Eric frowned.

One of Peter's excellent qualities was his patience. "You'll be in the gunship with the two bots with whom you've trained. One of the astronauts will be in the freighter ship, along with two bot pilots. If it becomes necessary, our new spaceships will be manned by an astronaut and two bot pilots each. NASA is sending two more astronauts, as backup, to the Center for training."

Eric remained perturbed, "That means that I'll be in space for six months minimum. I'm not sure I want to do that and what about the risk involved?"

"The risk is the same as before. The only difference is the time factor." Peter knew that they were placing a huge burden on Eric, but there seemed to be no good alternative at this late date. He was worried about Eric. At times he was gung-ho on the project. At other times, like now, he was indecisive. He knew that Eric was emotional, but he was well organized, too. It seemed like he had difficulty accepting a sudden change in plans. Peter was a detail nut. He and Maxid had planned for the eventually that Eric might drop out, so they had planned to substitute an astronaut, if that became necessary, but he wasn't about to make that move yet.

Brandy piped up. "Why can't we have just bots in the spaceships? Do we need to endanger humans? The bots seem very proficient."

"We have debated with Defense the use of bots versus humans. Some in the Cabinet, Herbert in particular, are still wary of the bots in spite of what they've seen them do. I, myself, am a little wary about leaving the fate of our civilization in the hands of some inanimate objects." Peter looked apologetically at Cephid, who nodded.

"Why not use just the astronauts and leave Eric out of it?" Robin said, backing up Brandy.

"We've been over this before. First, we all agreed that a human has to be along on this venture. Herbert wants someone he knows up there. Though he has not met Eric, he knows of him as part of this team, and that I have the utmost confidence in him. Eric has previously agreed to take part in this mission, though the time period has changed. So, Eric, do you want out or do you want time to think about it? We need a decision shortly."

Being a fast thinker, his calculating left brain over-ruled his emotional right brain, and without hesitation, "Sir, I'm going, sorry about the indecision." Eric looked chagrined at having let everyone see this weakness.

"Know that we all hold you in high esteem and appreciate what you're doing for your country, in fact for the world."

Led by Brandy, the entire team stood up and gave Eric a big round of applause.

"Then, I assume that the team is in favor of the new plan. Are there any dissenters?" There were none. "Eric, let me see you for a minute after the meeting."

Peter led Eric into his office, and asked him to sit down. "Again, we appreciate your sacrifice. The President would like to meet you, and asked me to set up an appointment. When would be a good time?"

"I'm at your disposal. When do you think we'll be taking off? I'd like to make some preparations."

"Soon. I'll talk to Maxid and Defense and see what date they have in mind. I already have an appointment with the President for tomorrow at nine, so I'll meet you here at 8:30. OK?"

"That'll be fine sir."

Over the rest of the day many of the team came in to talk to Eric in his office. He was getting the feeling that they were saying goodbye. He knew the trip was risky, and that he would be away for six months, so maybe that was appropriate.

Eric stopped by Brandy's office to thank her for her support. After a brief conversation, she got up and gave him a big hug. He knew she could tell how obviously grateful he was for that.

He stopped by Robin's office too. She said that she still felt guilty about dropping out of the competition for the mission he was going on. "Robin, it all turned out for the best. I have no regrets." He received a hug from Robin, too. These were the two most important women in Eric's life. He *hoped* that later he would have time to get to know each of them better.

The next morning Eric was at the office early to meet Peter. They both went to meet the President. Eric was surprised to see Herbert there too. They stood by the coffee urn and talked while eating donuts and drinking coffee. The get-together was to meet, and thank Eric for participating in the mission, and to wish him good luck. At the end a red-faced Herbert grasped Eric's hand in both of his, "Son, I'm the one to blame for getting you into this predicament. After reading your résumé and knowing that Peter thought so highly of you, I knew you were the one to lead the attack on the Shepherd ships. I trust you. I can't say the same for the bots, but maybe that'll change in time."

Eric was a little taken aback by the emotion shown by this blustery titan of the cabinet. He thanked him. The President shook Eric's hand and thanked him too, and then asked to be excused as he had to attend to other business.

It was now necessary for Eric to see his parents to say goodbye. They didn't really understand the situation, and Eric wasn't allowed to brief them in detail, but they realized the risk involved. So, while they were proud of their son, they were worried as well.

Next, he returned to Cal Tech to brief his group on what he would be doing for the next half year, and how they would be staying in contact with him. Not surprisingly, this was the part of the trip he was most excited about. He would be learning things that he could not hope to have learned in his lifetime. They would all be making history.

Eric was now checking into CEAF. He had been notified that the date for takeoff was in three weeks. He had brought the few articles he wanted to take on the flight with him, and he would likely remain at CEAF until take off. Eric was a little dismayed, as he thought that he would have time to say a few more goodbyes, but then, it was time to get the show on the road. He was not unhappy.

He noticed that Maxid had posted a training schedule for the next several weeks. Tomorrow was to be spent on 'Reflexes and Response

Time.' Interesting—it gave him food for thought, and he wondered if this applied to his robot partners too.

The next morning four bots—including Eric's flight mates, Torbid and Rubid—were in the spaceship hangar along with, Arnie, the astronaut who would be flying in the space freighter with the other two bots. They had built a training module of the spaceship's operations area. This morning they would be measuring response times in a simulated enemy attack.

Torbid started the exercise. He sat at the operations panel. A spaceship was flying on the monitor. It suddenly changed direction. Torbid responded with an almost simultaneous counter move. Software embedded in the system measured his reaction time, and also, determined the correctness of his move. He repeated the same exercise two more times.

Rubid followed doing the same exercise. Eric marveled at their response times, and knew that he would not be able to match their proficiency.

Eric followed. He had recent training in maneuverability and counter moves to an enemy on the simulator, but he knew that he was still at a novice stage. He hunched over the panel board, obviously anxious to respond rapidly to the enemies change in position. His arm on the joystick jerked suddenly. He waited for the second and third tries. Afterwards he looked up at Maxid for some sign. He got a half smile which told him nothing. Eric gave a sigh and got up so Arnie could take his place. He had prior experience in the simulator at NASA, so seemed right at home. Eric could tell that he was fast, but noticeably slower than the bots. He seemed satisfied with his performance.

The two other bots followed. Eric felt that their response times were in the same ballpark as their bot teammates.

Next was the test for response time to enemy gunfire, including correctness of aim. The six of them followed the same order as before. Here Eric felt nervous. He couldn't fire until he had the enemy in his sights. In his first try, he was sure he had fired before he had sighted the enemy ship. In his last two tries he was afraid he waited too long to fire, wanting to insure that he had the enemy in his sights. He realized that he needed more practice. He felt the others had done significantly better than he.

They then returned to Maxid's office for a debriefing. "This little exercise," began Maxid, "was to decide who should be manning the ship and guns once we are in battle. *Clearly* the bots have the edge in reflex time which isn't surprising and what we expected. They were also more proficient in maneuverability and correctness in their decision-making. We felt the need to *demonstrate* that to you *humans*. Arnie was a tad behind the bots in all responses, but good overall. I was impressed".

"Eric, you were only slightly behind in maneuverability, which was quite good. While on the guns you were hesitant. You'll need more practice. In particular, you need to cut down your response time between aiming and firing. But considering your experience, I think you did well. Use the next three weeks to become faster and more accurate in all these areas."

"When going into battle, the *bots* will be in charge and will man the cockpit and one gun station. A human will man the other gun station. Questions?"

Eric piped up, "Do bots ever make errors? What if their batteries start running down? Does that slow their response times?"

'Bots are error free unless something breaks. We have built into the spaceships, testing equipment so that the bots can be checked weekly to make sure that all their elements are working. Spare parts are stored on board in case some part needs replacement. The bots will be charged each month. They can be recharged earlier, if that becomes necessary."

Arnie asked, "What exactly will be *our* job on this mission?"

"You and Eric will each take one eight hour shift every 24 hours to pilot the ship. There will always be two positions to cover, pilot and copilot seats. The bots will each cover two eight hour stints with one session just with bots on duty. Following the same routine should keep you from becoming disoriented by any time change. As I mentioned, in battle, a bot will be piloting the ship. He can be spotted by a human, if that becomes necessary, say from an injury or a malfunction." There were no further questions so Maxid ended by saying, "I want you all to spend the remaining weeks practicing maneuvers and gunfire in the simulator."

That evening Eric had dinner with Arnie whom he had not had the chance to converse with previously. He was impressed by his credentials—having done a mission to the Space Shuttle. He was obviously better trained than he. It bothered him that the main reason he was going on this mission was because of Herbert. Eric couldn't see why the astronauts weren't considered sufficiently trustworthy. He felt he needed to explain to Arnie why he was here.

"You're probably wondering why I'm here, and why I'm flying instead of one of your fellow astronauts." Arnie raised his hand.

"Eric, my boss at NASA explained the situation to me, and I understand. I sympathize with you and realize the difficult position you're in. I'll support and help you in any way I can." Relief showed on Eric's face.

The ensuing weeks were spent in training with a lot of repetition. After two weeks, they were given a takeoff date—five days hence. During that time, Eric had no contact with the outside world except calls to and from team members.

He received an important call from Peter. While in flight, Eric was to query Torbid about his prior remarks regarding the armada waiting to be sent from Xyrpta upon the signing of the space exploration agreement. This was to be done as discreetly as possible.

Back to QCOM

Robin and Ed were to meet with Peter at CEAF, so Ed could see first-hand where and how the bots were constructed. Only the first part of the mission was revealed to Maxid—seeking to discover how the bot mind worked—while leaving out their intent to surreptitiously discover what undisclosed plans the Xyrptans might have in store for Earth.

Maxid had already contacted his superiors on Xyrpta to confirm that the Earthlings were to have access to all information related to the construction and operation of bots including their minds. At the meeting Robin asked, "Maxid, I'd like to have direct contact with a human on Xyrpta who's involved at a high level in the bot development process."

Maxid asked, "Why?"

Not wanting to hurt Maxid's feelings, though she knew he had none, "I want input from the creative source—what problems they've encountered in the past, what they're currently working on, and what are their future plans."

Ed interrupted, "Max, I'd like see more than just the end result. I'd like to see the algorithms that were used in your AI, the step by step process in how the bot mind was developed."

"The name is Max with an 'id', Maxid." This was said flatly.

"Sorry Maxid," and Ed showed a faint smile of embarrassment.

Their requests were beyond what Maxid could grant. "I'll contact the bot works on Xyrpta to see what they say," but he sounded dubious.

Ed wasn't going to let this chance go by without squeezing out every bit of information he could garner. He asked Maxid several questions relating to how his own mind worked, ending with, "Being a bot, are you aware of the mechanisms by which your own inner mind works?"

Here, Maxid became very wary. "As I said, I'll check with my superiors on Xyrpta and get back to you." Though bots don't show emotion, his voice implied that he didn't like this inquisition.

This ended their first meeting. Unusual for Peter, he had sat through the whole process without saying a word. He was proud of his new QCOM staff, particularly Ed Ackerman. He might even ask him to join the XCOM team. They could benefit from his expertise.

The rest of their trip was spent in the bot lab with Robin and Idid explaining and demonstrating the physical workings of the bots to Ed.

Not long after their return to the East coast, Robin received a call from Maxid indicating that she would have access to a human bot expert on Xyrpta. Fortunately, NASA had a direct line so she would have easy access from her work site.

All communications were to be recorded. Ed had software that could scour communications for subliminal messages. Also, Ed would give Robin questions for her to ask that would help him in his investigations. It had been decided that Robin would have sole access to their Xyrptan source—at least for now— to avoid any conflicts. Both were eager to get started, and within a few days Robin had made her first contact. This had gone well, primarily being to become acquainted with her human bot expert.

Mission Day

Mission or M Day finally arrived. The bot pilots, Eric, and the astronaut, Arnie, were up at five and ready for takeoff by eight. The bots wore their XASA jump suits, while Eric and the astronaut wore gear similar to that used at NASA.

There was no fanfare. An announcement of their departure was to be made after the fact.

Both ships took off, and with an ear splitting roar, they were off into space. The conversion to disc-shape occurred without incident once they were out of Earth's atmosphere.

On preflight planning, they had decided to follow a trajectory most likely being followed by the Praetorian Shepherd ships and missiles, the shortest distance between the two planets. It would be like looking for a needle in a haystack. As they drew nearer to the vicinity of the Praetorian ships, they hoped to pick up transmissions from the enemy which would help pin-point their location. Right now they were too distant to pick up any message— that likely would have to wait until the last month before interception.

Eric was anxious to begin his theoretical studies with the Xyrptans. They required that he start the trip before they would commence instruction. Now he contacted the Center and asked for the first series of documents from the astrophysicist on Xyrpta. These had been downloaded to Earth several days prior to take off, so Eric wouldn't be disappointed by having to wait. His expectations were met. He remained thoroughly engrossed in his work until his shift at the controls occurred some eight hours later.

Their ship was small, no more than 50 feet in diameter. The pilot and copilot seats were six feet apart with the copilot's position also serving as one of the gunnery posts and navigation center. Both sites had a bank of monitors mounted in front of them, allowing for 360 degree vision in all directions. A myriad of switches covered the panel boards in front of them—extending onto the wall. Both posts had joysticks that were directly in front of the seats, but below the counter level, the elbows remaining at a right angle to provide more comfort and maneuverability. Being a gunship, this was important during battle when sudden, rapid changes in position would be required. The joystick had a locking mechanism. Flying, as they were now, would require infrequent changes in direction, so there was no need to hold the joystick.

To the left of the joystick, at the pilot's seat, and at a lower level, was a keyboard connected to a built-in computer, allowing for computation while in flight. This was the communication center for all operations.

Distant communication, such as contacting CEAF, was available by just toggling a switch. Onboard, both human and bots wore helmets, the latter only for communication, while Eric's also contained his breathing system.

At the opposite end of the ship was another gunnery post.

Almost a third of the space in the center of the ship was a floor to ceiling core that contained the engine, fuel source, and other machinery.

On one side, between the two gun posts, was an open kitchen area with everything attached to the wall—sink, cabinets, microwave, and drawers for eating and other utensils. Next to this were a hinged table and chair that lowered from the wall.

More toward the pilot's station was an open workshop area with cabinets and a working surface.

Opposite of this, against the other wall, was an enclosed bathroom that contained a toilet—with thigh restraints to prevent floating—and a sink and counter with mirror. There was no shower, but Eric could take a sponge bath. The equipment for his private needs had been copied from NASA's provisions for their spaceships.

Lastly, Eric's sleeping quarters were between the bathroom and the lone gunnery post. This was a bunk, hinged to the wall. Like the toilet, it had restraints to hold him in place. Adjacent to this, Eric had a cabinet in which to store his personal things, a few books, and his study materials.

This would be his home for the next six months. He was not unhappy and he was adapting to his new environs quite well.

Several weeks out, Torbid indicated that they were coming upon Saturn. They were going to do a gravity assist that would slingshot them further into space at twice their present speed. He took over from Eric until the maneuver was completed. They were on their way out of the Solar System. After the gravity assist, Rubid, who had been doing the navigation, came over to assure them that their new course was correct.

Seeing Saturn close-up with its red rings and all was the highlight of Eric's trip so far. He used the ships built-in telescope to get a closer view. They were on the inside so the sun was reflected off the surface which gave him an excellent view. He was able to discern the A, B, and C rings with the Cassini division showing between the A and B rings, and he thought he could see the two outer, G and F rings faintly. He was familiar with the Voyager explorations of the planet, and had seen the many images of the planet and its rings from these sources, as well as from the Hubble Space Telescope.

Otherwise it was pretty boring, sitting and looking into the blackness of space, seeing only distant stars. However, he was impressed by the density of stars in the Milky Way.

The twenty four hour schedule was working well, and Eric kept a calendar so he was well aware of the passage of time. He took an eight hour work shift, while the bots alternated the pilot and copilot seats, excluding him from the latter.

The accommodations for his personnel needs were working out well, and even his dry good meals, while not great, were acceptable.

The solitude helped Eric think. Originally, he had thought that worry over the upcoming battles with the enemy gunships would hinder his concentration, but this was not the case. Several questions had arisen in his work, but he was able to send queries back to the Center. They, in turn, sent them on to Xyrpta for his mentor to answer. It took at least two days to get a turn-around, but that didn't bother him. He had plenty of material to keep him busy. During his work shift, both bots offered to cover at least a portion of his shift; however, he wanted to do his share, even though he realized that they did not tire, and it was no chore for them. Too, he felt more comfortable maintaining a twenty four hour schedule.

A month and a half out, they received a communication from Maxid. The Chinese Center had received a communiqué from Praetoria that suggested that a large spaceship had taken off following the Shepherd ships and missiles by several months. There was no proof so they were going to try and verify this information. This, perhaps, would yield information on the position of the shepherd ships, too, and their ETA to Earth.

Eric kept in touch with Peter through Maxid who would tie their respective lines together.

"How are you doing Eric? Do you need anything … not that we can get anything to you now?"

"I could use a pillow, something we forgot to install but that's ok. My helmet works just fine." Eric was being facetious. He had padding in his helmet that made sleeping more comfortable. Then, too, there was no gravity to weigh his head down.

Speaking to Maxid, "Sir, we're doing well, no unexpected incidents. I want to thank you for the information coming from Xyrpta about my project. It's fantastic. I'm forwarding the information on to my team at Cal Tech, so they can follow along with me. Is there any reason for them not to make this information public?"

"Taking the information public is OK, as long as you indicate the source." There was a little pause after Maxid's statement, perhaps he was rethinking his statement, but there was no follow up.

"Changing the subject,"—Maxid was back to his usual self— "you've heard the rumor that a large spaceship may have taken off from Praetoria months after the shepherd ships left their planet, presumably following in their wake. We're in the process of trying to verify or negate this rumor."

"Sir, that's bad news if true. For all we know they could be sending a *squadron* of spaceships. After all, if they're trying to destroy us, it would make sense for them to send an army to mop up after the attack. If there are more spaceships coming, perhaps we could ramp up our spaceship program. That would give us a buffer if the rumor's true. We're always playing 'catch up.' Isn't there some way that we can become more aggressive? Put a little fear into them?"

Both Peter and Maxid were online, Peter answered, "Now that we have the logistics figured out, we've had the same thought. You can be sure that we'll be going ahead *full* steam. If we can manufacture four or five ships, we'd be doing very well, but more realistically, we're aiming for two ships to be ready in time. We'll keep you posted on the rumor."

The days stretched into uneventful weeks. Eric kept busy with his studies. There being no interruptions, he was realizing that this period was the most concentrated studying he had ever done. It brought to mind England's astrophysicist, Stephen Hawking. ALS was a terrible disease to have, but he had mentioned that the privacy it provided had given him the time for concentrated thinking without interruption from the outside world. Eric could relate to that now.

On their seventieth day out, the Chinese Center received a message, which Maxid relayed to Torbid. One of the shepherd ships had broken radio silence. They were making good progress, and were only three months away from their goal. They were initiating contact now, so they could get an idea of what kind of reception they might encounter on their arrival. The news was chilling, but it allowed them to pinpoint their enemy's location. Torbid could expect to intercept the shepherd ships within days now. Radio contact was to be suspended until contact was made, so as not to alert the enemy.

Torbid was the navigator at the time they received the message. He made the appropriate calculations, and gave the information to Rubid at the controls to make the course correction. He gave a burst from one of the thrusters, which put them on a track to intercept the Shepherd ships trajectory.

Not long afterward, Torbid picked up a transmission that appeared to be coming from one of the shepherd ships. Estimating the enemy gunships position, Torbid verified that they would likely be going into battle within a few days. "When the enemy is sited," Torbid said, "I'll take the controls. You two will man the guns." Rather than sitting at a gun ready to pull the trigger, the gunner had his own set of displays, and from his panel he could maneuver the guns remotely and pull the trigger by pushing a button. That way each gunner manned two guns. If, in his maneuvering, Torbid felt that he could come in for a shot, he would warn the appropriate gunner. Of course, each gunner had the same views as the pilot, but, being at the controls, Torbid could fore-warn the appropriate gunner of a sudden change in position. He wanted everything to be clear. The margin for error would be very small. None of them had prior experience in a gun fight, but then, it was likely that the Praetorians were 'in the same boat.'

Torbid made brief contact with the freighter ship that had been fol-lowing them. He hoped that they would first meet just one spaceship in which case he wanted the freighter to stay out of the way and let the two gunships fight it out. He felt that they were set for whatever was to come.

It was two days later that they first saw a shepherd ship with its accompanying missiles on the horizon. There was only one ship. However, it was likely the other ships weren't far behind. At least, this first battle would be one-on-one.

Torbid warned. "There they are guys. Hold onto your hats. Here we go." A burst from one of the thrusters put them on a collision course. They had obviously been spotted as the shepherd ship was altering course too.

Rather than attacking the enemy directly, Torbid had the idea to attack the missiles first which would draw the enemy in. "Eric, Rubid, we're going to attack the missiles first. Shoot down as many as you can, and remember to shoot *only* behind us. We don't want to incinerate ourselves by flying into an exploding missile. I'll let you know when we have to break away. He maneuvered the ship over the missiles so that both gunners would have shots at the missiles. There was no noise except for clicks that indicated that a shot was being fired. However, on the outside it was different. One missile after another was hit and exploded. It looked like the Fourth of July a thousand times over, and fortunately they were not part of the fireworks.

"OK guys, he's coming after us. Listen for my warning for a shot. It's going to take split-second timing." Torbid began using his thrusters to maneuver the ship. Both Eric and Rubid had their screens locked onto the enemy ship, so they could see, as well as Torbid, what was going on. Eric could feel his muscles tightening up. He tried to relax. If they thought this was going to be over quickly, that idea was soon erased. An hour later they were still trying to out-maneuver one-another. Torbid said, "Patience is the name of the game."

They had gotten off an occasional shot but nothing damaging. The enemy had been more successful in hitting them, indicated by the loud pings of beams glancing off their ship's skin. These blows initially made Eric nervous. He realized that he had to concentrate on his job now if he was to be successful. He managed to clear his mind and focus solely on the enemy. Then the shepherd ship broke away.

"Oh, oh, he's going after the freighter. It's a sitting duck. This may be the time for our best shot. Stay alert."

The enemy ship traveled some distance, then maneuvered itself over the freighter, which was flying like a lumbering ox. The gunship slowed momentarily to take its shot. At the same time, Torbid came up over the enemy ship. "ERIC!" Almost simultaneously there was a click as Eric got off his shot. The enemy gunship was hit. It slowed. Smoke trailed its course. But the enemy had gotten off a shot too. The freighter was hit in its mid-section, but apparently not fatally so. Torbid swept underneath the enemy, which allowed Eric to get off another shot. There was a flash and then the ship exploded. Eric breathed a sigh of relief. One down; two to go.

"Good shot Eric. You get a spaceship painted on your helmet for that." Now there was a serious matter confronting the freighter. Torbid contacted them. They were functional but were still assessing the damage. After seeing that they were OK, at least temporarily, Torbid told them that he was going to do a little cleanup work and would be close by. He wanted to clear out as many missiles as possible before another shepherd ship appeared on the horizon. "OK, guys, let's get rid of the rest of these missiles. While you're cleaning up, I'll be contacting the Center to tell them of our recent adventure." Several hours later they had cleared out all the missiles and headed back to check on the status of the freighter.

The news wasn't good, but could have been worse. The freighter would be able to fly and make it back home. However, the oxygen supply system for the astronaut on board was damaged. It didn't look like it would hold out for the trip back to Earth. The only solution was to see if they could transfer the oxygen system from the gunship to the freighter. This would require that Eric go with the freighter, and they would head back to Earth. Torbid would take one of the bots from the freighter so there would still be three of them. He needed two gunners.

The spaceships were built so that they could attach to each other, enabling the transfer of personnel or equipment while traveling in space. The hatch on the top of the freighter was damaged from the hit. Fortunately, there was a secondary hatch on the underbelly of the freighter to which Torbid now headed. After the two ships were coupled, Rubid opened the hatch between the two chambers connecting the ships. Rubid then took control of the ship from Torbid who headed up into the freighter to assess the damage. Eric tagged along. If he was going to be transferred to this ship, he wanted to check it out first, not that he had much choice. It was the first time in almost three months that the two crews had seen each other.

After brief greetings, Torbid checked out the damaged oxygen system. He thought that they might be able to bind the parts together with duct tape, but he knew this wouldn't hold up for the trip back. The only safe solution was to transfer the gunship's oxygen system to the freighter. Turning to Eric, Torbid explained the situation, and that they were going to make the transfer.

This would necessitate Eric transferring to the freighter. This was the only solution that could guarantee the safe return of the humans to Earth. Eric understood and nodded his agreement.

The parts for the oxygen systems were identical for both ships, as they had been installed at CEAF after it was decided that a human would be on each ship. The transfer took a few hours, but the end result yielded a well-functioning oxygen system. Eric collected what little gear he had and transferred to the freighter. The bot who would take his place on the gunship did the reverse. By the end of the shift, the installation and transfer of personnel was completed and the two ships disengaged. The freighter began its trip back to earth.

Fortunately its engine, fuel supply, and thrusters had not been damaged so the trip should take no longer than the one out. Eric now had a chance to talk to the astronaut on board to get his take on the trip. "Arnie, how did you spend your time when you weren't piloting?"

"I brought a lot of Sci-Fi books with me, but that only lasted so long. Then I thought I'd get some information on Xyrpta from the bots, but they were made in the USA and knew little of their 'homeland.' Then I picked their brains on what knowledge they had about CEAF. They were pretty forthcoming. I bet I know more about CEAF than any of your team members," and Arnie showed a little smile of satisfaction.

"Did you learn anything important?" Eric felt the need to pry a little.

"Bots have a memory of which you're aware. The longer they've existed, the greater their storage of past events. Periodically, these events are censored and some memory is erased. What determines what is kept and what is not, they are not aware, but it's safe to guess that the remaining memory is pretty *sterile*."

"We'll have to talk more. That's very interesting." Eric wondered if all astronauts read science fiction. He left to store his gear.

Torbid now headed the gunship toward where he expected to find the other two shepherd ships. He wondered if he would meet the larger spaceship that was rumored to have left Praetoria. That would be an imposing enemy, and not one to look forward to. On the other hand, the large ship was *likely* a cargo ship, or perhaps even a transport vehicle filled with bots or even Praetorian humans. It would be presumptuous of the Praetorians to think that they could damage Earth sufficiently from their missile attack and then land and expect to take over the planet without any resistance, but then, the Praetorians weren't noted for their logic.

Torbid felt that the two remaining shepherd ships were aware of the recent battle, and that the absence of any message from their sister ship indicated its likely demise. He expected that they would now close ranks, and he wouldn't have the chance to meet them separately. It was just as well that Eric had left. He was more valuable back on Earth. Torbid felt that he was just as well off with a fellow bot on board.

Back at the Center, Maxid was about to call Peter and inform him of the battle and the subsequent events revolving about repair of the freighter. He knew the humans were safe and on their way back home.

Elation was evident in Peter's voice. "I'm happy to hear that Eric's OK, the astronaut too, and that there headed back home. Having shot down a shepherd ship is frosting on the cake for Eric. That should earn him a Presidential Medal of Freedom. Herbert should be happy too. What about the two remaining shepherd ships and their missiles? Can we expect to take them out as well?"

"I don't know. We have a ship with a good crew, but I expect the Praetorian ships are well-manned too. My worry is that the two remaining shepherd ships will team up now that they know their sister ship is gone. We're in contact with Torbid, and I expect that he'll make contact with the enemy in the next day or two. I'm just glad that the other shepherd ships weren't able to come to the rescue of their sister ship. That would have been real trouble."

"Well, Maxid, it looks like we're coming to the final chapter in our tale. Do you have any suggestions or additions to make to our plans?"

"Get those gunships off the assembly line as fast as you can. I suspect that we might need them—the sooner the better. We'll have at least six astronauts trained and ready to man the ships along with our bots. I think that'll be enough to handle the job. What do you think?"

"The contractors are working 24 hours a day. They have the help of the bots who have made a big difference. Keep me posted on the progress of our gunship and freighter."

The team was called together for a meeting the next day. Peter described in detail the battle that had occurred the day before. The response was enthusiastic. He then warned them of the impending battle that would occur in the next day or two. He asked that they pray for the success of Torbid and his crew. This was the first time Peter had invoked anything of a religious nature into his government dealings. He wasn't a particularly religious person, and he didn't go to church, but he had a sense of spirituality and he occasionally prayed, but he had always kept this to himself before.

There were many questions asked beginning with Brandy's. "How has Eric held up on this mission?"

"I understand from Maxid that he is doing well. I believe that he's been able to conduct his studies all the time he has been up there. So, along with shooting down an enemy space ship, I would say that he has had a very successful trip. We should all be proud of him."

Robin, not wanting to be outdone by Brandy said, "I think we should have a welcome home party for Eric. I'd like to be in charge of it."

"Good idea Robin, you're in charge."

Peter then brought the group up-to-date on the construction of the new gunships. "We have to be prepared for the worst, which right now would be that Torbid is *not* successful in destroying the two shepherd ships and their accompanying missiles. According to our calculations, we should have two gunships ready to go *several* weeks *before* the enemy arrives, presuming that they survive the battle with Torbid. That's calling it very close, but that's the best we can do. That battle would occur *within* our solar system. Any questions?" There were none so the meeting was adjourned.

The President and Defense had been informed of the recent events. Defense released a press statement documenting these events. The next day The New York Times screamed, "Astronaut Downs Enemy Spaceship and Missiles in Space." The article detailed the exploits of Eric, Torbid, and Rubid in downing the enemy space ship. It concluded with the warning that the battle had just begun. Peter thought that the article was satisfactory. They did mess up by calling Eric an astronaut. That was not technically correct, but this astrophysicist was acting the part of one.

There was now frequent contact between Maxid and Torbid. A big question was what tactic to use if Torbid should encounter both enemy spaceships at once, a likely and not appealing probability. Torbid expected that they would take advantage of the simplest of strategies: while he was defensively edge-wise to one ship, the other would maneuver for a belly or top shot to where he was most vulnerable. He could hardly avoid that likelihood. Maxid suggested that he put the missiles between him and at least one of the gunships. Perhaps his gunners could hit a few of the missiles while maneuvering and provide a distraction. That made sense to Torbid. Neither one could think of another strategy at the time.

Continuing to think along the line that Maxid had suggested, Torbid constructed a grid on his computer screen, putting the missiles at the crosshairs of each intersection. He knew roughly the distance between the missiles and their speed, enough for him to maneuver amongst them safely as long as he was careful. He then plotted several different pathways he might take going above and below them and moving forward or diagonally. He would have to be moving in the same direction as the missiles to avoid one of them hitting him. In turn, he would have to be careful to not run into one of the missiles. He was assuming that the missiles would be going at a constant speed and direction. He thought it unlikely that the shepherd ships would think to alter the course of the missiles, but he had to be alert to that possibility. That would be a calculated risk.

He gave himself several choices of pathways, so he could switch depending upon where the enemy gunships were located. He stored these pathways in his computer. By putting these on automatic pilot, he would be able to maneuver much faster than the enemy gunships that would have to alter course manually with each of his changed positions. However, would this allow him any shots at the enemy gunships? They would all have to be alert and take shots whenever possible. He could deviate from any pathway on a moment's notice if it looked like he could get in a good shot. The other question was, would the enemy gunships be willing to shoot at him, taking the chance of hitting their own missiles. Lastly, he figured that his gunners could fire at the missiles as they passed them. He was glad that he had all bots on board. They could multi-task whereas this would be mostly impossible for humans, particularly for fast thinking and reaction. He knew that his gunners would be able to not only shoot down the missiles but simultaneously keep track of the enemy ships for possible shots.

Later, he again talked to Maxid and passed his grid plan by him. He thought it was excellent. Another thought came to Torbid's mind. "If the chance should occur, should I try and crash into one of the gunships?"

Maxid thought for a moment. "That should be done only as a last resort. It would be better to fight and destroy as many missiles as possible and go down that way rather than knocking out one gunship and leaving the missiles and one shepherd ship left to complete their mission." Torbid agreed.

It was some twelve hours later that Torbid picked up the shepherd ships on his screen. As he suspected, they had closed ranks, and he would have to fight both of them simultaneously. He alerted his crew. He again mentioned that they shoot at the missiles behind them while keeping a sharp eye out for a possible shot at one of the Shepherd ships. "Good luck guys!"

The enemy gunships and missiles were closely in tandem. This played into Torbid's plan as he would start at the rear missile pack and work forward and then jump to the front pack. Instead of aiming for the shepherd ships, he went straight for the missiles. By the time the enemy gunships figured out his strategy, Torbid was already on automatic pilot and zooming through the missile pack with his gunner's blazing away. The enemy gunships held off, apparently trying to decide whether or not they should shoot and chance hitting a missile. This is what Torbid had been hoping for, but he doubted it would last for long. He was already halfway through the rear pack, and he could see that they were destroying a good number of the missiles. So far, so good.

Torbid could hear the pilots in the other ships talking in Praetorian. There languages were sufficiently similar that he got the gist of what was said. They were going to split up, one covering the upside and the other the downside, so each would be on either side of the missiles. If they hit a missile, that was a small price to pay for eliminating the enemy who was destroying their missiles anyway.

Torbid alerted his crew to the change in the enemy's tactics. He had just made his way through the rear pack of missiles and was entering the front pack. Hopefully they could make it through this pack, too, before having to deviate away. Torbid now changed to one of his alternate automatic pathways, as he was sure the enemy had deciphered his prior pattern and would be playing off it to nail him. He didn't expect that these maneuvers would be much of a deterrent for them. He had one more trick up his sleeve, and he would wait for the right opportunity to use it. This last option came to him just moments ago while his brain was multitasking for another solution. He would bide his time for now.

On his new pathway, he placed the ship edgewise to his enemies above and below him to make their shots more difficult and less effective. This posture made it a little more difficult for his gunners to hit the missiles, but they were doing a good job. They occasionally got a shot off at the other gunships but nothing that appeared successful. They had shots zinging by them now and they could hear the *pings* when the beams bounced off their *skin*. For anyone other than the bots, this would have been a harrowing experience as Eric had noted. They took it all in stride. There was no fear.

They were almost through the front missile pack. Now was the time for Torbid's new tactic. He estimated that they had destroyed almost half of the missiles—not a bad day's work considering the circumstances. Even if they were downed by a Shepherd ship, the more missiles they destroyed meant less damage to Earth if they should get that far.

Now he reverted to manual control and zoomed upward with all thrusters and engine going full throttle to obtain maximum speed. He went away from the missiles now intending to put as much distance as possible between him and them. He could see that his enemies were following, but they couldn't catch him. They were all in the same type of gunship, all made in Praetoria, although Torbid's had been captured at the Chinese Center.

Hours later, Torbid put the second part of his plan into motion. He called Maxid at CEAF, who was staying in close contact. "It's safe to send the freighter back to destroy the remaining missiles now. I've drawn the shepherd ships away, so they should have time to finish the job." He was relying on Maxid to read between the lines and get the real message that he was sending—'Draw one of the gunships away—thinking that the freighter would be attacking the missiles—when in reality the freighter wouldn't be returning.'

"Message received. I'm contacting the freighter now." Maxid had understood his message. Torbid could hear the pilots in the two gunships jabbering away. He got the gist of their conversation which was laced with frustration. Torbid and Maxid had conversed in Xyrptan and it was presumed that the Praetorian bots got the gist of their conversation too.

One of the gunships peeled off and appeared to be returning to check on the missiles, just as Torbid had hoped. His plan was working. Once the other ship was out of sight, he turned. Now the odds were even.

Torbid had another trick up his sleeve. He called Maxid, "Sir, when the freighter takes care of the missiles, they can take care of the one gunship that should have arrived back there too. Another problem; we've been getting some jamming of our radio reception, if you can take care of that," and he signed off. Torbid thought that Maxid would understand his cryptic message. First, worry the two enemy gunship crews. Then he expected that Maxid would jam the radio contact between all three gunships, so that the enemy ships couldn't communicate with each other. He didn't want the ship that had left, to notify his current opponent of the prior false message that had been sent. He was afraid that, if his present opponent found out about the false message about the freighter, he would rush back to the other ship and the missiles. He would lose his one-on-one battle.

The enemy changed course. Torbid felt that he was considering his next move. Then he turned and headed straight for them.

Torbid was wary of his new foe and warned, "Guys, the ship is headed straight for us. I don't know his intent, so stay alert. He should be on us in a few minutes." Torbid saw no reason to change direction, so he remained on a collision course. A minute went by. "Guys, I think he's going to zoom right by us at full speed, trying for a shot as he passes. We'll try the same. I think he'll veer upward or downward. I'll counter his move.

Another minute went by. They were still on a collision course. The thought of an actual collision finally occurred to Torbid. That would allow the remaining ship and missiles to complete their mission unimpeded. But then, the enemy doesn't know what resources we have available. So, he doubted that possibility, though he didn't rule it out.

They were just seconds from colliding. Torbid veered to the left. The enemy turned downward for a belly shot.

'Bam!' That was more than the ping of a glancing shot. Torbid knew that they had been hit—but how bad? He saw that the two ships were distancing themselves from each other. It gave him a minute to check his monitors and switches for any mal-function. He found none. He would have to assume that they had no serious damage and continue the battle.

Torbid turned as did the other ship. They were now miles apart. Torbid know knew that he was facing a formidable enemy, someone much smarter than the pilot he had faced earlier. So far, the enemy had been the aggressor and Torbid the defender. He'd have to change that pattern. Unfortunately, he had no preconceived plan for attack. His original thinking had been that he and his foe would be maneuvering in response to the other, much like a dog fight.

The enemy was coming toward him again. At first his course made no sense. Then he deciphered what he was doing. While keeping his edge to him, he was going in circles while speeding toward him, similar to following the course of wire in a coil. He would be encircling Torbid when he got this far. It would be hard to predict where he would be when he came abreast of them. "Guys, this is one smart pilot. We're in a real duel. I've got to come up with something fast, or we're in big trouble."

Torbid felt that right now he needed time to figure out his own game plan. He turned—keeping in mind where the missiles were—and sped in the opposite direction with his enemy in pursuit.

He knew he had little time. The grid plan he'd used that morning came to mind. Could he use it again? He had Rubid take control of the ship. Then he worked out a plan on the computer. He created a three dimensional maze by placing one grid on top of another, the total package being a cube, 100 miles on each side. At their speed that was a tight space. On automatic pilot, when the ship hit a cross hair, it would change direction randomly either up, down, right, or left. So, his course would be unpredictable, but he could go back on manual control on a moment's notice, when his enemy was in a vulnerable position.

Rather than being the attack dog, he figured to be the spider in the web, enticing his victim into his trap.

Not on purpose, but Torbid had done nothing to show his smarts. Instead he had come off as a dullard, not creative on defense or on offense—so far. Torbid would use this to his advantage, feeling that his enemy would be overconfident.

"OK, guys, this is what we're going to do," and he explained his maze plan. "Because of our frequent turns, he won't be able to make a beeline for us. He shouldn't be able to figure out our path, since our turns will be random. That should confuse him. While he's trying to figure out what to do, I'll be looking for a weakness. When I do, I'll try and turn so you both get shots simultaneously. Be fast— be accurate— good luck."

Torbid started his maze pattern. The Praetorian ship started circling, likely trying to figure out Torbid's strategy. Then he darted in one direction, then another. He was working his way closer. He appeared to make a decision, and darted apparently to where he thought Torbid was going to be next.

A sudden turn to the left and upward put Torbid on edge to the enemy who had veered downward. Both bot gunners got him in their sites simultaneously, and fired. The explosion shook their ship violently. Torbid wasn't sure, but what they had been hit too. Looking on their monitors, there was little to see—just chunks of metal and smoke dispersing in all directions. The enemy had been blown to smithereens.

Bots don't show emotion, but if they did, there would have been a sigh of relief. All we heard was, "Good job guys. Now let's get the last one."

A surprise had been concocted by Torbid for meeting his last opponent. He had taken some chances, so far, but for the most part he had fought conservatively. His next plan would be one of deception, some risk, but he felt that the benefit far outweighed the danger involved.

It took them four hours to get back to the missile pack. The enemy gunship could be seen off to one side, escorting the remaining missiles, which had been consolidated into one group. Torbid approached his opponent straight on as if he were friendly. He was counting on the two gunships being identical. Both were built in Praetoria, probably in the same factory. The Praetorian insignias had been left in place on his gunship, so they were identical in every respect to his enemy. This had been decided back on Earth, the thinking being that changing the insignias would be of no benefit to us, whereas it might be confusing to the enemy if we appeared identical to them in every detail. If he acted friendly, it would appear that his cohort had downed the Earth gunship and was returning to help guide the missiles to their destination. As he got closer, Torbid even wiggled his ship side-to-side, similar to a plane tipping its wings, in a salute as a friendly gesture. Radio contact was impossible due to the jamming. Torbid alerted Rubid. He suddenly sped up and veered upward. Rubid got off a top shot. There was a flash. The enemy ship slowed and wobbled, trailing smoke. Torbid went in for the kill; his other gunner inflicting the kill shot. An explosion ended the conflict.

Sometimes a wounded opponent is the most dangerous enemy. As they had gotten off their last shot, simultaneously a beam escaped the stricken spaceship. It struck home, and with a jolt, Torbid and crew knew that they had been hit. There was no explosion but a hole was showing in their floor near their fuel source. Worried, Torbid tried his thrusters and discovered that they were working only minimally. He feared that they were losing their fuel source. He called for Rubid to take the controls, so he could examine the damage. Fortunately there had been no harm to the bots. On checking the equipment, he soon realized they had major breakage. The bad part was that he couldn't see any way to repair the mess of jumbled, broken pipes and wires. They were lucky to have not exploded; their fuel source lay in a tank to the side of the debris. His next thought was to contact CEIF. Unfortunately they were still under radio blackout, so he would have to wait for Maxid to resume radio contact.

After reclaiming his seat, Torbid began thinking about what he could do before their fuel system failed completely, which was what he felt was going to happen. A human thought came to mind … survival.

What would the worth be to anyone to rescue them, considering the risk involved? He knew that without their fuel source, they would not be able to recharge themselves, nor would they be able to alter their course. They would become inoperative— *a derelict drifting in space for eternity.*

Bots have no fear or worry. They are programmed to make the best of any situation even though the end result might be meaningless, but the latter could not always be determined at the time a decision had to be made.

One maneuver that made sense was to put the ship on a predictable course, one that could be tracked by CEIF. Torbid was barely able to place the ship parallel to the missiles. No fuel would be necessary to keep apace.

He then cut their fuel use to a minimum, waiting for Maxid to resume communication.

Several hours later CEIF called. Torbid related the course of events to Maxid and indicated that they had eliminated all enemy gunships. Torbid said, "Unfortunately, as many as 1000 missiles remain. While our power lasts, we might be able to eliminate missiles in our neighborhood, maybe as many as a third."

Maxid wondered if the remaining missiles would still be a danger to Earth. Their chance of entering the solar system from this distance was still possible, if they continued on their same track. He couldn't change the course of the missiles. He would have to get the input of Peter and his Xyrptan superiors. It would be their decision to determine the next step.

Maxid said to Torbid, "The three of you are to be congratulated. You've accomplished three quarters of the mission for which you were sent out, against great odds. For now I believe you have made the correct decision. Rid space of as many missiles as you can before your fuel system fails. When the latter happens, you should remain on the same course as the missiles. I don't know what decision the higher ups will make, but I suspect that they will want to get rid of the remaining missiles. Hopefully, the new spaceships being manufactured here on Earth will soon be functional and can be sent to finish the job. Whether they'll decide to rescue you, as well, is questionable. In any case I expect that you'll have become inoperative by the time they arrive. If you're rescued, we'll be able to recharge you and return you to an operational status. Personally, I would like to see you all return to Earth and a hero's welcome. OK, get on with your job. I hope to see you in the near future. Again, you did a great job."

Rubid and his coworker finished off as many missiles as they could. Before they disconnected, Torbid had given Maxid their global coordinates and their course, so they could be easily found by the spaceships they expected to arrive some time in the future. Torbid then turned off all fuel use and the ship kept pace with the missiles. He was hoping that they would have enough fuel to be able to communicate with CEIF in the future. Now, all three bots remained at their posts, motionless, but still able to think. In several weeks or less, with recharging their system unavailable, they would all become completely inoperative.

Maxid called Peter first. "The threat from Praetoria is practically over. Torbid and his crew have destroyed the last two gunships. There was one complication. In shooting down the last gunship, Torbid's ship was hit, and their fuel supply was severely damaged. Their power is waning rapidly and they are drifting along with the missile pack. The missiles are still on track to reach Earth. Or course, being that far out, they likely would have to correct course to actually *hit* Earth, but I don't think we want to take that chance. You need to decide whether or not you want to go after the missiles and get rid of them once and for all, or let them go, in which case they might take a path that would take them out of our solar system. I think your team and Defense should make this decision soon. I can get the Xyrptan opinion, too, if you like."

"Well, Maxid, that's an interesting situation. I feel relieved that the main threat from the Praetorians is gone, but I think we need to deal with the remaining missiles and take zero chance of there still coming our way. It would be terrible if these missiles arrived on schedule. I think we can get a couple of our new spaceships operational within a few weeks. Then it could take a month or so for our ships to reach the missiles and destroy them. That doesn't give us much leeway, a pretty tight schedule. I'll convey this information to the President, Defense and our team and get back to you as soon as possible. For once I don't think we'll need to bother your fellow Xyrptans. I presume that we have enough astronauts and bots to man two spaceships."

"We'll have two teams made up of both astronauts and bots available for takeoff within the month." Maxid had planned for this need all along, preparing for the worst of all outcomes.

Next, Peter called the president and informed him of the situation, and requested that he and his team be the ones to confer with Defense in making the decision on whether or not to intercept the missiles. George agreed with this rationale, but insisted that he be kept informed in detail of the progress of their discussion with Defense. He would make the final decision.

Having been apprised of the situation, Herbert said that he would need a day to confer with his staff. Then he would like to meet with Peter and his team to make the final decision. Speed was paramount.

The next day, the president released a statement to the press describing in detail what had transpired in space. Reaction of the populace throughout the world was mixed—on the one hand relief that the enemy gunships had been eradicated but others worried about the missiles still out there.

Later that day, Peter conferred with his team by conference call to inform them of the outcome in space. He said that they were to meet the next day, followed by a meeting with Defense the following day to make a final decision on solving the remaining missile crisis.

The entire team was present, Robin having flown in the night before. Peter explained in detail what had occurred in space, the present situation with the missiles, and the predicament of Torbid, his crew, and their ship. Peter presented two realistic options—do nothing or send their new spaceships out to remedy the problem.

Michael was the first to speak. "I think the choice is obvious, we send up our new spaceships to do the job. It will be a first—the birth of our galactic exploration program. I would send up two ships, one to destroy the missiles, and the other to rescue the bots in their now derelict ship."

"I'm touched by your caring for my fellow bots," Cephid said, "but you realize that we are not human and are expendable. In fact, Torbid and Rubid could be recreated at CEIF and you wouldn't be able to tell the difference between the original and the copy. You don't need to risk that recovery. I feel confident that I speak for Maxid and the Supreme Council on Xyrpta on this matter."

"Damn it Ceph, you guys are as real to me as any of my human friends. I can't believe that you would desert your fellow bots in this way." Brandy bristled at Cephid's comments. This was as emotional as anyone had ever seen her.

Peter jumped in, "I think that Cephid is being practical, considerate, and unemotional with his words. I think that the decision regarding rescue should be made by us, since there's an emotional component involved. The three bots drifting out in space saved our world from catastrophic destruction. They're heroes. I believe that the majority of the people on Earth would not forgive us if we didn't make an *attempt* to recover them, particularly seeing as we are going out there anyway to destroy the missiles. I agree with Michael and favor rescuing the bots."

The meeting with Herbert and one of his staff the next day was short. Everyone agreed with the conclusion the team had reached the day before. The president was informed of the decision and he gave his consent for Peter and Defense to move ahead with the project with as much haste as possible.

Maxid made final preparations for the mix of astronauts and bots to man the two new spaceships. One would contain two bots and one astronaut and be under the command of a bot. The other ship would be manned by two astronauts and one bot and be under the command of an astronaut.

The new spaceships were actually ready in two weeks and were shipped down to Cape Canaveral for takeoff from the Kennedy Space Center. A shift in management was already being undertaken, and NASA was readying itself to take charge of the galactic space exploration program. This venue would allow a large crowd to see the initial flight of the new spaceships.

Three weeks later a large crowd was present to see the takeoff of the new spacecraft. The President gave a short commemorative speech. The specter of death-carrying missiles still pervaded the atmosphere, so festivities seemed out of order. He emphasized that this was the creation of a new space age, coming just some fifty years after the first American space flight by Alan Shepard in 1961.

Only a few minutes later, the countdown for liftoff began. With a roar and then another, first one and then the other ship arced into the heavens. This was the first time that two ships had been launched from the same area on the same day. Peter and the President looked at each other—a smile of relief showing on both their faces.

It was estimated that the spaceships would make contact with the missiles in about four weeks.

The lead spaceship was directed by an astronaut, Zach. All the astronauts on both ships had shuttle experience. The new ships were larger than the Praetorian gunship used on the first mission, largely to accommodate the humans on board.

Each day they tried to communicate with Torbid, but there was no response. Then, 22 days out, they sighted the missiles. The course mapped out by Torbid before his communication ceased was accurate. Alongside the missiles was the old gunship occupied by Torbid and his crew. Zach delegated the other ship to clean up the missiles while he checked out the gunship.

Going underneath the ship they could see it had been hit squarely in its midsection. Zach went topside where he saw no damage. This would allow them to connect port-to-port which maneuver they accomplished without incident. They were unable to unlock the port on the gunship, so they got out their welding torch and cut a hole around the lock. This accomplished, Zach took it upon himself to be the first to enter the ship followed by a bot. Zach felt the need for the bot to accompany him as he would best be able to assess the status of the bots on board the vessel. They both stood in the small quarters looking about. The three bots were motionless, Torbid at the pilot controls and Rubid and the other bot at gunnery posts. There was nothing to do but to bring the three bots on board their ship. This was accomplished uneventfully.

They disengaged from the derelict ship. Zach had been instructed to destroy the ship once they had achieved their goal. This was a policy that had recently been established for nonfunctioning objects within the solar system. Clean up as you go. The other astronaut on board was given the honor of demolishing the ship, which he did with several hits until the ship disintegrated.

Meanwhile, the other ship was doing a good job in ridding the heavens of the missiles. Zach's ship joined the fireworks.

With the mission accomplished, they headed back toward Earth. Zach had been given permission to revive Torbid but not the others. They didn't want six beings floating around in the small spaceship.

On being recharged, Torbid slowly awoke. "What took you guys so long? I've had enough sleep to last me a lifetime."

Zach laughed; he didn't know that bots had a sense of humor. "Well Torbid, if you don't appreciate our efforts, we can put you back to sleep. I don't think that Maxid and we Earthlings will miss one less hero." Everyone laughed at this dialog. Torbid gave Zach a weak thumbs up.

They all settled down to hear Torbid describe his duel with the enemy gunships. During this period, Zach radioed Maxid that their mission was accomplished, that they had retrieved Torbid and crew, destroyed the missiles, and were heading back to Earth. Maxid congratulated them and said he would relay the information on to the president, Peter and the others.

On relaying the news to Peter and describing the mission's accomplishments, Maxid was initially met with silence.

The silence was broken when Peter said, "Thank God! It's going to take a while for it to sink in that this is all over. Let me call the President and Defense and tell our team. I'll get back to you later."

Peter sat for a while, tears rolling down his cheeks and his hands shaking. He regained his composure after a minute or so. He asked his secretary to get the President on the line.

Shortly afterward, "George, I still don't believe it, but the threat is over. The spaceships destroyed the remaining missiles and recovered Torbid and his crew. They're headed home." There was a moment's silence.

Peter presumed the President was feeling, as he had, and needed a moment to compose himself. "Peter, that's the best news I've heard since I assumed the presidency. The stress and strain has been enormous. I feel like the weight of the world has been lifted from my shoulders. That's hard to say with two remaining wars facing us, but destruction of our civilization was the biggest threat ever. I want to thank you and your staff for all your hard work. We'll have to get everyone together and have a celebration."

Defense was next on the list to call. Herbert was elated but a little more reserved, as if he knew this would be the outcome. He wondered if they should now slow down and cut back on building the satellite system and more spaceships. Peter disagreed. The immediate threat was over, but there was no telling when another threat might emerge. Was there still a large spaceship on the way from Praetoria as had been rumored? He urged Herbert to maintain the existing schedule.

Next Peter called an emergency meeting of his staff and told them the good news. Half of them wept while the other half consoled them. Robin wasn't there but Brandy was. She held her head high and let the tears roll down her face. She hugged Michael who was sitting next to her.

A lot of hugging went on. A great weight had been lifted from their shoulders. After things settled down, Peter reminded them that there was still work to do, with the Chinese Center being one of the foremost problems. And was a large spaceship from Praetoria still out there?

The President's office released the news to the press. No one could remember a newspaper extra coming out since World War II, but it did the next day. There was wild celebration throughout the world. Preparations were begun for a ticker tape parade down Wall Street once the astronauts and bots returned to Earth. By the following day, the newspapers tried to bring people back down to Earth, reminding readers that there were still two wars, a recession plus the recent uprisings in North Africa and the Middle East. There were remaining problems in the world that still had to be dealt with. That hardly dampened the celebration.

The freighter and gunships were making their way back to Earth. The crews bided their time, Eric still working on his theories, the astronauts reading paperbacks, and the bots running the ship or sitting, staring into space.

QCOM's Queries and Response

Maxid called Peter, all upset. "I've just talked to Torbid, and he told me some disturbing news. During their space flight, Eric tried to interrogate him. It was a conversation that Torbid overheard between Cephid and me. It's something that should have been filtered out of Torbid's brain. Our filtering software is not perfect which allowed the slip."

"If you have any questions in the future about Xyrptan events or something a bot said, please come directly to me or Cephid. Don't try to interrogate one of our lesser bots." Maxid's voice was intimidating.

This riled Peter, but he realized that getting into an argument with an inanimate object, even though intelligent, was beneath him, so he remained calm. "Maxid, to hear that an armada of spaceships was ready and waiting to take off for Earth sounded threatening, especially when the news was inadvertently mentioned by a supposedly reliable source. "

"We've just been through a world-threatening scare. For all we know, there could be collusion between you and the Praetorians. It seemed like you were leaving us in the dark about your plans concerning Earth. How much else is there that we don't know? If we're going to be partners with you in space exploration, there needs to be openness and trust on both sides."

Maxid had calmed down. "Our intention was to send an armada of various types of spaceships; leisure, transport, and military to Earth after the battle with the Praetorians was won. It was to show you what you could expect in the future. It was of a completely peaceful nature. We saw no need to inform you ahead of time. I'm sorry about the misunderstanding. I have to reiterate though—if something like this should happen again, please come to me—don't interrogate a lesser bot."

Peter called Robin to apprise her of this conversation. "When I asked Eric to feel Torbid out about the armada set to come to Earth during their space flight, I didn't realize that Torbid would go directly to Maxid which he did." Peter then relayed to Robin the gist of their conversation. "Perhaps it's just as well that this occurred, because it raises an important question. Are the Xyrptans going to place a limit on what we can ask a bot in our research and development? We were told originally that we would have unlimited access to them. So, I asked Maxid if he was now placing a limitation on what we could ask a bot. He appeared flustered, and at a loss for words. Then he said that he would have to check with his superiors in Xyrpta. That left me feeling uneasy. It's the first time that I've seen a crack in the Xyrptan fabric, but then Maxid is a bot and not a human."

Robin was a little unnerved. "Wow, that's a lot to digest, particularly after we've gotten this far. What do we do now?"

"We'll just have to wait until Maxid hears back from his home. I think it's likely that they're going to place some restrictions on our study of the bots. I don't think it will effect building our own bots, but it may restrict asking existing bots about their past and particularly about information they may have obtained from outside sources. We'll see."

The Chinese Center's Future

A team meeting was called for several days later. Was there any reason to continue the deception of pretending to be Praetorian bots communicating with their homeland? Should they come clean, say who they are, and open a dialogue with the Praetorians? Or should they just shut down the site?

In the subsequent two days, there was considerable discussion among the team members as to what should be done, but there was no clear consensus. Perhaps the meeting would bring about agreement.

Peter called the meeting to order. He outlined the possibilities for the Chinese Center. He then introduced the Chinese ambassador, Chang Ho, who had been invited to participate in the discussion. He might even have the last word in making the decision. After all, the Center was on Chinese territory. When asked if he would like to speak first, the ambassador deferred, indicating that he would prefer first to hear some of the other opinions.

Cephid spoke up. "The Supreme Council in Xyrpta has discussed this topic, and I am giving you *their* recommendation. They see no reason to maintain contact any longer with the Praetorians. They, themselves, have held off making any contact with them. They had considered opening negotiations with Praetoria, as part of their helping in the defense of Earth, but since the threat has been averted, they reverted to their prior stance of avoiding any formal contact with that nation. Why open relations with an enemy who had tried to destroy your civilization? We were exactly in your position after we had defeated them. Since deporting them, we have left them isolated and dependent on themselves for their own survival. This policy has served us well."

"They pose little threat to you now. We are alert and will police them from our planet, and if there are any activities pointing in your direction, we'll let you know. In the near future you'll have an adequate defense against hostile alien invaders, and we'll work with you to bring this up to our standards. We recommend that you *desist* attempting to communicate with Praetoria and leave them *isolated*." There were murmurs from the group showing both concordance and disagreement.

Peter's cell phone buzzed. It was his office. They were not supposed to call during a conference unless it was an emergency. He asked to be excused and he left the conference room. Waiting for his return, the team broke up into several groups to debate the Xyrptan's recommendation.

On his return, Peter had a serious expression on his face. "Our troubles may not be over. Perhaps not as bad as before, but right now we don't know. That was Maxid. Zach is still out in space. He's picked up signals from a ship not far behind him. It seems they've been trying to contact their gunships, and of course, there's no response. For now, we have to presume that this is the large spaceship that was rumored to have left Praetoria after the missiles and shepherd ships."

"Maxid has put our ships on standby alert. He feels that we should send Zach's ship back to check this out." There were startled expressions of remorse. "Now we have even more to discuss. Cephid had you finished?"

Taking his time while thinking, Cephid replied, "Yes I'd finished my talk. As to this new information, I'll contact my superiors to get their views. I should be able to get back to you in a few days."

Michael was next. "I think that we should make the Praetorians aware that we took over their outpost some time ago, and that we have been able to deceive them ever since. Furthermore, I would make *clear* that we have destroyed their gunships and all their missiles. However, I would wait before contacting them until we hear from Zach and know more about the spaceship still out there."

"We don't know what the contents are of that ship. It seems unlikely that it would be a war ship, more likely it's a transport with troops. I can't see what purpose would be served by letting them continue to Earth. We should tell them to turn around or face destruction. However, the problem with that is that they most likely don't have enough fuel to return to Praetoria. I think it unlikely that they would send just a ship of bots. If there are humans on board, the humanitarian thing to do would be to let them land, refuel, and then send them on their way. I would make it very *clear* that we are in control and they have few alternatives. Lastly, if we can't agree on terms beforehand with the Praetorians, we should destroy the ship and *whatevers'* on board."

"That's a very strong but thoughtful statement, Michael," commented Peter. "I like your thinking. Any other opinions?"

"We don't know these people other than that they wanted to destroy us," said Brandy, "but they couldn't be more foreign to our way of thinking. We're likely to discover other aliens out there. I feel that we should learn as much as we can about them. The Xyrptans know them and have given us their opinion, but we need to find out *firsthand*, not just accept the word of an alien race that we have known for just a short time. So, I agree with Michael, but further, I would like to talk to them before sending them back. Through the Chinese Center, we'll have plenty of time to discuss with the Praetorians the ultimate fate of their ship and its contents."

The Chinese ambassador nodded to Peter, indicating that he was ready to speak.

"First, I bring you greetings from President Lintao and Prime Minister Yiabao. They both send you their congratulations for a job well done in eliminating the threat to our world. I like your words, and I agree with both Michael and Brandy. We should let the Praetorians land. We can accommodate them at the Center. Already, we are rebuilding the structures that were destroyed when the p-bots tried to retake the Center. Enlarging the landing field will be necessary. We can add other accommodations."

"I bring you another message. We believe that now that the threat is over, you should allow us and other nation's access to the new technology that you are receiving from Xyrpta, so we can build our own robots and spaceships. Thank you."

"We appreciate your remarks Mr. Ambassador. Our government has talked with the Xyrptans about disseminating their technology. This depends upon whether or not we are going to support their mission and help them explore the galaxy by serving as a satellite station. If we are agreeable to helping them, which appears likely now, then they would like to establish a consortium with all interested countries participating. This would control the dissemination of information flowing from them to Earth. Our Secretary of State would be the one to contact for further details."

Feeling that they had reached a decision, Peter concluded by saying, "I'm in agreement with Ambassador Hu, Michael and Brandy. So, unless there is some disagreement, I'll take this information to the President. Let's meet in two days to discuss this matter further. I'll tell Maxid to inform the lead spaceship to change course, track down the new Praetorian ship, and gather more information as to its contents and mission. I thank you all for a good days work."

A short meeting of the team occurred two days later. You could feel the exuberance in the room, a far cry from the depressing atmosphere that clouded the room just weeks ago. Peter began, "The President wants us to make contact with the Praetorians through the Chinese Center before we make any decision about the spaceship. I've talked to the Chinese and Maxid, and we'll plan together on how to approach the Praetor. We're going to meet in two days at the Chinese Center. Michael, I'd like to have you and Cephid join me. I expect that we'll come to some agreement and may well send our first message to the Praetor at that time. Are there any questions?"

Cephid rose. "I contacted my people about the spaceship. They recommended that you just *shoot it down*. That will send the clearest message to the Praetorians that you are not to be trifled with. You *can't* trust them. If you do contact them, make sure you stay in control, and don't agree to *anything* that has even the *remotest* danger for you. Let the Supreme Council know what you decide, so they can protect you from their end."

Communication with Praetoria

The next day Peter, Cephid, and Michael flew to China. On landing, they were whisked away by helicopter to the Chinese Center. They could see several structures going up with one almost finished, probably where they would be staying. Their host said that this was a barracks, and the other structures would be finished shortly. Maxid had flown in the same day, as had two representatives from the Chinese government, one in military uniform.

The dining facility was unfinished, but open for business. The Chinese officer apologized profusely for the status of the building, explaining that this was the best they could do under their present circumstances. Peter explained that he preferred to meet here, where they would be taking action, rather than in a more remote place.

The Chinese dignitary wanted everyone to understand that they would be depending upon the two Praetorian transmitter bots to translate and send their document accurately. Would there be anyone available to listen in and confirm that this was done correctly? Cephid indicated that he understood enough Praetorian language to do the job. They had been depending upon these two bots to transmit accurately for some time and there had been no problem. As far as they could tell, the recipients on Praetor had no suspicion that they had been deceived. This should attest to the trustworthiness, reliability, and accuracy of the two radio transmitters. Also, both Maxid and Cephid had been in close contact with the Chinese Center since it had been taken it over, and they were unaware of any untoward events.

The group met the next morning to create the substance of the document to be sent to the Praetorians. Michael and Cephid were chosen to write up the final draft. Both assented to do this job and everyone would review the document in the evening after dinner. Then, one of the transmitter bots would translate it into Praetorian. The last step would be for Cephid to go over the translation for accuracy.

All of this work was accomplished on schedule. The final draft stated:

To The Praetorian Supreme Council:

We are communicating with you from the radio transmitter center that you established in China on Earth several years ago. We became aware of this entity two years ago when we discovered your robots on Earth. It was then that we captured this site. Rather than close it down, we decided that we would continue transmissions as if there had been no change in control. To accomplish this purpose, we indoctrinated your two radio transmitter bots to our way of thinking by electronically altering their mental processes. Thereafter, they did as we bid. We believe that you were unaware of this change. We have benefited greatly from this deception, and we thank you for your cooperation in this endeavor.

From your transmissions we were able to confirm that you had sent three sets of missiles accompanied by shepherd gunships toward Earth with the intention of destroying our civilization. We are informing you that all missiles and their accompanying shepherd gunships have been destroyed. You grossly misjudged our capabilities.

We consider your threat toward us was an act of war. Understand that the government of Xyrpta is our ally and is in agreement with the contents of this transmission.

We demand an explanation of your act of war against us as a basis for any further communication.

Now we are aware that a large spaceship from Praetoria is coming our way. We intend to destroy this ship, as we did the others, unless you can give us a good reason for not doing so.

We will keep this line of communication open if it will be to our benefit. For the sake of your spaceship and its contents, we believe that you should respond. If we do not receive an answer to this document within fourteen days, the ship will be destroyed.

The United Nations Security Council
The President of the United States

The next day the draft was sent out to multiple sources for their approval; the United Nations Security Council, the President of the United States, and the main countries that had been involved in the defense of Earth. A copy was sent to the Supreme Council in Xyrpta, since they were referred to in the document with the presumption that they agreed with its contents.

All parties met the time frame of 48 hours that had been set for approval of the document. Both Maxid and Cephid were delegated to be present when the document was to be sent to Praetoria. Cephid listened in on the transmission sent by one of the bot radio transmitters, and he was satisfied that the contents of the transmission were accurate.

It was only a week later that an answer was received from Praetoria.

To the United Nations Security Council and the President of the United States:

Our endeavor to visit your planet was instigated by our need to find a new home for our people. We presently live in a harsh environment. We have been looking for another planet that would better suit our needs. To this end we discovered your planet, Earth, with its ideal climate and environment. It then became our intent to colonize your planet. We concluded that this would be impossible by peaceful means. Therefore, we decided to subjugate your population by military means. We believed that by this method you would be more amenable to our terms for cohabitation. Our purpose was not to destroy your entire population, but rather to make clear that we were coming irrespective of your wishes.

The fact that you destroyed our missiles and gunships shows us that you are a more advanced people than we believed. We misjudged your capability.

We would like to continue a discourse with you via our communication center on Earth, and we desire that this be of a peaceful nature. There will be no further military action directed toward you.

You are correct in believing that one of our large spaceships is in your vicinity. We calculate that they are now 30 days out from Earth. This is a friendly and not a military ship. It contains 50 young Praetorians along with ten robots. They were to set up our first colony on Earth. The ship cannot return to Praetoria without first refueling. Also, they have been short of food and on rations for the past year. We ask that you let them land and feed them. Then we can discuss what their future might be. The humans on board are not military personnel, but young, intelligent, resourceful youths whom we chose as good candidates for starting life in a new land. They are in no way a danger to you.

Lastly, we would like to sincerely apologize for our hostile actions. We hope to repair the damage we have done to our relationship. We will strive to do better in the future.

The Supreme Council of Praetoria

The document was distributed to the UN and appropriate countries— the Americans and Chinese receiving the initial copies. The Xyrptans were sent a copy as well.

Peter called a meeting of his team to discuss the document. "I presume that you've all read the reply. I'd like to get your comments. Also, I want you to know that we have sent one spaceship back to meet the Praetorian ship. Once there, it will contact the ship, evaluate the situation, and get back to us with the information and await further instructions."

"They're doing no less than what I thought they would do," began Michael. "Obviously they're trying to repair the damage they did. Then, too, they're trying to protect their spaceship. It's rather brazen of them to think that they can almost annihilate us and *then* expect us to communicate with them on a friendly basis. I agree with the Xyrptans, they aren't to be trusted. I would keep communication to a minimum. For humanitarian reasons, we need to let their ship land and care for their people, at least on a minimal basis. I would send them back to Praetoria as soon as their ship is refueled and restocked with food. I can see *no* circumstance where we would allow these people to stay. That would accomplish their purpose of starting a colony on *our soil*. They would be slyly accomplishing by peaceful means what they couldn't do by an act of war. It would be expecting too much of the new immigrants to not communicate with their own people and encourage more of them to follow in their footsteps."

Robin commented. "I agree with Michael. I have sympathy for the youth they've sent here, but the larger message must be sent that they aren't welcome, and we won't tolerate any further incursions. I believe the Xyrptans are a good guide. If they'll have nothing to do with these people, and they're stronger and more advanced then we, why would we want to chance another encounter with them?"

"I would like to meet and talk with their youth before deciding what to do with them. Otherwise, I agree with what's been said." Brandy got only unfriendly glares from the others in the room for expressing this sentiment.

The consensus was entirely in agreement with Michael's remarks. There was little else to say about the document. Peter narrowed the subject to what to do with the space ship arriving in just a matter of weeks. Was there something to be gained by keeping it and its contents for a while?

Brandy said with some confidence, feeling that she had got some backing from Peter. "It's hard for me to believe that an *entire people* are bad. I'm acutely aware of the Xyrptan's experience with these people. I would think that they have DNA and genes similar to ours. I can't believe that they are all *genetically predetermined* to be sociopaths. That's something we could investigate from interviewing those on board the spaceship. At this time, I wouldn't feel bad if we sent them all back to Praetoria, but I'd rather give them and us a chance to get to know each other first." Brandy got no support. No one said a word.

"Cephid, do you want to make a comment before we close?" Peter asked with raised eyebrows.

"My thoughts coincide with that of our Supreme Council that I stated earlier and they haven't changed. I agree with Michael's comments, except for one thing. I would shoot down their spaceship *as soon as possible*. That will send the strongest message to the Praetorians that you'll not tolerate any interference whatever from them." Cephid had a stern expression on his face at the end of his comment.

"Your comments are duly noted, Cephid. That may yet be the end result, but first we need to determine the status of their ship before making a final decision. I agree with Brandy that we need to be *humanitarian* about this affair. The freighter should be back in several weeks. Our spaceship and the Praetorian ship should not be far behind. That's it for today." Peter closed the session, but not before he said to Robin that he would like to speak with her in private.

Back in his office, Peter asked Robin to have a seat. "I've heard back from Maxid. He's received a directive from his superiors regarding how we can research their bots. They'll construct a bot at CEAF and turn it over to us. It *supposedly* will be identical to the product coming from their bot lab. You can take him to NASA or anywhere else and do with him as you wish, take him apart, put him back together. His intelligence will be at the same level as a pilot, comparable to Torbid and Rubid. This is a high level but not the highest. We don't have permission to query *any* of the other existing bots. I presume that this bot will be "sterile" in the sense that he won't have been exposed to any other bots or any human. I believe in this way they are insuring that no restricted information will leak out. I'm somewhat disappointed, but I guess, this is about the best that we could hope for."

"I'm not disappointed. We still have access to the AI human on Xyrpta, and hopefully Ed and I can extract some information from him on their near future and long range plans. As an afterthought, could you ask if we could have two bots? I'll take mine back to NASA so my team can help in the research, and I'm sure Ed would love to have a bot to study at his lab too."

"One other thing, Robin, these are research robots, and there's to be *no* fraternization among bots. I'll check with Maxid about the extra bot, but I don't imagine that'll be a problem."

Spaceships Return;
Praetorians Land on Earth

Three weeks later, word spread that the freighter would be coming in the next afternoon. A small crowd gathered to great the returnees. The ship came in slowly and hovered. Its spider-like landing legs sprouted and it slowly descended with its thrusters blasting away until it gradually sat down on the field. The hatch opened. Stairs were rolled up to the ship. Eric was the first to appear. A cheer greeted him as he stepped down. Robin ran out from the crowd and was the first to give him a big hug. He was then surrounded by the throng who threw congratulations and questions at him. The others then descended— Arnie and the two bot pilots. Retreating to the conference room, they all celebrated the return of the crew and partook of the drinks and snacks that Maxid had provided.

A week later, Zach sent word that they had found the Praetorian spaceship. He had contacted their crew and was told that the humans on board were in bad shape due to starvation. They would need emergency help when they landed.

Taking it upon himself, Peter instructed Zach, through Maxid, to bring them to the Chinese Center where they would have emergency vehicles waiting to treat them and take them to hospitals if necessary. Maxid and Cephid were *adamantly* against this decision, but Peter felt that this was the only humanitarian thing they could do.

The Chinese had enlarged the landing area at the Center to accommodate the larger ship that would be coming in. A new, paved highway had been laid down to the nearest town to replace the dirt road. An extra contingent of soldiers was added to the guards to be prepared for whatever might come off the ship. On the day the ship arrived, a large gathering was in place including Peter, Maxid, Eric, Michael and Cephid. UN, US and Chinese dignitaries were present to greet the newcomers. No one was quite sure what to expect, but they were prepared. If a medical emergency unfolded, ambulances and EMTs were standing by.

Zach, in the lead spaceship, came in first and hovered over the site, showing the way for the Praetorian ship. He then scooted away, on his way home to CEAF. The behemoth of a ship slowly descended, hovered overhead as it lowered its landing struts, and then came in for its landing. It shut off its engine. There was silence, as if the throng was holding its breath. The hatch opened and steps were lowered.

An individual appeared in the doorway. The only distinguishable features from that distance were metallic—they were bots. Several like individuals began descending with him.

A Chinese military officer and Cephid left the crowd to greet these strangers. No one was sure whether they would speak English or Praetorian, thus Cephid's presence. Surprisingly, their leader spoke fairly good English, though with a fixed expression on his face. He explained that he and the other bots were in good shape. He invited the two of them to come up with him into the ship to see the status of the Praetorians. On entering the ship, the military officer stared at the scene and then bent over and puked; the stench was nauseating. Being a bot, Cephid was unaffected. The humans were lying either in bunks or on the floor. They were skin and bones and barely able to move. There greenish faces showed desperation. Some raised their arms in a pleading fashion. Some were still conscious and aware that they had landed in unfriendly territory. The p-bot explained that they began to run out of food about a year ago, and they had severely rationed their food ever since.

Cephid ran down the stairs to explain to Peter, Maxid, and the others the terrible sight within the ship. The Chinese dignitary ran over to the emergency crews standing nearby and quickly explained the situation. The Praetorians would need help exiting the ship and clearly would need to be taken to hospitals at once. Little happened for a while thereafter except for the EMT's racing up and down the steps with stretchers and carrying the ill to the waiting ambulances. This happened over the next hour. At the end, the head EMT said that there were still ten bodies inside, of those who had expired. There were no humans in good enough condition for anyone to speak to, which left only the bots for interrogation.

All ten p- bots were led to the new housing. Two p-bot pilots and the navigator were asked to join a small party in a conference room, while the remaining p-bots—who had been used to service the humans—were placed in a separate room under guard.

The inquisitors were Peter, Maxid, Cephid and UN and Chinese dignitaries. They all deferred to Peter, who asked the p-bots if they understood and could speak English. The lead pilot said that everyone on board had attended classes in English throughout the trip. Peter wanted to get as complete a story from them, as possible, about their trip from beginning to end. "Why did you come here?"

The lead pilot became the spokesperson for the others. "We were told that our humans were to establish a colony on Earth and that others would follow later. We were to help in any way requested. The three of us were to arrange refueling of our ship and then return to Praetoria."

"Were you aware that missiles and gunships preceded you and were to destroy a large part of our civilization in order to make us more accepting of you?"

"Yes, we were aware of that fact, but we were given no details. We have no military people on board. In fact, the young people who volunteered for this project were all students from good families who were looking for a better life. Classes were held throughout the trip, at least until their health deteriorated. When we started, they were children—mostly in their mid-teens— peaceful, intelligent, and outgoing."

"I can't see how you could send such a group and not expect to find a *hostile* reception. If we hadn't been able to destroy your missiles and gunships, and you had decimated our cities and people, I am sure you would have all been killed on landing here. I just don't understand your logic."

"We're just the pilots. We did as we were told. You'll have to ask those who sent us here that question. I don't have an answer."

"Why didn't your people stock your ship with sufficient food for the trip? That shouldn't have been difficult to do."

"Again, I don't have an answer except to say that we took a year longer than planned."

"Did you bring any tools and necessitates to start life from scratch along with you?"

"Yes, we brought some tools, but mostly we were depending on the bots that preceded us to help us get established. We were planning on getting started here at the Center."

"Does anyone else have any questions?" Peter looked around and nodded at Maxid who had raised his hand.

"I would like to know who your contacts are on Praetoria. Have you kept them abreast of the status of your humans? Did you tell them that you were landing?"

"They are aware of our dire straits. I last contacted them just before we landed, but I couldn't relate as to what our reception would be other than that I saw a crowd of people—including soldiers—waiting for us. Our only contact has been with Praetoria, except when I recently tried to contact our gunships. Our humans communicated with someone at home every six months or so, but this was mostly with family."

The Chinese official had a query. "Did your people in Praetoria communicate with you about the battles that occurred in space just ahead of you?"

"Yes, they kept us abreast of what was happening. There was little we could do other than continue our journey. We didn't have the capacity to turn around and return home."

"Did your officials give you any indication of what to expect on landing and what might lie in store for you after doing so?"

"They said that we should not expect friendship, but they did not feel that you would harm us."

Peter took over, feeling that they had obtained about as much good information as they were going to get for now. He knew that there would be further extensive interrogation of all the p-bots, and when they recovered, of the humans as well. But before he ended, "I have one last question. Who are the leaders among your humans?"

"Two teachers, Durst and Eta, a student leader, Rhee, and the head is Zeta," replied the pilot.

Before breaking up, Maxid informed the three bots that they would be held under guard in this building with their cohorts pending a determination of their and their humans' future. Peter indicated to the Chinese representative that the Praetorian humans that had been taken to various hospitals should be placed under guard as well. He agreed and said that he would take care of that immediately.

Several days later, the President told Peter he wanted to have a ceremony to celebrate the return of the spacemen and to honor them. It was to be held on Friday. The day after, there was to be a ticker tape parade down Wall Street. Both events were widely advertised in the newspapers, and both were expected to draw huge crowds.

Eric, Zach, the other astronauts, the bots, Maxid, Torbid and Rubid gathered at the National Mall on a cold but sunny Friday morning. They were humbled by the scene that lay before them—an assemblage later estimated to be more than a million people, stretched as far as the eye could see. After the singing of the Star Spangled Banner, the President addressed the throng, and retold the exploits of the freighter and its survival after being hit, of Eric in the captured gunship shooting down the first enemy gunship, and then of Rubid shooting down the other two gunships under Torbid's command. In particular, he emphasized Torbid's ingenuity, valor and his ability to out-think and out-maneuver his opponents. He related the ordeal of the three bots after their ship had been hit, and then, of their rescue by our new spaceships under Zach's command.

He then called Eric to come up and receive the Presidential Medal of Freedom, the highest honor that can be bestowed on a civilian. A deafening roar erupted that lasted for minutes. After pinning the medal, the President gave him a strong handshake and a heartfelt hug. Both appeared on the verge of tears.

Torbid followed to receive the same honor. President West explained that he was a robot and as intelligent, skillful, and reliable as any human being. He, more than anyone else, was responsible for shooting down the three gunships and destroying the missiles that were headed toward Earth. The President didn't know how to show his deep appreciation for what Torbid had done, so, after pinning the medal on him, they shook hands and then he gave Torbid a hug. Torbid bowed to him and then waved to the crowd that again erupted in wild cheering. The other spacemen received lesser medals.

The President said that he had a further medal to bestow and asked Peter to step forward. This was unexpected and Peter hesitated at first.

President West explained that Peter, in addition to his job as National Security Advisor, had headed up XCOM, the commission that led the defense of Earth, the planning of the satellite system of lasers networked around earth, and the spaceships that had accomplished the job of eliminating the missile threat. They had a long handshake after the President pinned the medal on Peter. He then whispered in Peter's ear, "Dear friend, I'm eternally grateful for what you did. Words can't express my feeling of gratitude," and he gave Peter a long, heartfelt hug. The thunderous applause was repeated.

There was one last medal to be pinned. President West called for Maxid to come up. "Americans, Maxid is a robot who was built in Xyrpta, a planet 24 trillion miles from Earth. He arrived here 35 years ago, and built a center where they eventually were able to build the bots we have seen and heard about in the last few years. Unfortunately, they inadvertently led their neighboring Praetorians here. However, they fought the Praetorians by our side. Without them, our civilization, as we know it today, would not exist. They have shown us extraordinary friendship. We, in turn, will reciprocate by joining them in their space exploration program." The president was announcing this prematurely, but he had the assurance of the congressional leadership that his would be approved. "I want everyone to realize the significance of this event for our future."

He pinned the medal on Maxid's chest, and shook his hand. Deafening applause followed. The ceremony ended with the singing of God Bless America.

The following day the ticker tape parade down Wall Street was a wild celebration with well over a million, cheering people honoring their heroes as they passed by in open automobiles. It was said to be the largest parade ever held. Peter and Maxid sat side-by-side and waved to the crowd. Maxid made it known that he wanted to be able to send a video home about the events of the past two days so that the Supreme Council and the Xyrptan population would see that their efforts had been appreciated.

The team's meeting had been postponed for the celebration, but the day now arrived for them to get-together. Robin indicated that the ceremony that she had planned for Eric would occur after the meeting.

They had a lot to discuss and they had to make some serious decisions. This team, that had earned a reputation for sound judgment, were now listened to by many groups. Peter wanted to discuss what should be done with the Praetorian immigrants.

The team first received news on the condition of the Praetorians in the hospitals in China. Peter said that there had been two further deaths, and that there were several still in critical condition.

Brandy was concerned. "I now realize that with their markedly different appearance the Praetorians wouldn't fit into our society. In fact, they would likely be racially discriminated against, particularly with the animosity now felt toward Praetoria. However, it might be worthwhile to have them attend a special school for a year to teach them our history, culture and way of thinking. They then could act as ambassadors when they return to Praetoria."

She felt that they should be sent home after the year in school. The team agreed with sending them back to Praetoria, but they were divided on supporting them for a year of schooling. Michael pointed out that having them schooled, in isolation, without contact with our people, would leave a bad impression. Peter inserted his agreement with Michael, and added that if they were treated poorly by fellow students, they would not make goodwill ambassadors. A consensus appeared to be forming for sending the Praetorians back home as soon as they recovered and their ship could be refueled and restocked with food. Brandy became incensed, "I think that you're being cruel to these innocents who are victims of their own people through no fault of their own. Showing a little kindness won't cost us anything. Let's not take our anger against the Praetorians out on these kids."

At this point, Peter called a halt to the meeting by saying, "I think we all need to think on this matter further, and keep our emotions in check."

As the meeting broke up, Robin announced that the luncheon celebration was to be held in the auditorium down the hall. She said that she had invited many of those that had participated in the defense of Earth, so there would be a quite large assemblage of guests. Maxid, Torbid, and Rubid would be coming, and there was even a chance that the President would stop in.

Robin smiled to herself feeling that she had done a crackup job with balloons everywhere and crepe paper hanging from the ceiling and walls. She even had large posters of the heroes on the walls. There were tables of food and beverages, and a large ice carving of two spaceships gunning for one another over a globe.

Brandy had not had a chance to talk to Eric since his return from space, so she sought him out. She found him waiting in line to get food. He appeared to be deep in thought. She sidled up to him and gave him a hug. He didn't respond, so she asked what was wrong.

"Brandy, I have a problem. Let's get a drink and sit down where we can talk." There was no quiet corner, so they left and found a small adjacent room that was empty.

After getting comfortable, Eric began. "While I was in space, I had a lot of time to communicate with the astrophysicists on Xyrpta. They downloaded information to me as fast as I could handle it. At first I was delighted to discover answers to problems that I had been working on, and I forwarded these to my colleagues at Cal Tech. Then my elation gradually turned to a feeling of uneasiness, and then, finally, to depression. I realized that I was no longer being creative and trying to discover answers to the origin of the universe. Instead I was reading the works of others and doing *nothing* creative myself. It's like all my goals had already been reached by someone else, and there was nothing left for me to do. Being a millennium ahead of us, there's a ton of information to catch up on. That could take a good part of the rest of my life. Perhaps in a few years, I could reach the level of some of the astrophysicists on Xyrpta, and *then* be able to make a contribution in my field. In the meantime it feels like being back in school. Not surprisingly, when I contacted my colleagues, some of them had the same feeling." He shook his head. "I've always admired your intellect, Brandy. Do you see an answer to my dilemma?"

"I can see that this could be a problem in many fields where creative work is necessary, particularly in the sciences. I don't have a ready answer. Maybe you should just dig in your heels, and assume that you'll be back in school for a while. Or, maybe you should take a break. The time away might make things clearer for you. Or, you and your colleagues could get together and have a barn storming session. I think that a few hundred or so good minds would stand a better chance of coming up with a solution than any single brain."

"I like your last thought." Eric finally smiled. "We could have a convention, the aim of which would be to evaluate the information we're getting, how to handle it, and what part each of us could play in going forward. I *really* like that idea. I think I'll try and get a meeting started. That would occupy me for a while and might make me less depressed. I knew I could count on you, Brandy."

"One other thing you might consider is seeing a doctor and getting an antidepressant for the short term."

"Well, I've gone that route before. One doc thought I was bipolar. I have mood swings, but I've never thought that they were to the degree to warrant that diagnosis. I think I can work it out myself. Thanks, though. You've made me feel better." They both stood up. Eric hesitated. Briefly, he remembered how Brandy had rebuffed him in the past. It was dawning on him that his feeling for Brandy was mainly one of admiration. She was a remarkable woman. They looked at each other and smiled. Eric gave her a big bear hug and she reciprocated. Eric said, "We better get back to the celebration."

As they entered the auditorium, Robin saw them and locked eyes with Brandy. Robin's eyes narrowed, and her lips pursed. She would have to speak to Robin about this. She and Eric were just good friends, nothing more. Obviously Robin had feelings for Eric. Brandy saw Ingrid who was talking to several of her fellow bots, so she went over to converse with some friendly faces.

Eric was besieged by well-wishers. Herbert was there and gave Eric one of his hearty handshakes. "My boy, you did us proud. I knew you were the one to lead us." Eric hesitated but kept quiet. Torbid and Rubid had done more than he, but he saw no purpose in putting Herbert down. "Sir, we all did our part. Thank you."

Herbert even went over and spoke to Maxid and the other bots as if they were old friends. "I've been hard on you bots. I was angered by your leading the Praetorians here. I have to say, though, that when the chips were down, you came through in spades. One good thing that came out of all this is that we got our galactic space program started. I thank you for that." This is about as close as one could expect Herbert to go in apologizing for his earlier behavior.

Robin came over and grabbed Eric. "Come over here hero. We want to get some pictures of you guys. She had gathered Torbid and Rubid and some of the astronauts and now arranged them in different groupings for the photographer. Eric could feel that Robin was being impersonal, not showing any of her usual friendliness toward him. He would have to fix that.

To top off the afternoon, Peter escorted the President in for a short visit to congratulate Eric, the astronauts, and the bots on a job well done. The President then grabbed Eric by the arm and led him aside for a private word, "Son, you've done a great service for your country. I don't think you realize yet the *enormity* of what you and the bots achieved. If there's anything I can do for you, please let me know. I'd be happy to help you in any way I can."

Eric was overwhelmed and felt a lump in his throat for a moment.

"Sir, there's one thing you could do … not just for me, but for my fellow astrophysicists too. We've been inundated with a *wealth* of information from Xyrpta, so much so, that it's been hard to know in what direction we should go. I'd appreciate your help in setting up a conference for my colleagues to decide what we should do. I'm sure that many of the other sciences will be feeling the same way, and they may need similar guidance in the future."

"Eric, I'll give you all the support you need. Let's work through Peter. That'd be the best way to get this started. Good luck with your endeavor."

The President left and the party gradually wound down.

Eric sought out Robin. "This's been some party, Robin. You really went out of your way. I'm sure we'll all remember this for many years to come. Thanks!"

"I saw the look you gave Brandy, when we came back in the room. I wanted to share a problem I had with her, and it was too noisy in here, so we went to a room down the hall to talk. She helped me. I admire her, and she's a good friend. I hope to keep that friendship, but I want you to know that we are just friends, nothing more."

Robin showed a half-hearted smile. "Brandy's my friend too. I think you may have misinterpreted my look." Robin made it clear that she wanted to change the subject.

"How about going out to dinner tomorrow evening?" That returned a real smile to Robin's face, and if she had any doubts about Eric, these seemed to abate, at least for now.

Among the last to leave were Eric and Peter who stopped to talk.

"Eric, the President spoke to me just before he left and mentioned your request. Why don't you formulate a plan for your convention, and bring it to me? I'll help you set it up. I think we can find funds to meet your expenses."

Eric, with an almost embarrassed smile, thanked Peter and they parted.

Preparing for the Future

The team met a week later to discuss what their future might be.

Peter, with a dejected expression on his face, limped up to the head of the table. "I'm sorry to say that my arthritis is acting up again in my hips. My orthopedic doc has been encouraging me to get hip replacements which I've put off until now. Since our immediate problems have been mostly solved, I think it's time for me to get this surgery done. I go in next week for the first hip, and six weeks later I'll have the second one done ... but that's not the reason for our meeting."

"I've talked to a number of sources, including the President, and we've made a decision. We're going to continue with the team, but we are going to make a few changes. We're leaving Washington and we'll be moving over to the jurisdiction of NASA, actually to the Johnson Space Center in Houston. We'll be a separate division. I'm leaving the post of National Security Advisor and will be heading up this new division. This is a chance to get in on the ground floor of a new and exciting adventure—a new era of space exploration in association with the Xyrptans. We expect to get congressional approval for the program shortly. We'll be working closely with Maxid at CEAF. I'll be moving to Houston as soon as I've healed and have completed my rehabilitation. Those who decide to stay with us will need to make this move, as well, and I encourage you to do so. "

"I know that gives you a lot to think about. I'd like to have your decisions about moving within the week. While I'm out on medical leave, Michael will be in charge, so please go to him with your decision and any questions. I expect to be back at work in three months." Peter rose and limped out accompanied by several, "Good luck," wishes.

Michael took charge and asked if there were any questions. A number of the team members were upset by the need to move from Washington.

Brandy voiced her feelings. "I've loved working with this team. I've been excited by the endeavor, but I hate to think of leaving where I have my family. Is there any way I could commute or be a consultant?"

Michael answered, "Brandy, I think that'll depend on what your job duties are going to be. I want to defer answering your question until we have a better grasp on your job. I presume that you'll continue working with Ingrid. This goes for a number of others as well. While Peter's away, we can flesh out what the jobs will be. Offhand, I would think that any job that's full time will require moving. I want to set up interviews with all of you, so we can get a handle on your individual futures. I'll contact you soon, so we can get started." That pretty well squelched any further questions and the meeting broke up.

Robin and Eric had their dinner date that evening. Their conversation eventually drifted around to what each would be doing in the future. Robin reiterated her intention of continuing to work at NASA in robotic engineering, and she expected that she would be traveling to CEAF frequently to benefit from their robotic expertise. Her main interest going forward was to be able to create her own bots in the image of those from Xyrpta and then extend their use to industry.

Eric mentioned his depression, as he had related it to Brandy, and how she had suggested that he convene a convention for astronomers and astrophysicists to discuss their future. At the mention of Brandy, Robin crinkled her nose, which didn't go un-noticed by Eric. So he interrupted his monologue to assure her, again, that he and Brandy were just good friends but that it didn't go any further. For her part, Robin didn't feel reassured, but she wasn't going to let that be evident. She gave Eric one of her text book smiles and asked him to get back to discussing his future.

He indicated that he had been doing some lateral thinking. "I've already made some significant contributions in my field. I'm almost thirty. Maybe I've already done my best work. I could follow the traditional role and teach and supervise a bevy of younger scientists, but I'm not sure that's what I want to do. Working at NASA might be interesting and helping develop the program with the Xyrptans for further space exploration, but that's a big change from doing theoretical physics. I just don't know."

Robin asked if he was interested in actually being involved in exploring space by being an astronaut. "I've thought of that, but I've already had enough flight time in space to last a lifetime. I'm not so much interested in exploring the solar system, but galactic exploration sounds more intriguing, especially when we have intelligent robots available to do the travel. I think we should call them *astrobots.*" Eric smiled at his new characterization. Robin was very supportive, realizing that this would bring Eric from Pasadena to Houston.

Robin, quite independent and bold, asked, "Eric, do we have any future together—of a serious nature?" Eric was taken aback. He had been thinking of himself and his problems and not of any romantic involvement. But he was no shrinking violet either. "I just don't know. I've been *consumed* by my work for years. In the past I've never seriously thought of settling down. I've had affairs, but nothing serious. My long term goal has always been to get married and have kids. I guess I need to insert that into my decision making process now. I'm going back to Pasadena tomorrow. I'll be doing a lot of talking to my coworkers and a lot of thinking about what we've talked about. So, to answer your question, I don't know now. You're the only one I considered myself as romantically involved with in the last few years even though that's been pretty minimal. I hope that isn't too lame an answer." Eric gave Robin a weak, apologetic smile.

With a poker face she said, "Well, I was bold and asked the question, and you gave me an honest reply. That's all I have a right to expect. Let's stay in touch. I hope you'll be coming to Houston to consult and that we can get together. Perhaps you'll decide to join us at NASA. That would be great." Robin put her napkin down on the table, and rose, a disappointed expression on her face. Neither was happy about the way the dinner ended.

Several weeks passed. Michael called a meeting to inform them of their current status. "I've talked to everyone on the team. About half of you have agreed to move to Houston. Some are leaving us, and some will remain as consultants. I originally had an IT job and took leave when I joined the team. I'm leaving that job and will become a permanent member of the team, and I'll be moving to Houston. Robin is already at NASA. She'll continue her robotic work, but she'll be available to consult on a moment's notice. Brandy has decided to stay in D.C. and will serve as a consultant. Her main job for the foreseeable future will be working with Ingrid. Cephid has his duties as ambassador but will serve as a consultant too. We'll need a full time bot to replace Cephid, and Maxid will supply that individual. Eric is returning to Cal Tech, but he'll serve as a consultant too. Our new quarters should be ready in about six months, so that'll be when we expect to move and be ready for work. I'll inform you of the exact date as soon as we know."

"Moving on, it looks like we have a decision on what to do with the humans from Praetoria. I'll let Brandy inform you on this issue, since she's been key in solving this problem.

With a smile of satisfaction Brandy began, "The Praetorians were all children when they started their trip to Earth. Now most are in their late teens or early twenties. Toward the end of their journey they suffered a terrible experience, some dying from starvation. So my heart's gone out to them. As I mentioned before, they were nothing more than vassals being exploited by their government. So, I've worked *hard* to see that they are treated humanely and not just put back on their spaceship and returned to Praetoria. I worked out a plan with Peter and Maxid and presented it to Doug Black at Homeland Security. He, in turn, modified it, and talked to several other groups before we all came to an agreement. We're going to set up a special school for these people, which will be located near CEAF. For one year they'll attend school. They'll learn of life on Earth and be taught by our teachers. At the same time, we plan to open the school for a similar number of our own students. These students will be specially picked to make sure that they're tolerant and will be kind and understanding of our guests. They'll spend a year being taught by our and the Praetorian teachers to learn of what life is like on Praetoria. There'll be interchange between the two groups of students, which should be a great learning experience for all. After a year, we'll return them to Praetoria via their spaceship. We'll make sure that it's amply stocked with food, so that there won't be recurrence of the starvation they incurred on their trip here. They should then be able to act as goodwill ambassadors from us to their people on Praetoria. Any questions?"

"I think that's a great solution. I commend you for your creativity and hard work on this issue," Eric said. "Have you broached this plan to the Praetorians?"

"We have, and there's been universal agreement, not a single dissenting vote. They were delighted. In their present circumstance I don't think any of them were looking forward to starting a colony from scratch which was their original mission. Also, they have no stomach for *immediately* climbing back into their spaceship for a return trip to Praetoria."

"Thanks Brandy. I think you've found a solution we can all be happy with." Michael was all smiles, as was Brandy who had finally won.

"There's one other subject we should mention, although there isn't any general agreement yet—what should the status of the bots be? This includes both Maxid and Cephid, our 'brothers.' It's been decided that bots will have their own special category in the immigration service. Any bot that doesn't have a brain will be considered a piece of machinery, while those with thinking skills will be considered humanoid. The latter will have to register with the government including those already in the country. We expect that other countries will do the same. It's also agreed that bots will have to be *easily* distinguishable from humans, but that's where the disagreement lies—what should be the differentiating characteristics."

"We've had some guidance from the Xyrptan government, and we expect more help from them. Although we've had no problems so far, we've been communicating with the Xyrptans on how to control the manufacture of bots, particularly their mental capacity. As Herbert pointed out, they're smart enough to take over their own manufacture and destiny. We can't have bots running wild. So, their manufacture will have to be under some licensing regulations. We'll have a further discussion on this subject when we know more."

"For the few remaining p- bots on Earth, we'll dismantle them except for the two radio transmitters who will remain working at the Center." Michael nodded. "Let's call it a day."

A day before he was going in for surgery, Peter asked that Maxid stop by his office. Maxid was in town visiting Cephid so this was convenient. Peter and Maxid had become close friends in the last several years, and Peter wanted Maxid to know how much he appreciated his help in defeating the Praetorians. Maxid brought with him a desktop model of one of their new spaceships. "We made this model in our shop. It's a token of our appreciation for all the good you have done, and for your efforts in bringing our planets together for space exploration."

Peter was touched. "Maxid, through the difficult times in the last few years, you've become one of my best friends. I want you to know that, and I expect we'll have many more years in which to work closely." Peter was not one to usually initiate a hug, but now he rose, came around his desk, and gave Maxid a big hug.

Many of the team came in the next few days to give Peter well wishes on his surgery. Michael dropped in for the same reason. Peter mentioned, "Michael, I've been thinking of my deceased brother recently, and it made me realize how proud he would be of you, his son. You've made us *all* proud."

Eric called Cephid and asked if he would stop by his place to say goodbye before they parted. After all, they were practically brothers, Cephid sharing a portion of his brain functions. Eric recalled how he had discovered, several years ago, that Cephid was the one chosen by the Xyrptans to receive some of his brain functions in return for his receiving some astrophysical knowledge from the Xyrptans. He briefly thought, maybe they could embed enough new information into his brain now, so that he could rise to the level of one of *their* top astrophysicists. Eric was a dreamer. He always thought that a good part of his creative skills came from this source. However, he dropped this thought. This wouldn't satisfy his creative urges. He would just be a living library of other's creative knowledge.

He and Cephid spent the evening reminiscing about the events of the past few years while sipping from Cephid's new brandy snifters. Cephid even swirled his glass of brandy. Eric filled Cephid in on the details of his excursion into space, ending by telling Cephid of his dilemma regarding his work. He didn't think that Cephid could help him, but then perhaps he knew of similar situations on Xyrpta.

Cephid was sympathetic but unfortunately of little help. "Eric, I strongly urge you to move to NASA, and engage in the greatest adventure of the twenty first century—participating in the physical exploration of the Milky Way galaxy—what could be more exciting?"

Richard W. Blide, M.D. graduated from the University of Rochester and Albany Medical College. He attended the University of Maryland Medical Center in Baltimore for his residency and fellowship training. A pulmonologist, he practiced academic medicine at the latter institution for seven years before becoming medical director at the Will Rogers Hospital. Later he practiced preventive medicine until his retirement in 1999.

His lifelong interest in writing did not come into fruition until retirement. This latest book, *Alien Threat*, is the result of his interest in science, especially astronomy.

His first book, *Heartfelt: a Memoir of Political intrigue, Passion and Perseverance*, is about his challenging political efforts in a small Colorado town to help the local health district dig out from years of incompetence to achieve a first-rate health care system and a new hospital, the first for the area.

Dick and his wife Patti now reside in Ashland, Oregon and enjoy hiking, gardening and the many cultural offerings of the area.

Made in the USA
Charleston, SC
03 April 2013